Scan to listen
TEGAN'S ROAD TRIP

HELLO, BARNES & NOBLE READERS!

I'M SO THRILLED YOU'VE PURCHASED THIS SPECIAL EDITION OF THE CRASH, WHICH INCLUDES A THEMED PLAYLIST TO ACCOMPANY THE BOOK!

AS A NEW ENGLANDER, I HAVE LEARNED THAT SNOWSTORMS CAN HAPPEN AT ANY TIME BETWEEN OCTOBER AND APRIL (NO FOOLING), SO SNOW IS A FREQUENT OCCURRENCE IN MY BOOKS. THERE'S NOTHING LIKE LOOKING OUT THE WINDOW AND SEEING THOSE BIG WHITE FLAKES FALLING OUTSIDE—AS LONG AS YOU'RE NOT TRAPPED IN AN ISOLATED CABIN WITH A BROKEN ANKLE AND NO PHONE OR ELECTRICITY. WHENEVER IT'S SNOWING, I FIND IT FUN TO LISTEN TO A PLAYLIST OF WINTER SONGS, SO I HOPE YOU ENJOY THE SONGS ON THIS LIST THAT CELEBRATE THE COLDEST SEASON!

OF COURSE, WHEN YOU LIVE IN A PLACE WITH SNOW, YOU QUICKLY LEARN THAT THE WEATHER MAKES DRIVING TREACHEROUS—SOON AFTER MOVING HERE, I TRADED MY SEDAN IN FOR AN SUV WITH FOUR-WHEEL DRIVE SO I WOULDN'T KEEP GETTING STUCK IN THE PARKING LOT AT WORK. MY PLAYLIST ALSO INCLUDES SEVERAL SONGS ABOUT DRIVING, ALTHOUGH NONE ABOUT DRIVING IN THE SNOW, BECAUSE AS TEGAN QUICKLY LEARNS, THAT'S A DANGEROUS TOPIC THAT YOU MIGHT NOT WANT TO SING ABOUT!

HAPPY READING AND DRIVE SAFELY!
JUST REMEMBER TO TURN INTO THE SKID!
FREIDA

ALSO BY FREIDA MCFADDEN

The Boyfriend
The Teacher
The Coworker
Ward D
Never Lie
The Inmate
The Housemaid
The Housemaid's Secret
The Housemaid Is Watching
Do You Remember?
Do Not Disturb
The Locked Door
Want to Know a Secret?
One by One
The Wife Upstairs
The Perfect Son
The Ex
The Surrogate Mother
Brain Damage
Baby City
Suicide Med
The Devil Wears Scrubs
The Devil You Know

THE CRASH

FREIDA McFADDEN

Poisoned Pen Press

For my father

Published by Poisoned Pen Press, an imprint of Sourcebooks
P.O. Box 4410, Naperville, Illinois 60567-4410
(630) 961-3900
sourcebooks.com

Cataloging-in-Publication Data is on file with the Library of Congress.

Printed and bound in the United States of America.
LB 10 9 8 7 6 5 4 3 2 1

PROLOGUE

AFTER THE CRASH

I've never killed anyone before.

I'm not a murderer. I'm a *good* person. I don't lie. I don't cheat. I don't steal. I hardly ever even raise my voice. There are very few things I've done in my life that I'm ashamed of.

Yet here I am.

I expected a struggle from the person beneath me. But I didn't expect this much of a struggle. I didn't expect this much thrashing.

Or the muffled screams.

I could stop. It's not too late. I have fifteen seconds left to decide if I want to be a murderer—thirty seconds, on the outside.

But I don't stop. I can't.

Then finally—*finally*—the struggle ends. Now I've got a limp, motionless body lying before me. I don't need to be a doctor to recognize a dead body.

What have I done?

I bury my face in my palms, choking back a sob. I'm not a crier—never have been—but in this moment, it feels appropriate. If I don't cry, who will? After a moment, I force myself to straighten up and compose myself. I did this for a good reason after all.

It was the only way.

PART 1

ONE WEEK BEFORE THE CRASH

CHAPTER 1

TEGAN

I'm not sure I'll make it to my front door.

It is approximately fifty feet from my little Ford Fusion to the entrance of the apartment complex where I live. Fifty feet isn't far. Under the best circumstances, I could run it in seconds.

But not tonight.

I live in a studio apartment on the second floor of a small apartment complex in Lewiston, Maine. It's a terrible neighborhood, but right now, I can't afford better. My shift at the grocery store ends after dark, which means that it's pitch-black outside right now. There used to be a streetlight illuminating the path from the parking area to the complex, but the bulb blew out a month after I moved in, and nobody has bothered to fix it. Once I kill the headlights, I won't be able to see two feet in front of my face.

I turned off the engine in the car soon after parking because I can't waste any gas right now. It's cold enough that even within the car, I can see the puff of air from my own breath. In Maine, the temperature in December is always well below freezing. I peer through the windshield, and I can just barely make out the entrance to the building. There's no streetlight, but there's a tiny light just above the doorway that will make it possible for me to see the keyhole to unlock the door.

It's also just enough light to see the man lingering in the shadows near the doorway.

Waiting.

I'm shivering as I shift in the driver's seat, which isn't easy to do these days. A sharp, electric pain shoots down my right leg, which has been happening to me more and more lately. The doctor told me it was something called *sciatica*, caused by an irritated nerve in my spine. I thought my life was about as bad as it could get, and then I went and irritated a nerve in my spine on top of everything else.

I squint into the darkness at the man by the entrance, wondering what his business is here. It's too dark to make out any of his features, but he's relatively tall and lean. He's wearing a long, dark trench coat, which doesn't make me feel any better. His face appears menacing, but to be fair, everyone looks menacing when cloaked in shadows.

His intentions could be entirely innocent. Maybe he's visiting a friend in the building. Maybe he's an undercover cop. (Not likely.) Maybe he's... Well, I can't think of what else someone might be doing here at nine thirty in the evening. My point is he isn't *necessarily* here to mug me.

Anyway, I can't sit in my car all night.

I reach into my purse and remove the bottle of pepper spray I've taken to carrying around, and I relocate it to my coat pocket. If this guy wants the meager contents of my wallet, I'll make sure to give him a run for his money. I move my house keys to my other pocket for easy access, and then I grab the bag of groceries on the passenger's seat and heave it into my arms. Mr. Zakir always gives me a massive discount on soon-to-expire groceries, and I refuse to leave them behind just because of some creepy man outside my building.

That lightning bolt shoots down my right leg again as I climb out of my Ford. My coat hangs open, but there's not much I can do about it, because it doesn't zip closed anymore and hasn't for several months now. There's nothing functionally wrong with the zipper, although a broken zipper would be fairly consistent with the state of my life these days. No, the reason my coat doesn't close anymore is that it no longer fits over my distended belly.

I am nearly eight months pregnant.

As soon as I step out of the car, my swollen feet scream in protest. Over the course of a double shift at the supermarket, they have expanded to nearly twice their original size and barely fit in my sneakers anymore. I straighten up as best I can, and the cold air smacks me in the face. I've become increasingly fatigued over the course of my pregnancy, especially later in the day, but that ice-cold wind wakes me right up.

I slam the car door behind me, and the man leaning against the front of the building jerks his head up. I still can't make out much more than a silhouette, but he's now staring directly at me. My arm holding the bag of groceries trembles, and I reach with my other hand into my pocket for the pepper spray.

Don't even try to take my expired bread, you asshole.

I suck in a mouthful of chilly air and walk purposefully toward the entrance of the building. I avoid looking at him, like I've learned to do over the years with dozens of other creepy men, but I can feel his eyes following me. My fingers encircle the pepper spray, and I am close to whipping it out when a familiar voice breaks into my terrified thoughts:

"Tegan?"

I pivot my gaze in the direction of the voice. The light from the doorway is bright enough now to make out the man's features, and all the tension instantly drains out of me.

"Jackson!" I cry. "Oh my God, you scared the crap out of me!"

The man in front of me, who I now recognize as Jackson Bruckner, is wearing a trench coat over his usual rumpled white dress shirt, gray tie, and gray dress pants underneath. He's not local, and I'm assuming he's driven at least two hours to get here, but he always looks bright-eyed when he shows up at my door.

Without my having to ask him, Jackson heaves the bag of groceries into his arms, which makes my aching feet hurt a tiny bit less. "I'm so sorry," he says. "I was going to go to the supermarket, but my GPS said it was closed, so I came here instead. I figured you'd be home any minute, so I was waiting."

"You could have texted me," I mumble, now slightly embarrassed by how frightened I was of this man wearing coke-bottle glasses, with big ears that stick out on either side of his head. Now that he's not cloaked in shadows, he's pretty much the least threatening man I've ever seen. He's cute, but in a dorky sort of way.

He is not, by the way, the father of my unborn child. He's not my boyfriend either.

"I did text you," he says.

I reach into my purse for my phone, and sure enough, there are a bunch of text messages from Jackson that I hadn't seen. Of course he texted me. Jackson is responsible. He works as an attorney and graduated summa cum laude at his Ivy League law school. He didn't tell me that, but I googled him.

"I guess you did text me," I admit.

He glances at his watch. "I also ordered Chinese food, which will be here in a few minutes."

My stomach growls at the mention of food. I'm supposed to be eating for two, but I'm barely eating for one. "Chicken lo mein?" I ask hopefully.

"Of course." He grins at me. "Let me carry these groceries up for you, then I'll come back down to get the delivery."

I want to protest, but carrying groceries up the stairs has gotten progressively harder as my belly has grown larger. If he's willing to do it for me, I'm nothing but grateful.

"Thank you," I say.

His eyes meet mine under the dim light over the entryway. "Of course."

Jackson waits patiently while I fumble to get my key in the lock. It always sticks in cold weather, and around here, that's ten months of the year. When I finally get the door unlocked, he holds it open for me like a gentleman.

I really like Jackson. I like it when he comes over with an offering of dinner, which has been happening with increasing frequency lately.

But in actuality, this is not a social call. Jackson and I have important business to discuss.

Soon, I'm going to be rich beyond my wildest dreams.

And it's all because of the baby growing inside me.

CHAPTER 2

Once Jackson and I get inside, I bypass the mailboxes. I'm not excited to see the bills that await me, and I don't have money in the bank to pay them anyway. Instead, we climb up the two flights of stairs to my apartment. The bulbs in the stairwell are low wattage, and the paint on the walls is badly chipped, but nobody here would complain. My feet throb with each step, but soon I'll be home.

I stop at the second-floor landing, taking a few seconds to catch my breath. I'm always out of breath these days. I assume it's because of the fetus growing inside me, keeping my lungs from expanding as much as I would like. Or it could be something terrible. I asked Dr. Google, and I didn't like anything they had to say. It could be a blood clot in my lungs. It could be heart failure. It could be *tuberculosis*.

But my health insurance is awful, so I'm just going to keep my fingers crossed that it's nothing serious.

Jackson's brow creases in concern. "You okay?"

"Fine," I gulp. I nod at the stairwell. "Let's go."

As soon as we reach the top of the last flight of stairs, Jackson's phone buzzes in his pocket. He pulls it out and looks down at the screen. "Food is here."

I hold out my hands for the bag of groceries. "You go down and get it. I'll take it from here."

He looks doubtful. "You sure?"

I shoot him a look. "What do you think I do every day when you're not around?"

A flash of guilt passes over his thin face, but I don't know why. It's not Jackson's responsibility to babysit me during this pregnancy. It's nice of him to carry my groceries, but my baby and I are not his problem. And very soon—after the papers are signed—I'll likely never see him again.

Jackson passes the groceries back to me. I juggle them in my left arm while I walk down the hall to my apartment, digging around in my coat pocket for my keys. I almost get the door open when a sharp voice speaks up from behind me:

"*Another* man, Tegan?"

I swivel my head to meet the watery, bloodshot eyes of Mrs. Walden, my elderly next-door neighbor. I discovered her first name is Evangeline when I saw a package left downstairs, but on the day we met, she introduced herself as Mrs. Walden, and even though we have lived next door to each other for two years now, she has made it very clear that I am still to address her as "Mrs. Walden."

"Honestly," she says, "you're turning this place into a brothel."

I have no idea what she's talking about. In the entire time we have lived next door to each other, Jackson is the only man who has come to visit me aside from my brother. And the two of us aren't even sleeping together. But it would be pointless to argue. In her eyes, I may as well be parading around the building with a scarlet letter on my chest.

Mrs. Walden's eyes drop to my belly, protruding below my thrift-store black-and-green blouse with the empire waist. It has ruffles around the collar, and it's so tacky I could cry, but at the time I bought it, I was in no position to drop a bunch of cash on clothing I would need for only four or five months. Anyway, Mrs. Walden isn't judging me on my cheap, ugly shirt. She's judging me because I am twenty-three years old, eight months pregnant, and unmarried.

But honestly, it's none of her damn business.

"I meant to ask you, Tegan," she says in her crackly voice. "Will you be moving to other accommodations once the baby is born?"

I rest a hand on my abdomen and am rewarded with a hearty kick. One thing I can say for this baby is that she has a ton of energy. More than I do right now.

"Maybe," I say. "I haven't decided."

"You know, it will be quite disruptive having a baby around." She lifts her chin. "All that crying at all hours of the night! What a nightmare."

I put my hand back on the key protruding from the lock and turn it until I feel that satisfying click. "I've heard that babies cry a lot. It's because they don't know how to speak yet."

"Nobody will be able to sleep!" she continues. "It's

very selfish of you to bring a newborn into a community that is mostly adults."

"Well, it wasn't like I planned it out."

Her lips purse. "No, I don't imagine you did."

I want to snap at Mrs. Evangeline Walden that she's got me all wrong. She's made a lot of assumptions, and they are grossly incorrect. I am not the kind of girl who has a one-night stand and gets knocked up without even knowing who the father is, although now that it's happened to me, I feel guilty for all the other women I've judged for it. I had big plans for my life, none of which involved getting pregnant at age twenty-two.

But the fact is I did get pregnant at age twenty-two. It *was* a one-night stand. And up until recently, I didn't know who the father was.

So really, there's not much I can say to her that wouldn't be a lie.

Instead, I wrench open the door and offer her a smile. "Good night, Mrs. Walden."

"I'm going to speak to management about—"

Mrs. Walden is smack in the middle of a sentence when I slam the door closed behind me. If she wants to complain to the manager that I am illegally populating the apartment with my offspring, then she can go ahead and do it. I'm not going to suck up to her. Not anymore.

As soon as I get my money, I am out of here.

I flick on the lights inside my studio, which only illuminates how painfully dreary it is. The white paint isn't cracked, but it does have a dull, lackluster appearance, much like everything else in the apartment. It's like there's a layer of grime on every piece of furniture and appliance that I can't get off, no matter how much I scrub.

It wasn't supposed to be like this. I was working double shifts at the grocery store, desperately scraping together enough money to go to nursing school. And at the end of a shift, I could flop down on the couch and watch television to my heart's content while chowing down on my dinner for one. I wasn't supposed to get pregnant.

And in just over a month, everything will change. I'll have a *baby*. A living, breathing human being who will be my responsibility. This baby will not be allowed to be alone and will require clothes, food, and eventually an education. And will presumably keep me awake half the night so that I become a zombie during the daylight hours.

I slide into my small kitchenette, where I can barely fit now that I have reached my third trimester. I lay the paper bag filled with groceries on the kitchen counter. Before I leave the grocery store every day, I scrounge around for an assortment of items that are close to or past their expiration date, and today I've got a bunch of canned goods as well as some bread and cheese. I've also got a small carton of milk that's only one day over and will probably taste fine. And five cans of tuna fish.

Every woman has her own weird pregnancy cravings. Mine is tuna fish. Ever since my second trimester started and the nausea went away, I have been craving tuna. I can't eat as much as I want due to the mercury content, but if I could, I would eat tuna for every meal, including breakfast. As a result, I have informally named my fetus Little Tuna.

Tuna for dinner, Mama?

Okay, that's another weird thing. I often imagine that

my baby is speaking to me from within my womb. I'm not losing my mind, I swear. I know my eight-month-old fetus is not capable of speech. But sometimes her sweet little voice talks to me, clear as day. Even though I haven't seen her face yet, I already love her. I want her to have a better life than I've had and all the advantages I never got to have. And I'll do whatever I have to do to get it for her.

That's why I don't even feel one scrap of guilt about the payday coming my way.

CHAPTER 3

Jackson materializes at my door less than five minutes later, carrying a brown paper bag.

He would be happy to carry the food to the kitchen, but I'm too quick for him. I grab the paper bag from him while he trots after me, his ears still bright red from the cold. I rip it open, releasing a burst of tantalizing aromas, and yank out one of the white cartons. I tear the flaps slightly in my eagerness.

I don't even bother with a plate. I grab a fork from the drawer by the sink and eat it right out of the container. I'm not sure if *eating* is the correct term. *Inhaling* might be more accurate. I am always starving these days.

"Sorry," I say between bites. "I haven't eaten in a while. Double shift."

He frowns. "Is that okay for the baby?"

"I'll cut back soon."

Even though I'm too impatient to bother with plates, Jackson grabs two of them from the cupboard over the sink. He starts to grab another container out of the bag, but then he stops himself.

"Oh, hey," he says. "I brought you something."

I was so distracted by a tender piece of chicken that I didn't even notice the little gift bag Jackson had placed on my kitchen counter—he must have grabbed it from his car when he went down to get the food. It is pink and sparkly, which makes me laugh because he is the opposite of pink and sparkly. It's hard to imagine him picking it out.

Perhaps reading my mind, he smiles awkwardly. "It's for the baby."

As much as I enjoy stuffing forkfuls of lo mein noodles into my mouth, I am even more excited about the idea of a present. I haven't received any presents for the baby yet. Well, aside from a car seat my brother sent me, which is still in the cardboard box it was delivered in.

I grab the pink, sparkly bag and gasp at the contents. It's literally *the cutest thing I have ever seen*. It's a tiny little outfit, made for an impossibly tiny human being—I've learned they call it a onesie. And in pink lettering on the chest are the words that melt my heart:

My Mommy Loves Me.

Little Tuna kicks me at that moment as if in agreement. Even though I have just over a month left before Tuna makes her appearance, I have not yet started to stockpile baby clothes, so this is my first. I stare down at the outfit, blinking furiously. Despite my growing belly and the constant kicks to my ribs, there's something about this onesie that makes this all seem very real for the first time. I'm going to have a baby, and she's going to wear this.

Oh my God, I'm going to cry.

"Do you like it?" Jackson asks eagerly.

If I say anything, including "yes," I'm going to lose it, so I just nod. And his face lights up.

None of this is his job. His job is not to bring me Chinese food or adorable baby clothes. The reason he is here has nothing to do with any of that. It has everything to do with the contents of the leather briefcase that he left near my front door. That's the only reason he is here and the only reason he is *ever* here. And when all that is resolved, he won't be back here. There will be no more lo mein or egg rolls or surprise visits after a long shift at work.

Jackson does not come here for social reasons. This is his *job.*

"So," I say as I grab my box of takeout and carry it to the futon sofa, which doubles as my extremely uncomfortable bed. As I plop down on the futon, I prop my swollen legs up on the coffee table. The relief is heavenly. "What did you need to discuss with me?"

Jackson grabs his own box of food and joins me on the sofa. "Just a few minor details I want to go over in the contract. But next time I'm here, it will be ready for you to sign."

A fluttering sensation fills my lower abdomen, and I'm not sure if it is nerves or the baby. I can't believe I am about to sign a contract that will result in my receiving quite a lot of money. It will set me up for life.

It all started almost eight months ago.

I had driven up with a girlfriend to visit my brother, Dennis, at the ski slope where he works as an instructor, so we usually got a good discount. He was busy that night, so the two of us ended up going out to a local bar for drinks. That was when I met a man in a dark suit who offered to buy me a drink. He was handsome in a clean-cut sort of way with an expensive haircut and chiseled features, and his effortless charm convinced me to accept the drink. He told me he was in town for an important business deal—only there for the one night. While my friend was distracted by a guy with a mullet, I found myself flirting with this confident, attractive older man who was so different from anyone I knew back home.

Long story short, I must have had a few too many drinks. I don't remember much about that night, but I woke up with a splitting headache, and my mouth felt like an ashtray. I had only a vague recollection of coming back to my hotel room with the handsome businessman, but I was embarrassed to admit I couldn't even remember his name. I chalked it up to life experience and tried to forget about it.

Until I missed my period.

I wasn't even a party girl—I hardly went out and focused most of my energy on saving money for my dream of going to nursing school—yet I had become a cliché. I got pregnant while drinking, and I didn't even know who the father of my child was.

It was hardly the way I had planned my life to work out, but after a lot of soul-searching, I decided to keep and raise this baby. Maybe eventually the right guy would come along, but if he didn't, I would do it on my own. And nursing school—well, if it was meant to be, I would get there eventually. I was sure of it.

And then something unexpected happened.

I was watching the news three months ago, balancing a plate of food on my growing belly, when I saw a man on the television screen. The caption underneath his handsome face declared that his name was Simon Lamar. He was a local businessman who specialized in real estate development.

And he was the man I left the bar with the night I conceived Little Tuna.

What happened next was a little short of a fairy-tale ending. I wish I could say that I located Simon Lamar, that he was overjoyed if a bit surprised by my pregnancy and insisted on winning me over. I wish I could say that after a couple of months of courting me, he dropped down on one knee to ask me to marry him so that the three of us could be a happy family. That was the scenario I envisioned when I reached out to Simon to let him know about my situation.

It didn't quite work out that way.

Despite the fact that I didn't recall a wedding band on his finger that night, Simon Lamar was very much married. Not only was he married, but he had two little ones of his own, and he had absolutely no interest in any illegitimate children. Nor did he want his beloved wife of ten years to discover his infidelity—or the press, for that matter. He refused to even meet with me, even after the paternity test he demanded proved that he was indeed the father of my child.

However, he had Jackson reach out to make me a very intriguing offer. A boatload of money—enough to support me and our child and then some. I wouldn't have to worry about rent, about childcare, or even about college tuition for my daughter. Simon would pay for all of that. And all I would have to do was sign a nondisclosure agreement, promising that nobody besides Simon and me (and Jackson) would know he was the father of my child.

I said yes.

What else could I do? I *had* to do it. Simon was offering to secure my future and Tuna's for life. And as a single mother-to-be, I would have been stupid to say no.

Thanks to Simon's generous offer, I will still be able to go to nursing school on schedule or even sooner than expected. I'll be able to send my daughter to the best private schools. I won't have to raise her in a tiny studio. He saved me.

"Thank you for working so hard on this contract," I tell Jackson around a mouthful of noodles.

He waves a hand. "It's my job."

Is it though? Jackson has been driving out here as often as once a week to help broker the deal. A lot of things could have been done on the phone, but he always insists on coming here personally. Which is more than I could say for Simon, who I have not laid eyes on since that fateful night.

And I believe Jackson has my best interests in mind. There were clauses in the contract that I might have naively agreed to, but Jackson advised me against it. *This isn't a high enough cost-of-living increase. It's not fair to you.*

Jackson reaches into the inside pocket of his suit jacket and pulls out an envelope, which he places on the coffee table in front of us. Based on experience, I know it's filled with twenty-dollar bills—just enough to tide me over with food, groceries, and medical expenses. Even though there's a bigger payment coming, those envelopes of cash have taken a lot of the strain off the last few months.

"Thank you," I tell him.

Jackson pushes his thick glasses up the bridge of his nose. "No problem. The bank was still open before I got on the road."

He's never mentioned going to a bank before. When we began our negotiations, Simon was very clear about the fact that I was not to receive a penny until the contracts were signed, but then Jackson started showing up with those envelopes containing small amounts of cash, and I assumed Simon changed his mind. But now I wonder if Jackson has been giving me money out of his own personal accounts this whole time.

"By the way," he says before I can ask, "Simon will be coming down here to sign the final contract in a few days and discuss a few things with you."

"Oh." The thought of seeing Simon again makes me nervous, maybe because of how unenthusiastic he has been since he found out about my pregnancy. It's a stark contrast with how utterly charming he was the night we met. "Okay, I guess."

"I'll be here too," he adds.

He gives me a reassuring smile, and I can't help but think that I wish it had been Jackson I met that night at the bar by the ski lodge. I would happily give up the monster offer from Simon for a chance at starting a family with a great guy like Jackson.

But I can't look at it that way. I can't change the past. I should feel fortunate that I'm getting such a generous offer from Simon, one that will provide for my child for the rest of her life.

CHAPTER 4

I'm in the middle of folding laundry when I have a contraction.

It's not a real one. Not the kind that would knock the wind out of me every five minutes and send me running for the emergency room. But the kind that is just annoying enough that I have to stop what I'm doing for a split second and take a breath. I've been getting a couple of them every day. Practice labor, Dr. Hanson called it.

Which means this baby is coming. Soon. Maybe not today, maybe not tomorrow, maybe not even this month. But sooner rather than later, Little Tuna is coming.

I don't feel ready. First of all, I'm exhausted. I haven't quit my job yet, and I'm afraid to do it until the contract is signed, because I'm paranoid it will all somehow fall through. But the main reason I'm tired is that I'm barely sleeping.

I've been having nightmares. I don't remember

exactly what happens in them, but each one ends with Simon's handsome face hovering over mine. He stares intently into my eyes while his own flash with determination. I wake up shaking with fear that goes down to my very core. (And then I have to get up to pee.)

So yeah, my sleep is crap.

I lay a hand flat on my belly. I haven't picked out a name for the baby yet. Obviously, I can't *actually* call her Tuna. I hear about couples who argue over baby names, but I don't have that problem. I can call my baby anything I want, because it's just me.

Yet I can't think of a name. So she's still Tuna in my head.

Hi, Mama! Don't forget to buy me a crib, or else I won't have a place to sleep!

"Soon." I place a hand on the muscles of my uterus, which gradually unclench. "As soon as I get the check from your dad, I will get you a crib. And a lot more."

Right after the contraction passes, my phone rings somewhere in the apartment. I'm lucky I live in a studio, because if I didn't, I would never be able to find anything ever again. Does everyone have brain fog this bad when they're pregnant? Yesterday, I was looking for the paperback I had been reading to take my mind off everything, and I finally discovered it in the refrigerator.

I walk (no, *waddle*) around the studio in search of my phone. At first, the ringing offers me a clue as to the location, leading me in the direction of the kitchen. Then the ringing stops, and I don't know where to look anymore. My eyes scan the kitchenette, searching for my tiny little phone.

Oh my God, if I find it in the cheese drawer, I'm going to be so pissed off at myself.

But no, it's on the microwave, nearly blending into the black surface. I snatch up my phone, wondering if it's Jackson calling to firm up details about the final contract. We are supposed to be signing tomorrow, and I want everything to go to plan. I figure no news is good news, so I don't want any news right now.

But the missed call wasn't from Jackson. It was from my brother, Dennis. My shoulders sag in relief as I press the button to return the call.

"Tegan?" My brother's booming voice fills my ear. "You okay?"

There's something about talking to my big brother that always makes me feel like I'm five years old again. "Yes, fine."

Dennis lets out a long breath. "What's going on, Teggie?"

"I'm just..." I look around my small living space. "I'm lonely."

"When are you signing the contract with Lamar?"

"Tomorrow." I chew on my lower lip. "Any chance you could come out here?"

"I wish I could," he sighs. "You know I'm swamped right now."

I can't argue with that. Dennis works as a skiing instructor upstate at a resort aptly named Snow Mountain. He has loved to ski ever since I can remember. He almost became a professional skier—he's that good. But then he broke his leg when he was in his early twenties and instead fell into a cushy job working as a ski instructor. Unfortunately, December is one of his busiest months, leading up to the Christmas holiday season. He works his butt off during the winter, then takes it easy for the rest of the year.

"I'll try to come for a few days when the baby is born," he promises. "Unless you want to come here for a little while? I've got a spare bedroom."

It's not a terrible idea. "Let me think about it."

The invitation is tempting. Dennis always fusses over me when I come to visit him, and I haven't seen him since I got pregnant. Our dad was a workaholic businessman who had a massive heart attack at age forty when his company went under, so Dennis, who was twelve at the time, stepped up as the man of the house and then once again when our mom died of pancreatic cancer eight years later. He did everything you would expect a father to do, including approving or disapproving of my boyfriends. When one boy showed up at the front door stinking of alcohol, Dennis ran him off with a baseball bat before I could get in his car. Truth be told, most of my boyfriends were not good enough by his standards. He definitely does not approve of Simon.

I wonder what he'd think of Jackson.

CHAPTER 5

Today we are signing the contract that will cement my future.

I am a nervous wreck, even though all I'm doing is signing a piece of paper. I slept even worse than usual, waking from my nightmares practically every hour—it felt like every time I drifted off, Simon's face would invade my dreams and wake me up again. I just can't get him off my mind. At around four in the morning, I gave up trying.

Yesterday, I went to the thrift shop and bought a new maternity outfit—a flower-print dress. Unfortunately, the thrift shop didn't have a dressing room, so I just had to hold it up in front of me, and when I put it on at home, I looked a bit like a whale wearing florals. But it's still better than anything else I own.

I don't know why I dressed up though. Who am I trying to impress? Simon? Do I really think that he might take a look at me in my flower-print muumuu and decide to leave his family for me? Do I even want that?

No, I don't. The truth is I don't want to have anything to do with Simon Lamar. There's only one person I've dressed up for, and it's not Simon. It's a man I've been seeing quite a lot lately and have become quite fond of, who I'm worried I might never see again after I scribble my name on the dotted line.

I took the afternoon off from work, which stressed me out a lot because I need the money so badly. I keep having to remind myself that after this afternoon, I will have more money than I know what to do with. It's hard to wrap my head around that reality, considering... Well, I've never had money in my whole life. The first thing I'm going to do when I get the money is find a two-bedroom apartment in a better neighborhood. Or maybe even a house.

It's five o'clock when the intercom buzzes from downstairs, alerting me that Simon and Jackson have arrived. While I'm waiting for them to walk up the stairs, I pace the length of my studio apartment. It doesn't take long.

After the annoying buzz of the doorbell fills the studio, I fling open the door to reveal the two men in suits. Jackson looks his usual adorably rumpled self, his thick glasses perched on his nose. And then there's Simon standing next to him.

I haven't seen Simon Lamar in...well, not since the night my entire life changed. He's nearly two decades older than I am, but he's aged very well. I had forgotten how classically handsome he is, like his features were chiseled in stone by a skilled sculptor. I had seen photos of him since that night, but it's different in person—he's better-looking in person too. Seeing his face jogs a vague memory of that night, which is still so foggy for me. I try to grasp on to the memory, my mind straining to recall anything about the night I conceived my daughter.

But no. It's a blank. Almost like someone took an eraser to my brain. The only thing I can remember are the nightmares of his face that have been haunting me with increasing frequency. But I can't blame the guy for my nightmares, can I?

That night at the bar, Simon seemed warm and friendly with an easy smile. Tonight, he seems irritated to be here. The first thing he does when we see each other is look down at his watch and then down at my belly with undisguised disgust on his face.

"For God's sake," he says. "I should file a lawsuit against the company that made those condoms."

Jackson shoots Simon a dirty look while my face burns. I'm glad to know we at least used a condom. I did get tested for all the usual STDs, just to be on the safe side. I was clean.

"Well," I say brightly, "come on in."

The look of disgust on Simon's face does not waver as he steps into my dingy apartment. When I lead him to the futon, he is reluctant to sit down. I almost expect him to ask for a towel to put down beneath him. But finally, he perches on the edge, looking like he wishes he were anywhere but here. I sit at the other end of the futon, as far as I can get without falling off.

"The contract is just as we discussed," Jackson says gently as he sits on the only other piece of furniture in the room—a rickety wooden chair that I found on the curb. "As I said, you're welcome to review it with your own attorney."

"I trust you," I say.

I have to trust him, because I can't afford an attorney right now. But my statement makes Simon smirk, which makes me think maybe I *should* get one. The sardonic expression on his face jogs my memory again. It is so frustrating to try to remember something and not be able to. It must be terrible to have dementia.

"You discussed the exact terms of the nondisclosure, right?" Simon speaks up.

"Yes," Jackson confirms. "We did, right, Tegan?"

"Yes..."

The nondisclosure agreement is the part of this contract that makes me the most nervous. If I sign, I can never tell anyone that Simon is Little Tuna's father. It won't be on the birth certificate. I cannot tell a soul—not ever. I won't even be able to tell my daughter, or else Simon could sue my pants off. I'll have to tell her... I don't know... Her father died in a tragic accident.

"So you understand?" Simon presses, his gray eyes leveled at me. I jolt with the dissonant memory of thinking how soulful his eyes were that night. "You can't tell anyone about this. Not family, not friends, not your baby."

My baby. He has already relinquished responsibility. "I understand."

"Smart girl." He winks at me. "Let's get this signed then. Looks like you could really use the money."

I don't like this man, Mama. I don't want him to be my daddy.

Simon leans forward to pull out the contract,

reaching into the expensive briefcase he brought. As he gets closer to me, I catch a whiff of his cologne. It's the same cologne he was wearing that night.

It's an unusual fragrance. Vanilla. Oak. And a spicy undertone.

I close my eyes for a moment, and I see his face hovering over me like I do in my nightmares. But this time, it's different. Instead of just seeing his face, I can also see his naked body. On top of me. And there's a hungry look in his eyes that terrifies me.

No, I manage to say with a tongue that feels like dead weight. *I don't want to. No. No!*

Simon rolls his eyes. *Didn't you finish your beer? Go back to sleep, Tegan.*

No. I don't want...

And then...

My eyes fly open. That scene playing out in my head felt so real, and I know with a sick certainty that it *was* real. I had believed all those images of Simon in my nightmares were my imagination playing tricks on me, but it wasn't my imagination.

It was a memory.

And now it all makes a sudden horrible kind of sense. I knew I didn't have that much to drink that night. I have never been blackout drunk in my entire life, and certainly not after a couple of beers.

Simon slipped something into my drink.

And then when we got back to my hotel room, he...

Oh *God*.

CHAPTER 6

Simon flips through the pages of the contract as my heart beats so fast it feels like my chest might explode. For months, I have been trying to grasp any memory of that night. And now I can't stop seeing it. Over and over and *over.*

Simon on top of me as my slurred voice pleads with him to stop.

"You *raped* me!" I blurt out.

Simon freezes, clutching the contract along with the nondisclosure agreement. "Excuse me?"

"You put a roofie or something in my drink!" I cry. "That's why I can't remember anything from that night. But I remember now. I remember begging you to stop, and you wouldn't. You wouldn't stop." I cringe. "You told me to go back to sleep."

His eyes flash, which gives his face a terrifying edge. "That's absolutely preposterous! How could you accuse me of something like that, especially after how generous I've been?"

My temple throbs. "You mean after you raped me and got me pregnant?"

Simon looks over at Jackson for help. Jackson's mouth hangs open as he stares at me. "Jackson," Simon says, "do you hear this ridiculous accusation?"

"Yeah." Jackson rakes a hand through his hair, stopping halfway through so it sticks up in the air. "Tegan, what are you talking about? You never said anything like this before."

"It just came back to me! It was...it was his cologne." I think I might vomit.

And now it feels like the floodgates have opened. I remember more—Simon whispering in my ear that we should "get out of here," my head lolling in the back seat of his Porsche as he drove back to my hotel, him practically carrying me to the room. The terrifying part is that if I hadn't come face-to-face with Simon and smelled his sickening cologne, I might not have remembered any of it.

I feel so disgusted. *Dirty*.

I can't be near this man anymore, that's for sure. I jump off the futon and run for the only place where I can have some privacy in this tiny studio apartment: the bathroom.

I slam the door behind me, leaning my weight against it. A contraction seizes my stomach, like a giant fist squeezing my uterus. I do not want to go into labor right now. I can't even imagine having to deal with that with Simon still in my apartment. *Please, Tuna, don't do this to me. Not now.*

But then the fist around my womb loosens. The contraction subsides.

A fist raps gently on the bathroom door. "Tegan?"

It's Jackson's voice. I squeeze my eyes shut, wishing they would both go away.

"Tegan? Can I please come in? Please?"

I don't want him to, but then I remind myself that this is not Simon. This is not the man who assaulted me. This is Jackson, the man who has been fighting for me to get a good deal and has been giving me cash from his own funds and who bought Tuna a present in a glittery pink bag.

Slowly, I back away from the bathroom door and crack it open just enough to allow Jackson to slide inside. The bathroom is appropriately tiny given the rest of the apartment, and it's almost painfully cramped with the two of us inside. Jackson's warm brown eyes stare at me through his coke-bottle lenses.

"Tegan," he says, "what were you talking about back there?"

"I'm sorry," I say, although I don't know why I'm the one apologizing, because his boss is the one who is at fault. I am the *victim*. "Simon drugged me and he... Well, I told you what he did."

He shakes his head, like he doesn't understand what I'm trying to say. "Simon *drugged* you?"

"Yes, he did."

"I don't get it." There's a tremor in his voice. "All this time, you've been saying it was a one-night stand. And now...I mean, you really think he drugged and *raped* you?"

"Yes! I didn't remember until I saw him. Until I *smelled* him."

His mouth falls open. "*Smelled* him? Tegan, is there...

do you think there's any chance you could just be, well, *imagining* this?"

"No. I'm not imagining it." I swallow a lump in my throat. "It's *real*, Jackson."

I protectively hug my belly. I wish I hadn't remembered what happened. It was easier thinking my daughter was conceived during a wild night of consensual, albeit drunken, sex. Now I have to live with *this* for the rest of my life. I will never stop seeing the image of what Simon did to me.

"Tegan," Jackson says in an urgent whisper, "you need to sign that contract. Whatever you think happened, you need to put it behind you and sign the damn contract for your own good."

"Whatever I *think* happened?" I repeat. "So you don't believe me?"

"I'm trying to help you here. That contract will set you up for life. You have to sign it."

"Answer the question. Do you believe me?"

He looks at me for a long time. Long enough that it's clear what his real answer is even when he hedges. "What you're saying is terrible, Tegan. I know you're not making it up, but...I've known Simon a long time, and...I don't know. You have to admit, you're under a lot of stress right now..."

"He raped me, Jackson." My voice cracks. "And if he did it to me, I bet he did it to other women."

He drops his eyes, unable to look at me anymore. "Please sign this contract, Tegan. I'm begging you."

"Or else what?"

He doesn't answer me, but he doesn't have to. The answer is obvious. *Sign the contract, or else you and your baby will get nothing.*

I push past him, wrenching open the bathroom door. Simon—that bastard—is standing in the middle of my living area, still holding the contract in his right hand.

"I'm not signing a nondisclosure agreement," I say. "I'm going to the police."

Simon's gaze snaps over to Jackson. "You told me you were handling her."

I feel a surge of disgust for these two men. Simon for what he did to me. And Jackson for trying to cover it up. I thought at least Jackson was a good guy, but I was so wrong. All this time, he was just "handling" me.

I wonder if Jackson knew the whole time. I wonder if I'm one of a long string of girls who he pretended to be kind to in order to keep them from coming forward with the truth.

"Get out of my apartment," I say. "Right now."

Simon holds up the contract in both his hands. "I am going to give you one more chance, Tegan," he says. "I'm going to give you one more chance to accept this extremely generous offer for you and your child. But if you don't take it, you won't have another chance."

I would be lying if I didn't say I have a moment of hesitation. This offer is beyond generous. If I don't take it, I may very well be living paycheck to paycheck for the rest of my life. I won't be able to give Little Tuna the future I have dreamed for her. This money would change everything.

But then I think of my daughter as an adult. Twenty-two years old, enjoying a drink at a bar with a handsome stranger. And then his hand hovers just a little too long over her glass....

No, I can't let him get away with this. I have to do

something. For all the other women he might hurt in the future.

For my daughter.

"I'm not signing," I say again.

I wince as Simon tears up the contract right in front of me. He tosses the pieces back in his briefcase. "You are going to be very sorry, sweetheart," he says. "And even sorrier if you try to go to the police. It's your word against mine, and nobody will believe you. You don't have one ounce of proof, and I will make sure you get *destroyed* in court. When this is all over, I'll be suing *you* for defamation."

I glance over at Jackson, who is avoiding my gaze. I shouldn't be surprised though—he made his position known.

The two men grab their briefcases and leave my apartment without so much as a goodbye, taking the future of my little family with them.

CHAPTER 7

I can't stop crying after Jackson and Simon leave my apartment.

I have screwed up. This money was supposed to provide for my future and the future of my daughter. All I had to do was sign on the dotted line, and we would have been set for life. I would have been able to go to nursing school, I would have had childcare for Little Tuna, and we could've moved into a nice house instead of this studio dump in a scary neighborhood.

And now I am back at square one.

Yet I know in my heart that I didn't do the wrong thing. How could I let Simon get away with what he did? I couldn't. Every time I spent his money, I would feel sick. I had to turn it down.

About an hour after the two of them leave, my phone starts ringing. For a moment, I am hoping that it is Jackson, telling me that he believes me after all and that he's going to go with me to the police. That he wants to show me that he actually is the decent guy I believed him to be. That I'm not alone in this.

Apparently, I have become delusional. Anyway, it's not Jackson. It's my brother.

"Teggie!" His voice is jubilant. He has no idea what just happened. "I am popping champagne right now in your honor."

I flinch. "No need."

He laughs. "I know you're not going to have any champagne while you're pregnant. I'll save a glass for you for after the baby comes, okay? Or maybe we can get you some sparkling cider?"

"I can't afford it."

"Oh, come on! You're loaded now! Time to loosen the belt."

"No, it's not..." I close my eyes, not wanting to tell him everything that happened between Simon and me. God, what if *he* didn't believe me? It would kill me. "The deal... It didn't work out. I didn't sign a contract."

"*What?*" It sounds like all the air got knocked out of him. "Why the hell not?"

"It's..." I press two fingers against the space between my eyebrows, fending off an impending headache. "It's complicated. I really don't want to talk about it now."

"I don't understand. What happened? Lamar *owes* you that money. He's the father of the baby, isn't he?"

Using the word "father" to describe that man feels like a bastardization of the word. He isn't Tuna's father. He's *nothing* to her. "I can't talk about it now."

"But, Tegan—"

"I can't." My voice breaks on the words, and that's

when Dennis shuts up. He recognizes I'm serious. "I wish I could see you."

This isn't the sort of thing I can tell my brother over the phone. It's got to be face-to-face.

"I wish I could see you too, Tegan." He's quiet for a moment, probably trying to figure out what the hell is going on. I can't blame him. "Is there any chance you could come here? You could drive up here tomorrow, and you're welcome to stay in my spare bedroom as long as you want. Until the baby comes, if you'd like."

"I don't know," I say, thinking of all the miles between my apartment and Dennis's place up north. "It's a long drive."

"Of course, you're right," he acknowledges in that voice he always used when we were kids and he was about to refute what I had thought was a very valid argument. "But it'll be worth it. Because once you get here, I promise you won't have to lift a finger. I'll make sure the fridge is stocked, and I've got a wide-screen TV."

I grin. "Will you give me a foot massage?"

"*One* foot massage," he chuckles. "Redeemable at any time."

As much as I've always appreciated my own space, the idea of staying with my big brother for a few weeks and getting taken care of sounds like exactly what I need. Yes, my doctor is here, but I can find a new doctor. What I need is my brother. And possibly a foot massage.

"Actually," I say, "that sounds great."

CHAPTER 8

I'm driving out to see Dennis today, and it doesn't take me long to pack. After all, my maternity clothes fit in one small duffel bag. I had been hoping to buy more, as well as clothes for Little Tuna, but I'll never be able to afford it now.

I run into Mrs. Walden as I am carrying the duffel bag out of my apartment. She gives me her usual critical look. "I heard shouting coming from your apartment yesterday," she tells me.

Oh great. She overheard my argument with Simon and Jackson. Hopefully, she couldn't make out what we were saying.

"You know," she says, "if you entertain a gentleman caller, the polite thing to do is to keep the volume of your voice down."

"Sorry," I mutter.

I thought I wasn't going to have to live next door to this horrible woman anymore. Now all that has changed.

Actually, I'll be lucky if I get to keep living next door to her. She might get me kicked out for having a baby.

I wish I could have gotten on the road in the morning, but I couldn't afford not to pick up one last shift at the grocery store—after all, it will be my last until after I'm recovered enough from the birth to go back to work. Now the sun has dropped in the sky, and my phone says it will officially set in less than an hour. A few snowflakes have started falling, and there is a storm on the horizon, but I'm pretty sure I'm going to beat it.

My gray Ford Fusion has two hundred thousand miles on it and was owned by at least half a dozen people before I bought it at the used car lot. It has front-wheel drive only, but I'm used to driving in snow, so even if the storm picks up, it will be fine. Either way, I've got to get away this weekend. Maybe I will decide to stay with Dennis until the baby comes.

I climb into the driver's seat of the car, throwing my purse and the duffel bag into the passenger's seat. Every time I use the car, I need to adjust the seat and the steering wheel to compensate for my belly, like I'm expanding by the minute. I'm scared that in the next month and a half, I won't be able to fit at all anymore.

I punch Dennis's address into my maps app and get on the road. It's still just flurries, but it's beginning to edge in the direction of legit snow. But there's nothing I can do about it at this point.

Just as I merge onto the highway, my phone starts to ring. I glance down at the name on the display—it's Dennis.

"Hey, Tegan," he says. "Any ETA?"

"I'm just getting on the road now. I…I picked up an extra shift today."

"Just getting on the road now?" He doesn't sound thrilled. "Okay, well, don't make any stops. It's already started snowing, and you need to beat the storm."

"Don't worry. I'll be there soon."

"You got everything? Did you pack my flask?" he asks me.

"Got it in my purse."

When he turned twenty-one, his buddies bought him a titanium flask, which he managed to leave here last time he visited. When I shook it, the contents swished around inside, but the smell of anything alcoholic now makes me so ill, I couldn't bring myself to empty it out. Hopefully, it won't spill in my purse.

"Now, Tegan," he jokes, "you better not drink it all."

I manage a tiny smile, which he can't see because we're on the phone. The silence hangs between us.

"Teggie, you've got to tell me what happened yesterday," he finally says, breaking the silence.

"It's…it's a long story. I'll tell you when I get there."

"Whatever it is, I bet you can fix it. I bet it's not too late to sign that contract."

"No," I say firmly. "There's no chance."

"But—"

"*There's no chance*."

I can almost hear him frowning on the other line. "Seriously…what happened?"

I blow out a breath. "We'll talk when I get there, okay? I promise."

"You're scaring me, Teggie."

"Don't be scared. I love you, and I'll be there in a couple of hours."

Dennis doesn't push me harder. I'm glad, because it's hard enough to drive a car when you are thirty-five weeks pregnant, and it's even harder to do it while confessing that your pregnancy was the result of a rape. This will not be an easy conversation.

But I refuse to keep it to myself. I need to tell Dennis what happened to me. Because I'll need his support when I go to the police.

I tune the radio to a pop station, and with every mile I put behind me, I feel better about the trip. The snow is coming down faster, but it still doesn't seem to be sticking to the ground. And because of the storm, the traffic is much lighter than it would ordinarily be at this hour. At this rate, I might make the two-hour trip in only ninety minutes.

I glance down at the clock display and realize I've been on the road for nearly an hour. The GPS is directing me off the expressway to a smaller road that looks like a shortcut to a second highway. My stomach rumbles slightly, and I wonder if I should stop for food. Thanks to the pressure from my uterus, my stomach is about the size of a pea, so I'm forced to eat about a dozen small meals every day. Why didn't I grab some power bars from the grocery store for this trip? I'm starving.

But no. I can't afford to get off the road now. If I do, I have no chance of making it to my brother's apartment before the storm descends on us. I'm almost there.

When I get off the highway, I realize that I have officially lost my opportunity to beat the storm. The snow is now coming down hard, and my wipers are working at full speed to keep my windshield clear. I am starting to wish I hadn't taken that extra shift and instead gotten on the road this morning, like I'd planned to. It was one thing risking my safety when it was just me, but it was reckless of me to risk my daughter's safety. I have to start thinking about things differently now that I'm about to be a mother.

The road is thick with snow and ice, and I have to turn my wipers up to the fastest speed to keep my windshield clean. I've got to get back on the highway. I look up at my phone GPS mounted on my dashboard, but it seems to have stalled out. There's a message in the corner of the screen that says "connection lost."

Damn it.

Okay, I have a basic idea of how to get back to the highway. And after I get back on, I'm going to find the nearest rest stop to camp out. I squint through the windshield, and instead of seeing signs for the highway, all I can see are trees. Have I veered off the main road into a wooded area? As I'm navigating the best I can, the sound of my ringtone fills the car. My internet is out, but the phone still seems to be working at least. I glance down at the screen and see an unexpected name flashing:

Jackson Bruckner.

CHAPTER 9

Incoming call, Jackson Bruckner.

I should be focusing all my attention on the road, but after the conversation yesterday at my apartment, it's hard not to get distracted by a call from Jackson. I don't know what he could want. He made his opinion very clear: he did not believe me.

Despite my better instincts, I take the call.

"Hello," I call out into the speaker phone.

"Tegan?" Jackson's familiar voice fills my car. "Where are you?"

"What's the difference to you?" I say bitterly. I still can't believe how he spoke to me yesterday. *Whatever you think happened, you need to put it behind you and sign the damn contract for your own good.* I had thought that Jackson of all people would believe and support me. I thought he was a decent guy.

I feel so stupid.

"We need to talk. Are you home?"

"No."

"Well, where are you?"

"Actually, that's none of your business, Jackson."

"Tegan." There's a loud crackling noise on the other line. I wonder where he's calling from. "I need to…"

But before he can get any words out, there's another crackle on the other line, and his next sentence is inaudible.

"I can't hear you," I say. "What was that?"

"Tegan," he says, "Simon is…"

More crackles. I blink at the windshield, which has turned into a mass of blinding white. "What did you say?"

"Simon told…the police and…"

My heart speeds up. What is he telling me? Why would Simon be going to the police? What's going on? I've got to find a place where I can get a decent signal.

Except where the hell am I?

I press my foot against the brake to pull over and get my bearings, but the pedal doesn't respond. I press down harder, but there's no traction at all on the road, and all I've got is front-wheel drive. I'm pretty good at driving in the snow but not in what I'm quickly realizing is a blizzard and also with a beach ball between me and the steering wheel. I pump on the brake frantically, but it does nothing.

And I'm heading right for a tree. Fast.

I turn the steering wheel in an attempt to avoid it, but the road is too slick. Nothing I'm doing is having any effect on my inevitable trajectory toward that tree. In a last-ditch effort, I press all the weight of my right foot onto the brake. That familiar electric pain shoots down my leg, but nothing happens. I'm not stopping. I'm not even slowing down.

And then a second later, the hood of my car smashes into the tree and crumples like a tin can.

CHAPTER 10

Time stands still for a full second.

Everything freezes. The moment when my front fender makes contact with the tree seems to last an eternity, and the hood of my car crumples in slow motion. For a split second, I can make out every individual snowflake hovering in the frigid air outside my windshield. The airbag inflates gracefully, like a balloon.

Then time starts up again, and I realize I am completely screwed.

The airbag did not, in actuality, inflate gracefully. It blew up in a millisecond and smacked me in the face. I think my nose might be bleeding. And because the front of the car is crushed—and it wasn't a great car to begin with—the dashboard has pinned my thighs to the seat.

The crash itself was loud, but now everything has gone quiet. The engine is silent. The phone call has been disconnected, and there's no sign of the pop station that had been playing in the background just before I got the call. There's smoke billowing out from the hood, although it's hard to say with all the snow starting to accumulate on the windshield. The wipers are frozen mid-wipe.

I pause for a moment to take inventory of my situation. I glance up at the rearview mirror, trying to catch a glimpse of my face. I can see my forehead, and there is a large lump bulging over my right eye. I must've bumped it before the airbag inflated, or else the airbag did it to me. Either way, I got a good knock on the head.

What's your name?

I'm Tegan Werner. I am thirty-five weeks pregnant. I'm twenty-three years old. My birthday is on November 20.

Okay, I still know who I am. So I don't seem to have a severe head injury at least.

Next I check my arms. I curl my fingers into fists and open them up again. I can still move them. My arms still work.

Now the really scary part—my legs.

The dashboard collapsed slightly, and my legs are pinned underneath. I try to move them, attempting to free myself and…

Nope.

My right leg moves okay, but when I attempt to move my left leg, which is the one closest to the driver's door, a white-hot jab of pain shoots up from my ankle all the way to my spinal cord. I had been complaining about that electric pain in my right leg, but this makes that pain seem like a paper cut. This is *agony*.

This is really, really bad. My left ankle is injured, possibly broken. And as far as I can tell, there's nobody else on this road. Not for miles. If there were any chance of walking for help in this mountain of snow, I can't do it now. Not with an injured ankle and while heavily pregnant.

Several years ago, my brother was in an accident just like this—also on an icy road. He broke his leg in several places so that he couldn't get out of the car, and when I rushed to his side at the hospital, he recounted that it took an hour before someone found him. *It was the scariest hour of my life, Teggie.*

It took an hour for him to be found. And that wasn't even in a storm. It's far less likely someone will come upon me now, given the snow swirling around outside with increasing ferocity. I could be stuck here all night.

Another terrible thought occurs to me. Since the moment my car made impact with the tree, I haven't felt anything from within my belly. Up until now, Little Tuna has been so active, she keeps me awake at night, pummeling me in the ribs. But now she's not moving at all.

I place my hand on the bulge of my abdomen. "Tuna?" I whisper. "Are you okay?"

There's no kick in response.

Oh no. No, no, no... I could deal with a broken ankle. But if anything happened to my baby...

And then I feel it, that tiny little fluttering against the taut skin of my belly. I hear Little Tuna's baby voice in my ear. *I'm here, Mama. I'm okay! That was scary though, wasn't it?*

Tears stream down my face. Tuna is okay. I didn't lose her in this terrible accident.

I reach for my phone, which is mounted to the

dashboard. It's difficult to do much with my legs pinned down, and the pain is increasing by the second. But I manage to work it free without dropping it. I punch in 911.

Call failed.

"Damn it!" I want to throw my phone across the car, but that won't do me any good, especially since I can't move an inch right now. I type in the three digits once again, but the call doesn't connect.

All right. This is bad, but it could be worse. Dennis is expecting me, and when I don't show up, he'll try to reach me. If he calls me repeatedly and can't get through, he'll call for help. After what happened to him, an accident will be the first thought on his mind, and he'll be frantic.

Of course, I might not be so easy to locate. I have definitely veered off the main road, and my tire tracks are quickly being obscured by the rapidly accumulating snow. Best-case scenario, it will be hours before somebody finds me here.

I had been so focused on the pain in my left leg that I was not aware of another sensation. The cold. It's *very* cold in this car. Before the crash, I had the heat on. But now the engine is dead. I don't even dare try to start it up again, because if it catches fire, I am a goner.

Can a person freeze to death in a car? Considering how cold it is at this moment, I believe it could be possible.

I do my best to wrap my coat around my midsection. I curse the fact that I didn't bother to get a coat that could even close all the way. I've got a hat and a scarf, but they're useless to me right now, packed away in the trunk of the car. It may as well be on Mars.

Oh my God, I'm going to freeze to death.

I snatch up my phone one more time. My fingers are shaking badly from a mix of cold and adrenaline, making it difficult to type in the three digits of 911, and I can barely feel my fingertips. I say a little prayer that the call will go through.

Call failed.

The snow is now falling from the sky in clumps. How long will it take for my car to be completely buried? There's no way anyone will find me before the morning, even if Dennis calls the police right now. If I wait much longer, I won't be able to get out of the car at all.

I don't have any choice. I need to try to find help. If I can walk back to the main road, I can flag down a car to take me to the hospital. At this point, it might be my only hope.

I can do this. I'm a survivor. I made it through thirty-five weeks of pregnancy without anyone's help. I turned down a ton of money for my daughter and me because it was the right thing to do. I can do this.

For Tuna.

I squirm in my seat, trying to free my legs. I've got a little bit of give on the left, which might be enough to get free. I shift, trying to move my left leg and…

Oh my *God.*

The pain in my ankle takes my breath away—it's *got* to be broken. It is so unbearable that it brings tears to my eyes. It's the worst thing I've ever experienced—worse than any contraction I've felt. And that's when I realize the reality:

I can't get free from this car.

I can't walk.

I have no food or water.

The temperature is steadily dropping as my car becomes buried under a mound of snow.

I'm going to die here.

I don't want to die. When I'm old and gray, sure, but not here—not now. There's so much I have left to live for, including my daughter. I want to see her. I want to hold her in my arms. I can't go now. It's not my time. Please, *no*.

My chest feels tight. I've been having trouble breathing since the beginning of my third trimester, but this is something much worse. That was mild, but right now, I'm having a lot of trouble sucking in a breath. This could be a panic attack, but it could also be a punctured lung from the accident. Or worse.

I close my eyes, trying to calm myself down. But when I do, I see Simon's face. His gray eyes staring into mine as he climbed on top of me. *No, no. Please stop, Simon.*

I'm going to die out here, and my last memory is going to be of that man.

But then I see it.

A flash of light. It dances before my eyes. The thought occurs to me that maybe my lung really did get punctured and I am on the brink of death. Maybe this light is the light I'm supposed to walk toward.

No. It's not. It's a headlight.

Oh my God, it's another car! I'm saved! I let out a sob of relief.

I summon all my strength to slam the palm of my hand down on the horn of the car, and the sound blasts into the raging storm. No way I'm letting this car go by.

I hit the horn again, and the headlights grow brighter. The car is coming closer—they see me.

I can see in the rearview mirror that it's a green pickup truck. That's even more good news, because it doesn't look like it's going to get stuck in the snow like my Ford. The truck slows to a stop right behind my car.

I expect the driver to kill the engine, but instead, they flick on their high beams. Bright light floods the car, and all of a sudden, I get an uneasy feeling in the pit of my stomach. It's hard to see the truck anymore because of the bright light, but I can make out a shadow emerging from the vehicle.

It's a man. An extremely large man. And he's coming toward me, an object gripped in his right hand.

CHAPTER 11

This man is terrifying.

As he gets closer to my car, his features come into focus. He's well over six feet tall, and even with a coat hiding his body, I can tell that he's strong. He's got a black hat stuffed over his head, and most of his face is concealed by a thick beard. If you saw someone who looks like him hitching a ride on the side of the road, you would never, *ever* pick him up. He's the "murder you and dump your body in a swamp" type.

And he's coming right toward me.

He raps on my window with his knuckles, his dark eyes peering into my car. My heart is thumping so hard, I feel like I'm going to pass out. Tuna is kicking me hard in the ribs.

Mama, be careful! I don't trust that man!

I squint out the window, and the man holds up the object in his right hand to show me. I realize now it's a shovel. Without further explanation, he starts shoveling the snow that's apparently blocking my door from being able to open.

In the past, when I had to shovel my car out after a big storm, it would always take me forever. But this guy clears away the side of my car in less than a minute. He puts down the shovel and raps on the window again. It takes me a second to realize what he wants me to do.

He wants me to unlock the door.

Be careful, Mama!

I don't want to unlock the door. I'm completely helpless right now, and although I need to be saved, I don't want to be saved by this man. But at the same time, what am I supposed to do? Stay in the car and freeze to death?

So I hit the button to unlock the door.

The man pulls the car door open. As soon as the door swings open, the temperature inside the vehicle drops at least twenty degrees with the windchill factor. Snowflakes drop onto my face and hair.

"You okay?" the man asks me. His voice is deep, close to a growl.

I swallow. "No. I can't get out. And…" I take a deep breath, knowing this next admission will reveal how helpless I am. "I think my ankle might be broken."

The man's eyes sweep over the inside of the car, assessing the situation. When his gaze falls on my belly jutting out of my open coat, his eyes widen slightly, but he doesn't comment. He reaches down and presses a button that slides the seat backward. The pressure on my legs eases up.

Now that I'm free, I try again to move my left leg to get out of the car. Just like before, the pain is overwhelming. My eyes start watering. "I can't move my leg."

The man seems to be frowning, although it's hard to read his facial expressions with that huge beard covering his face. "I'll carry you back to my truck," he says gruffly.

I want to protest, but there's no other option. I can't walk. I can barely move. If he doesn't carry me, I'm not leaving this place.

"What's your name?" he asks me.

I consider giving a false name, but what's the point? He doesn't need my name in order to hurt me if he gets it in his head to do so. "Tegan."

"Hank," he grunts, although he says it as if slightly annoyed by the human tradition of assigning names to people and animals.

Considering the fact that a blizzard is raging around us, Hank is eerily calm. When he slides one of his beefy arms under my legs, I nearly scream with pain. So he stops. He waits for the wave of pain to subside before he attempts to lift me again. He finally raises an eyebrow at me, and I nod to give him permission to keep going.

The good thing about being rescued by a man who is so terrifyingly large is that he has no problem lifting me along with the five gallons of fluid my body is retaining as well as Little Tuna. He doesn't even grunt. I feel 100 percent secure in his arms, like there's no way he could possibly drop me. He carries me through a snowdrift that looks several feet high, and he wrenches open the passenger door of his truck.

"Could I lie down in the back?" I ask.

"No," he says without further explanation.

He helps me get into the passenger seat, and as awful

as the pain in my ankle is, the worst part is knowing that I am going to have to do this again in reverse when I get to the hospital. But I can't think about that. I'm not going to die buried in my car in a blizzard—I can handle some pain.

"Can you grab my purse?" I ask Hank. "It's in the front seat of my car."

He glances back at my car, which looks like it had an avalanche fall on it. No wonder he brought a shovel to get me out. "Yeah, okay."

"And my duffel bag?" I add.

He has every right to tell me to go to hell, that he's not trudging back to my car to get all my crap, but he just nods.

The car is blissfully warm, and some of the sensation returns to my fingertips. My toes start to tingle and then burn, although the sensation is largely overwhelmed by the throbbing in my left ankle. I watch as Hank carries my luggage and my purse back to his truck, and he dumps them roughly in the back seat before climbing into the driver's seat next to me.

Inside the car, Hank pulls off his waterproof gloves and tugs off his hat, which is wet with snow. The hair on his head is clipped short and not nearly as unruly as his beard. And he's slightly younger than I thought too—maybe late thirties. He has no expression whatsoever on his face, which makes me very uneasy.

"You buckled?" he asks me.

"Uh-huh."

Without further comment, he gets the car moving. He navigates slowly and carefully through the mounting snow. I wonder how far we are from the hospital. Now that the cold isn't distracting me anymore, the pain in my legs is escalating.

"Which hospital are you taking me to?" I ask.

He doesn't answer me. And now I realize that the trees surrounding us are growing thicker by the second. It doesn't seem like we're going back to the main road. It seems like we're going deeper into the woods.

"Which hospital are you taking me to?" I ask again, more insistently this time. I try not to let a note of alarm leak into my voice.

"I'm taking you to my house."

My stomach drops. "Excuse me?"

"It's just up the road. We'll be there soon."

"But..." I squint through the windshield at the increasingly dark and desolate stretch of road that we're driving through—barely even a road anymore. "I'm injured. And...and I'm pregnant. I need to go to the hospital."

He doesn't answer this time. He just keeps driving deeper and deeper into the woods, to a place where nobody will ever find me.

Panic mounts in my chest. I should never have unlocked the door for this man. He's taking me up to his deserted cabin in the middle of nowhere, and the surrounding area is now buried under two feet of snow. And with my injured ankle and giant belly, escape will be near impossible. I'll be his prisoner as long as he wants me to be. I thought what Simon did to me was bad, but what is about to happen will be far worse.

This man is going to kill me.

But not before he does whatever he wants to me.

CHAPTER 12

I've got to get away from this man.

My life and the life of my unborn child depend on it. But since I'm in his truck, in the middle of a blizzard, while my ankle is possibly broken… Well, I am completely at his mercy. The only thing I can do is try to appeal to him.

"Please take me to the hospital." My voice is edging on hysterical as tears well in my eyes. "I…I have money I can give you…"

I don't have money. Well, I have a few dollars but not enough to tempt him. But I'm desperate.

"Try to stay calm." Hank's eyes are pinned on the road, his expression unreadable under that huge beard. "We'll be there soon."

"Please!" Tears jump into my eyes as I clutch my belly. "Anything you want. I swear. I need to go to the hospital…" I glance back at my purse in the back seat. I've got my bottle of pepper spray in there, but it doesn't do me any good up in the front seat. I bet he knew it when he threw it back there. "Please. *Please* don't hurt me."

He doesn't answer me. He keeps on driving, his expression eerily blank.

I shift in the seat, which sets off another wave of pain in my ankle, and I have to breathe through it. I stare at Hank's profile, wondering if I have any chance of defending myself against him. If there were ever a time to do it, it would be now, while he's distracted by the road. But if I attack him now, we'll crash again, and then I'll be just as bad off as I was before he pulled me from my car.

No, it's hopeless. I clutch my belly, my breaths coming faster and faster. This man is going to hurt me, which is bad enough, but what about my baby? She's counting on me to protect her, and I have screwed up royally.

I don't even realize I'm hyperventilating until my fingertips start to tingle. Oh God, what am I going to do to get away from this man? I've listened to enough true crime podcasts to know where this is going. Soon we'll be in his dungeon, and then it will truly be hopeless.

The truck skids to a halt in the slippery snow, although I don't see anything resembling shelter. Why did we stop? Where is this secret den that will serve as my torture chamber? Wherever it is, it's clearly very well hidden from view. Nobody will ever find me there.

Oh God. Oh God oh God oh God oh God…

Hank throws the truck into park. Slowly, he swivels his head to look at me. In the shadows of the vehicle, with half the beard obscuring his face, he is nothing short of terrifying. He could strangle me right now, dump my body in the snow, and nobody would know.

"Tegan," he says in an even voice, "the nearest hospital is ten miles away. If I try to drive you there, my truck is going to get stuck, and then both of us are going to be in big trouble."

I stare at him.

"I'm going to take you to my house," he continues, "and we'll see if we can call for an ambulance from my landline." He levels his eyes at me. "I won't hurt you."

I don't know if he means it or if he's just saying it to lull me into a sense of false comfort. It's not like I can trust the word of this giant man I met in the woods. But I have to go along with this—I don't have a choice. "Okay."

"Now can you let me focus on driving safely?"

"Yes."

Without further discussion, Hank puts the car back in drive. He does have a point that the road is completely covered in snow, and even his big pickup truck is struggling. We really need a snowplow. Hopefully, they can send one with the ambulance.

A few minutes later, a house comes into view. I had expected a tiny one-story shack that was barely a single room, but this is a real house, with two stories and a chimney blowing smoke into the snow-streaked sky. It's definitely not some cave where he'll violate me and leave me to die. That said, it's not a *nice* house. It looks old, and the wood on the outside is splintered, and it could use a good coat or two of paint. This cabin looks like it's seen better days, although it's hard to tell what kind of shape it is in, given the amount of snow caking nearly every inch of it.

Hank pulls his truck up right in front of the door and kills the engine. "I don't know if the power is still on, but my wife is keeping the fire going, so it'll be warm."

I feel a sudden rush of relief. "You have a *wife*?"

For the first time since I met him, a smile twitches at the corners of Hank's lips. "I sure do. And Polly used to be a nurse, so she'll make you feel comfortable until the ambulance gets here. Now just wait here a minute, and I'll tell her what's going on."

Hank climbs out of the car and goes up the five front steps to the porch and fits his key into the front door. I wait there for a moment as he disappears inside the house. I wonder what he's telling his wife. I wonder what sort of woman is married to a man like that and what she'll think of him bringing home a pregnant stranger with a possibly broken ankle.

A minute later, Hank comes back out of the house but this time with a woman at his side. His wife—*Polly*. She's wearing a pea-green woolen coat paired with a white beanie with a puff ball at the top. She steps into the snow in her knee-high boots, and when she gets close to the window of the truck, I can make out the braid swinging behind her back, her green eyes, and the freckles sprinkled across the bridge of her nose. Her face is very pale, which I assume must be from the cold.

Maybe this will be fine. After all, I won't be here long.

CHAPTER 13

Hank carries me out to the sofa in their small living room and sets me down as gingerly as he can. I have to hand it to him; he's making an effort to be gentle, although the pain is still horrible. It's so bad that a sweat breaks out on my forehead, despite the fact that the living room is pretty chilly.

Polly crouches down next to me as I squirm to get comfortable. "Tegan, right?"

I swallow. "Yes."

"I'm Polly." She waves her arm around the room, which is illuminated only by the fireplace and the flickering candles. "As you can see, our power has gone out."

I wipe a strand of wet hair from my face. "What about the phone lines?"

She shakes her head. "Sorry. They're out too."

I groan. "Oh God, what am I going to do? I need to get to a hospital."

"The power and the phone lines will probably come

back in the morning," Polly says. "And the roads will clear out too."

Tears gather in the corners of my eyes. "I think my left ankle is broken. I need to go to the hospital. *Please*."

"We're not going anywhere in this storm," Hank barks in his gruff voice.

He's right, of course, but his declaration causes me to burst into hysterical tears. Hank's expression darkens—he's irritated with my reaction, but it's not like I can help it. Polly looks over at him with her lips pursed together. She seems like she wants to say something to him but then thinks better of it.

"Tegan, honey," Polly says, placing her warm hand on my ice-cold one, "I'm a nurse, and I'm going to make sure you're okay tonight. And then in the morning, we will get you straight to the hospital."

Polly's tone is calm and soothing. Immediately, my tears start to subside like a faucet is being turned off. She must be an incredible nurse.

"Hank," she says, "let's get some blankets for Tegan."

The giant yeti of a man stares at me, writhing on his sofa, before speaking. "We should put her in the basement."

An alarm bell goes off in the back of my head. "The *basement*?"

Maybe it's my imagination, but there's a flicker of fear on Polly's face, although it quickly vanishes. "We actually…um…we had the basement converted into a hospital room when my mother was sick. There's a great hospital bed in there, a bathroom, and everything you could need."

"I'd rather stay here," I say weakly.

Hank lets out an annoyed grunt. He shoots Polly a look, and she flashes me a plastic smile. "The sofa isn't very comfortable," she says. "You'll never be able to sleep here."

While that may very well be true, the thought of being taken underground in this already remote cabin makes me feel ill. "I'll be fine."

"Tegan, honey," she says in her soothing voice, "I know what you're thinking. But I promise you, by around midnight, you are going to *hate* this sofa. It's lumpy, and it's got springs sticking out of it. You'll never get comfortable, especially with that big old belly. We have an expensive hospital bed paid for by insurance in the basement, and that's where you want to spend the night. Trust me. And then first thing in the morning, we'll get an ambulance over here to take you to the hospital."

I bite down on my badly chapped lower lip. I've been on this couch for only a minute, but there's already a spring biting into my lower back. A jolt of electric pain shoots down my right leg. I hate to admit it, but she's right. "Okay, fine," I agree.

Hank has to carry me, because walking has become impossible. He mutters something under his breath before moving closer to me again. Now that he's not wearing his coat, I can appreciate how very large and strong this man is. And when he easily scoops me off the sofa, I catch a whiff of wet snow and something else. Motor oil, I think.

He carries me down the long flight of steep stairs to their basement. I am so utterly helpless being cradled in his arms, and despite having agreed to this, I feel a sense of doom as he descends each step. Even with a broken ankle and the snow outside, when I was upstairs, it felt like I could leave when I wanted. But now that I'm down in the basement, escape is much more difficult—if not impossible.

But I can't worry about that. Polly assured me in the morning they would call 911. Everything will be fine.

Polly follows us downstairs with a flashlight, which allows me to make out the contents of the basement. As promised, the room contains a hospital bed, reclining thirty degrees from an upright position. By the bed, there's a seat with a bucket attached, which looks like it could have been used as a toilet. She shines the flashlight to illuminate a bookcase filled with magazines and paperbacks—whoever last occupied this room must have liked to read. The scent of alcoholic sanitizer permeates the air.

But in spite of the innocuous contents of the room, there's something disturbing about this basement. It's so quiet and still. And *dark*—without Polly's flashlight, it would be pitch-black. And on top of the chemical smell, there's another odor that lingers in the room. One that's hard to put my finger on at first, but then I finally figure it out. It's the sickening smell of decay.

Like someone died down here.

Hank lays me gently on the hospital bed. It's much colder down here than it was upstairs, and a chill goes down to my bones. It's still more comfortable than the couch though.

"Are you okay?" Polly asks me.

"It's really cold." My teeth are chattering. "You don't have a fireplace down here, do you?"

She shakes her head. "I'm so sorry, no. But we've got tons of blankets."

Polly goes into the closet in the corner of the room and retrieves two heavy blankets—one down and one wool—and she sends Hank upstairs to grab more. "Can I pull off your boots?" she asks me.

I hesitate. "Yes. But please be careful."

She pulls off my right boot without much trouble. But the second she attempts to remove the left, the pain is like nothing I ever experienced. I let out an ear-piercing scream that echoes off the empty walls.

"Oh my God," I gasp. "That *hurts*."

"We need to get them off."

"No." I shake my head so vigorously the bed trembles. "Leave it."

Polly shines her flashlight on my left boot, her lips pressed together. The thought of her trying to take that boot off again makes me physically ill. I would rather be stabbed in the eye with an ice pick.

"I'm a nurse," she reminds me. "We need to see—"

"*Leave it*."

I don't care what she says. Nobody is taking this boot off. Polly finally sees in my eyes that I mean business and backs down. Her gaze softens as she looks at my bulging abdomen.

"How far along are you?" she asks.

I place a hand protectively on my belly. I feel a kick, reminding me that despite the sorry state of my ankle, my baby at least is okay. "Almost eight months."

"Wow," she says softly. "Almost at the finish line."

My chest tightens as it occurs to me that the stress of my accident could send me into early labor. What will I do if that happens here? Polly might be a nurse, but that doesn't mean she knows how to deliver a baby—especially one that is premature. And even if she could, the last thing I want is to give birth to a baby *here.*

"Boy or girl?" she asks, distracting me from my escalating panic.

"Girl. It…it's my first."

"How wonderful for you." Her face fills with tenderness. "What a blessing."

"It…it wasn't exactly planned."

"Still. I'm sure she will be very loved."

I shift in the bed. I hit a button that supposedly would make the head of the bed elevate, but then it hits me that it wouldn't work with the electricity out. I guess I'm as comfortable as I'm going to get. I attempt to shift again, which sets off an excruciating wave of pain in my ankle.

"Polly," I gasp, "do you…do you have anything for pain?"

She blinks. "I can give you Tylenol," she says. "Nothing else is safe to take in pregnancy."

Tylenol? For a broken ankle? Is she *out of her mind*? But then again, she's right. I'm pregnant—I can't pop a bunch of pills.

"Fine," I mumble. "I'll take the Tylenol."

"I'll go get it for you right away."

"Thank you, Polly." I manage a smile that I'm sure is crooked. "Also, could you bring me my purse? Your husband put it in the back seat of his truck."

She winks at me. "Sure thing. I'll be back in a jiffy."

"Can…can you please leave the flashlight down here?"

The smile on her face wavers for a moment. She looks up in the direction of the door to the basement, where her husband disappeared a few minutes ago, her lips turned down. “Of course,” she says as she hands it over. “I’ll be right back.”

And then Polly disappears up the steps to the first floor of the house, leaving me alone in the dark basement with only the glow of the single flashlight to keep me company. As I lie in the hospital bed, surrounded by that sickening stench of decay, I can’t help but wonder if Polly’s innocent story about her sick mother was true. I cringe, remembering how Hank insisted that I be brought down here and Polly reluctantly going along with it. I suddenly wish I had refused.

What if this basement was used for a different purpose? What if I am not the first visitor to lie in this bed?

I wonder if the last person to occupy this bed made it out alive.

CHAPTER 14

It's a relief when Hank drops off the extra blankets and then disappears upstairs. The man may have saved my life, but I don't feel comfortable around him.

There's something about the way he looks at me—I don't trust him. Or maybe it's the fact that he's so damn *big*. And he has that frightening beard concealing half his face. It's possible I'm being unfair to people with beards, but I always feel like they're hiding something.

Right now, I'm starting to doubt if there are any good men out there at all besides my brother, but either way, it's clear that Hank is not one of them. And the sooner I can get away from him, the better.

Polly comes down the stairs shortly after, shining another flashlight into the small basement room. She's got my purse slung over her shoulder, and she's got a bag of something else in her other hand. All I can think is that I hope she's got some Tylenol in the bag.

"How are you doing?" she asks me.

"Terrible," I say honestly.

I hate being in this basement. The windows are nearly blacked out with snow, and it feels a bit like I'm in a tomb. The room might be perfectly fine on a bright and sunny day, but it's nothing short of terrifying when every piece of furniture is shrouded in shadows. I can't believe I have to sleep here. All I want is to get to a hospital.

I push my hands against the mattress, trying desperately to get comfortable but only setting off another sickening wave of pain in my ankle. What are the consequences of not getting a fracture fixed right away? Does it mean that it will never heal right? What if I can't walk right again after this? What if it needs to be *cut off*?

I can't think about that. I will survive this. Tuna and I will be fine.

Polly fishes around in the bag she brought and pulls out a bottle of Tylenol. "I'll give you two of these. That should take the edge off."

I highly doubt it, but it's better than nothing.

She hands me my purse while she goes to the bathroom to fill up the glass she brought for water. I rifle around inside, dismayed to find that Dennis's flask spilled a bit and my whole purse stinks of whiskey. My heart sinks further when I can't locate my phone. I must've forgotten to put it in my purse after I tried to call for help. It's probably all the way back in my car, which is buried under several feet of snow.

The idea of being stuck in this basement and not having access to my phone makes me very uncomfortable. I feel disconnected. But there's nothing I can do. I'll be out of here by the morning at least.

"Here you go!" Polly sings out as she emerges from the bathroom with a big glass of water and two pills in her palm.

Even though I don't really believe it will help, I snatch the two tablets of Tylenol and swallow them with a big gulp of water. The meds might not relieve my pain, but the water feels really good sliding down my throat. I hadn't even realized how thirsty I was. I end up gulping down the entire glass.

Polly smiles at me. "My, you were thirsty, weren't you?"

"I guess I was."

"Better?"

I don't know how I could be when I swallowed the pills two seconds ago. "I could use a shot of whiskey," I say.

Polly doesn't quite smile back at my sorry attempt at a joke. I'm half tempted to chug from that flask in my purse just to ease the pain.

She reaches over to take the glass from me, and that's when her sleeve slides back to reveal a deep red bruise on her wrist. The appearance of it is shocking. It's the sort of angry bruise made by somebody clamping their hand around a wrist and squeezing as hard as they can. Polly notices me noticing the bruise and quickly pulls her sleeve back down, her face flushed.

Damn it. I *knew* Hank was a bad guy, and now I've got proof. That asshole beats his wife. How could he do that to her?

"I'm going to light some candles for you around the room." Polly avoids my eyes as she speaks, clearly uncomfortable. "That way, you won't have to use up the batteries in the flashlight."

"Thank you."

Like Hank, Polly appears to be in her late thirties or early forties. She is a bit too skinny for her frame, which makes me wonder if she gets enough to eat around here, and up close, the long braid running down her back looks dry and limp. Yet she moves around the room lighting candles with a determined efficiency, which reminds me of the sort of nurse I'd like to be someday.

How could her husband hurt her like that? I'll have to try to help her when I get out of here. Of course, it's not like I'm in any shape to help anybody right now. But maybe, somehow, we could help each other.

My thoughts are interrupted by a swift kick in the ribs. Little Tuna has woken up, and her foot is wedged firmly under my rib cage. Just when I thought I was as uncomfortable as I could possibly be.

Polly looks concerned. "Are you okay?"

"Fine..." I attempt to reposition Tuna's wayward leg with my hand. "The baby just likes to kick me right in my ribs."

"That just means she's healthy."

"Yes, but sometimes I wish she weren't *quite* so healthy, you know?" I laugh weakly, although the sound dies on my lips when I see Polly's expression. I make note of the fact that Polly is a no-nonsense type of nurse who doesn't appreciate joking around when it comes to health issues. She's a professional. "I just mean... This pregnancy has been so uncomfortable. You know what I mean."

"Mm-hmm," she says.

"Do you have children?"

"Oh, no," she says. "It's too busy for that right now. Maybe someday."

I think of the giant fists of her husband and the bruises on her wrist. I wonder if she's ever lost a pregnancy. Or more than one.

"I don't blame you for waiting." Tuna shifts in my belly, finally taking the pressure off my ribs. "Like I said, this wasn't exactly planned. I guess I'm ridiculously fertile."

I wish I weren't quite so fertile. As much as I know I'll love my baby once I hold her in my arms, this isn't in any way how I planned to become a mother for the first time.

"Your husband must be excited though," Polly says.

I almost tell her that I'm not married and that Tuna was the result of an unfortunate one-night stand. Or worse, that the baby's father drugged and assaulted me. But what if she doesn't believe me, the same way Jackson didn't believe me? I don't want this woman judging me like everyone else does. Just for tonight, I'm going to pretend I'm like everyone else. Married, with a loving husband who is excited to be having our first child together.

"Yes," I say dully. "He's very excited."

She smiles at me. "What's his name?"

Great. Now I have to come up with a name for my fake husband. "Jackson," I blurt out before I can stop myself.

I don't know why I said that. I'm still furious at him for the way he treated me. The way he *handled* me.

"I bet he's real handsome," she remarks. "After all, you're so pretty."

I manage an uncomfortable smile, because right now, I feel the opposite of pretty. "I guess. I think he is at least."

"What does he do for a living?"

Hmm, what sort of job should I give to my fake husband? May as well stick close to reality. "He's a lawyer."

"How wonderful! It's a very stable career, perfect for supporting a family."

"Yes. It's… He's great."

Polly squints through the darkness at my legs. "Would you like a pillow under your legs? The bed usually elevates them, but that's not going to happen with the power out."

"Um…" It would feel good to have my legs higher up, but the thought of moving them makes me almost nauseous. "I don't know…"

"They're going to swell up quite a bit if you don't."

"Okay. Sure."

Polly is very gentle about propping my legs up on a couple of pillows. It is intensely painful, but after she's gotten me elevated, I do feel just a tiny bit better.

"So," she says brightly as she fluffs my pillows, "where were you headed in this storm?"

I groan, angry at my own stupidity. "I was going to visit my brother. He's a ski instructor upstate. I was supposed to leave earlier, before the snow got really bad." I rifle around my bag one last time, hoping to find my phone stuffed in some pocket I didn't check before. "He's going to be worried sick when I don't show up."

"I'm sure the phones will be working by tomorrow."

I inhale sharply, taking in the vanilla scent of the candles. It reminds me vaguely of Simon's cologne, which makes me cringe. "Yeah…"

She frowns at me. "Have you eaten anything? Are you hungry?"

A minute ago, I would have said absolutely not. But now that I am a little more comfortable in the bed, an empty gnawing sensation in the pit of my stomach gets my attention. *I'm hungry, Mama! When are we eating?* "Well…I don't want to put you out…"

"It's no trouble! I'm not going to let you starve." There's a determined look in her eyes when she says that, which makes me wonder if her husband might feel differently on the matter. "I could fix you a sandwich."

"That would be great. Thank you."

"Of course. What would you like?"

All at once, I'm at the point where I could just about eat dirt off the floor. "Anything is fine. A sandwich, cold cuts, whatever."

Polly stiffens. "You shouldn't eat cold cuts during pregnancy. You could get a listeria infection that could kill the baby."

I knew that. Of course I knew that. But with all the horror of the last several hours, I just plain forgot. "Right. Of course. What about…tuna fish?" Even now, I'm still craving tuna.

She frowns. "Tuna has *mercury*."

"Yes, but my doctor said a little bit is okay…"

"Okay, I guess so," Polly says, but she sounds a bit disappointed, which makes me feel a stab of guilt. As a nurse, she's trying to give me advice for the sake of my baby. But a can of tuna should be fine—my doctor said so.

I hesitate. "Also…"

Polly raises her eyebrows. "Yes?"

"Would *you* bring it down to me, not Hank?" I smile apologetically. "He…he makes me a little nervous."

For a moment, I worry I've said the wrong thing. I have surely insulted Polly. Then again, she has to realize that her husband is terrifying. And from the looks of her wrist, he's got a temper too. I won't be here long, but I want to spend as little time as possible with that man.

Thankfully, she nods in understanding. She gets it. "No problem."

I let out a breath. This is going to be okay. I'll spend the night here, and then they'll take me to the hospital. The doctors will fix my ankle, and everything will be fine.

As Polly goes up the steps to make my sandwich, I rummage around in my purse a little more. My wallet is in there at least, as well as my credit cards—although they are all maxed out anyway. But as I search the depth of my handbag, I noticed one other thing that's missing.

My pepper spray.

CHAPTER 15

While I'm waiting for Polly to return with my sandwich, I try to ignore the thumps and thuds filtering through thc thin ceiling.

Mostly, it sounds like people walking around. I learn to distinguish Hank's heavy footfalls from Polly's lighter steps. Occasionally, I can hear voices, but they're extremely muffled. I can't make out any words, just that one voice is male and the other is female. They sound tense.

And then there's a loud crash.

I don't know what's going on up there, but I'm certain those muffled shouts and swears are coming from Hank. I brace myself, waiting for a female scream, but nothing comes. I suppose Polly is used to Hank yelling at her. God, I hope making me that sandwich hasn't gotten her in trouble.

When Polly returns with the tuna sandwich, the smile on her face is strained. She sets the plate down on a tray next to the bed. I'm absolutely famished, but unfortunately, there's a much more pressing need right now.

"Polly," I say meekly.

"Yes?"

"I…uh…" I avert my eyes. "I have to pee."

Polly steps back, her intelligent eyes assessing the situation. It takes her half a second to recognize how hard it would be for me to get to the bathroom. "I'll grab you a bedpan."

It's absolutely mortifying for Polly to help me with the bedpan, but she is professional about it, which makes it easier. She's obviously done this before. I thought it would be difficult to pee without gravity helping, but my bladder is so full, it doesn't end up being an issue.

"Thanks so much," I say when we're done. "I…I'm really sorry."

"Don't be sorry," she says firmly. "It's not your fault."

As she helps me get repositioned, that familiar squeezing sensation grips my uterus. I'm barely eight months pregnant, but I've heard trauma can trigger an early labor.

"Are you having a contraction?" she asks.

I consider the question as the contraction subsides. It doesn't feel any different from the ones I've been having for a while now. "No."

Her shoulders sag in relief. She's probably glad she won't be forced to help me deliver a baby tonight. *You and me both, Polly.*

She readjusts my legs in the bed, and I can't help but notice my knee seems swollen too. When she moves my left ankle even a millimeter, I clench my jaw to keep from crying out. There is no way my ankle isn't broken. I'll probably need surgery to fix it.

"Polly," I gasp. "Do you think… Could I have something stronger for pain? The Tylenol…it's useless. I might as well be taking sugar pills."

"You're pregnant," she says kindly.

"I know, but…" I squeeze my eyes shut. "You have no idea how bad this pain is." I swallow a lump in my throat. "I don't even know how I'm going to be able to sleep at night. And having this weight on my abdomen… I can't even *try* to reposition myself."

"I can help you. Do you want more pillows?"

"No. *No*." My words come out sharper than expected, and Polly jerks her head back in surprise. "I'm sorry, but this is *my* baby, and it's *my* choice. If you have something stronger, I want to take it. I'm going to lose my mind if I have to lie here like this all night."

Polly is quiet, looking at me thoughtfully.

"Please, Polly." My voice breaks as I imagine the endless night ahead of me—trapped in this bed with my giant belly weighing me down, my ankle in agony. "I'm begging you. Just…just one pill. You have something, don't you? You must…"

"Yes," she finally says. "I do."

CHAPTER 16

The room is very dark when Polly leaves.

There are small windows up close to the ceiling, but all of them are obscured by several feet of snow. I shine the beam of the flashlight Polly gave me at the white powder pressed against the solid glass, wondering if those windows even open. When the beam of light reaches the corner of the room, it reflects the web of a spider that is apparently sharing this room with me.

Lovely.

I don't like this basement and its antiseptic smell, which tickles my nose. The room is only partially finished, which means that while the floor has been paved, the walls are still naked brick. It makes me feel like I am being kept in a dungeon.

My left ankle throbs painfully, and I close my eyes, breathing through the pain. The boot is starting to feel uncomfortably tight, but I'm terrified of taking it off. Not just because it's going to be unimaginably painful but because I'm scared of what my foot looks like under there. Considering how much it hurts, I'm terrified we'll find a bone poking out through my skin.

Of course, if it is, it's better to take the boot off and let Polly try to clean it up and disinfect it, but I can't bear to do it. Anyway, I'll be at the hospital by tomorrow morning.

I'm itching for my phone. These days, I'm never without it for very long. I'm sure there are about a hundred missed calls from Dennis—he plays the part of a laid-back ski instructor, but he can be an anxious mama hen at times. Why did I take that extra shift at the grocery store? If I hadn't, I'd be sitting at his apartment right now, drinking a glass of… Well, not wine, obviously. Maybe some hot cocoa.

I wonder if Jackson tried to call me again. Not that I have any desire to hear from him.

I had thought I'd left my phone behind in the car by accident, but I'm not so sure anymore. I always keep that pepper spray in my purse, and the fact that it's gone means someone took it out. When Polly was down here talking to me, Hank must have gone through my purse and removed both my phone and my pepper spray. I don't know why he did it, but there's no *good* reason he would have robbed me of both a means of communicating and defending myself.

Although I can't hear what's going on upstairs, I can make out the thump of footfalls above my head. Every time Hank's heavy boots stomp on the floor, my body jolts.

The door to the basement finally cracks open, and footsteps descend the stairs moments before Polly comes into sight. I can just barely make her out in the candlelight, which makes her face seem even more drawn and tired.

"I have your pills," she tells me.

I feel a stab of guilt. Little Tuna and I are connected by our bloodstream, and anything I take, she'll get a dose of too. There is a small list of medications that are safe to take during pregnancy, and I'm sure whatever Polly has in her hand is not on that list.

But for God's sake, my ankle might be broken. I'm only human.

"What did you bring me?" I ask.

"It's Dilaudid."

Dilaudid. I don't entirely know what that is, but it sounds powerful. I imagine the horrible sharp pain in my ankle subsiding to a dull ache. A dull ache sounds like heaven right now. I only question for a moment why this couple has powerful pain pills stocked in their medicine cabinet.

"I'll get you some water," Polly says.

She goes to the bathroom with my water glass, her braid swinging behind her head. She emerges with half a glass of water and two little white tablets in the palm of her right hand. Her sleeve is rolled up just enough so that I can see the ugly maroon bruise peeking out.

"Thank you so much," I say as I snatch the pills from her hand. "I really appreciate it."

"Of course. You're clearly in a lot of pain, and you… you shouldn't have to suffer."

I had been about to pop the two pills into my mouth, but something stops me. Yes, I'm in pain. But Tuna isn't in pain. Tuna is counting on me not to put anything in my body that could hurt her, and here I am, popping pain pills like candy.

"What's wrong?" Polly asks. "Don't you want them?"

I do. God, I do. If it were just me, I would be swallowing them down and begging for more. I'm that desperate for relief. But it's not just me anymore. I have to protect Little Tuna. It's bad enough that being drugged is what landed me in this situation to begin with. How could I even contemplate putting something in my body that will alter my mental state? I need to stay sharp—for both of us.

"You know what?" I say. "I think you're right. I'm not going to take this. It's not good for the baby."

"You're not? I thought you were in pain." She seems surprised.

"Yes, but…" I squeeze the wool blanket on top of me, my fingers biting into the fabric. "I can handle it. I'll be all right."

She looks at me for a long moment without saying anything. Finally, she nods in approval. "Okay. You can keep them in case you change your mind again."

"I won't," I say as I drop the pills onto the dresser next to the bed.

"Is there anything else I can get you?" she asks.

Her tone is so gentle. I can just barely make out the freckles across the bridge of her nose. Once again, I cringe at the thought of that ogre upstairs grabbing her by the wrist hard enough to create those dark bruises. I hated the way he shouted at her loud enough for me to hear through the ceiling. Like me, Polly is the victim of a terrible man. I feel a sudden surge of kinship with this woman.

We have both been through something terrible. And for both of us, it is far from over.

"Actually," I say, "you haven't seen my phone, have you?"

She looks at me blankly. "Your phone?"

"My cell phone," I clarify. "It was in my purse, but I didn't see it when I looked through it."

"Oh." She tilts her head to the side. "Maybe it fell out in your car?"

"Maybe..."

Or maybe her husband went through my purse and took it. Right around the time he took my pepper spray.

"I could look for it," she offers. "I'll see if it fell out in Hank's truck."

"Thanks. I appreciate that." I hesitate, wanting to share something with her that isn't a lie about my fake husband. "By the way, I think what you do is amazing. I'd been saving up for nursing school."

Her eyes light up. "Oh?"

"Yes. I've wanted to be a nurse ever since I was a little girl, when I got the chicken pox and I was sick for weeks," I say, knowing full well that a lot of people look at me and still see a young girl. "Some kids want dolls to pretend they're babies, but I pretended my dolls were my patients, and I would nurse them back to health."

She laughs. "I can relate."

"I still want to do it, but..." I rest a hand gingerly on my abdomen. "It might take longer than expected."

That's an understatement. I can't imagine a time in the future that I'll be able to go to nursing school. Even before I totaled my car, it was a pipe dream. And now...

"It's hard to go through school when you have a baby," Polly acknowledges.

I drop my eyes. "Like I said, this wasn't in the plan. Unfortunately, babies happen." You can't always stop them, even if you're given half a chance, which I wasn't.

"Yes," she says softly. "I understand."

I can't help but wonder what trapped Polly in this marriage. She said she didn't have children, so it couldn't be that. But Hank must have some sort of hold on her. There must be a reason she stays, in spite of his abuse.

There's always a reason.

CHAPTER 17

I don't sleep well.

That's no surprise. It would be far more surprising if I did sleep well. Between the baby doing gymnastics in my belly and my injured left ankle, I basically just drift off for an hour at a time, then I jolt awake, squirming in agony. I can almost feel the bags under my eyes.

And every time I dream, I dream of Simon. After retrieving that memory, it's all I can think of, especially at night. I dream of lying in a bed, just as helpless as I am now, and begging him to stop.

Please. Please, no. Please get off. Please…

But in my dream, he never listens. And in real life, he didn't listen either. I have the proof of that growing inside me.

I wish I hadn't remembered. I was happier before I knew. Sure, I was having nightmares, but they would have gone away with time. Now I'm haunted by what he did to me. And the fact that Jackson didn't even believe it.

Will anyone believe me? As Simon pointed out, I have no proof it wasn't consensual sex.

But I have to do something. I can't let him get away with it. I can't let him do this to another girl if there's a chance I can stop it.

I almost took the two pills on my nightstand about a hundred times last night. I was that desperate. But I resisted. Those two little white tablets are still lying there. I'm proud of myself. One day, I'm going to tell Tuna about how I went through an entire night with a broken ankle and no pain medication and no nightlight—just for her.

But now it's morning—I can tell by the tiny bit of sunlight peeking through the snow-covered windows close to the ceiling. And there's another piece of good news. When I press the controls for the bed, it moves. And that means the power is back on. It also means I'm getting out of here.

"Hello!" Polly sings out as she flicks on the basement lights and descends the stairs. I don't know why she is so damn chipper, but I don't care anymore. "How are you doing?"

"Been better," I manage. My mouth feels painfully dry, but there is one physiological urge that is overwhelming all the others. "Can you give me the bedpan please?"

My bladder is about to burst. Well, maybe not burst, but I am definitely one sneeze away from soiling myself.

My leg is pulsing with pain as Polly helps me shift to get the bedpan underneath me. The last time I used it, I waited until she left the room, but the second the bedpan is in position, I let go. I can't hold it one more second.

Polly disappears into the bathroom to give me some privacy, and then she comes out to take the bedpan and empty it. She is humming to herself the whole time. As she reaches behind her head to smooth out her braid, I notice the bruise on her wrist has now turned a vivid scarlet.

"So should we call 911 then?" I ask her.

I hadn't realized in the candlelight last night how many freckles she has on her face, but they're more visible under the overhead lights. And under the freckles, she is almost deathly pale. "911?"

I swipe a strand of sweaty hair from my face. The heat must have kicked on during the night, and my entire body feels like it's covered in a layer of moisture. "I need to get to the hospital."

"Oh." She frowns apologetically. "Well, the phone lines are still dead."

What? It didn't occur to me that this was even a possibility. "What about your cell phones?"

"We don't get cell service out here!" She laughs as if such a thing were preposterous. "I'm so sorry, but I'm afraid you're stuck out here for a little bit longer."

"Can't Hank drive me to the hospital then?" I'm not excited to be alone with that man, but it's better than the alternative.

"I'm afraid not. There are several feet of snow on the ground, and we're buried. The plows won't get here till late this evening or maybe even tomorrow."

Oh no. No, no, *no*. I am not staying here one more day. Is she out of her *mind*? I look up at the windows near the ceiling, which are indeed still blocked off by snow.

"I'm just in a lot of pain," I say, more sharply than I intended. "Can't you hurry things up?"

Polly blinks at me in surprise, and I feel a stab of guilt. I didn't mean to speak to her so angrily. She already has a husband who abuses her—she doesn't need another person in the house who is pushing her around. We are supposed to be allies.

"I'm sorry…" I say quickly. "I just feel like that's a long time to wait for a plow to arrive. Can't they come sooner?"

"I…I wish it could be different, Tegan. I truly do."

"I don't mean to complain," I say again. "I'm just in so much pain."

"Yes," she murmurs, her brow wrinkling. "I can see that."

I open my mouth, not sure what to say. There's clearly nothing Polly can do for me at this point. She can't move mountains of snow. But I also know that I need a doctor to look at my ankle if I ever expect the fracture to heal right, and I need them to make sure Little Tuna is unharmed. At the very least, I need somebody to get this boot off my left leg.

"Look," she says. "As soon as we get our phone service back, we will call for an ambulance. Or if they plow before that, Hank will take you straight to the hospital. I'll make sure of it."

"Okay. Thank you," I murmur.

"And of course," she adds, "we'll be sure to let Jackson know you are okay if you can give us his number."

I look at her blankly. "What?"

"Jackson," she says again. "Your *husband*?"

Oh, right. I forgot all about my stupid story.

Jackson—my handsome attorney husband. Why didn't I just tell her there was no husband on the horizon? But now I'm embarrassed to admit it, so I have to continue the lie. "Yes, sorry. Thank you."

"Now"—she smiles at me, forcing on a mask of cheeriness—"what would you like for breakfast?"

I lie there for a moment, waiting for Tuna to talk to me and tell me what she would like to eat. But she is silent.

"Maybe just some toast," I murmur.

"Coming right up!" Polly chirps.

Polly darts up the stairs, taking them two at a time. It isn't until she disappears behind the basement door that I recall the pepper spray missing from my purse. And the phone that I couldn't find even though I'm sure I dropped it back in my purse.

What if the snow is already plowed? What if the phone lines are working?

What if Hank doesn't want me to leave?

CHAPTER 18

I've spent most of the morning crying.

Not continuously. I haven't been sobbing like a waterfall ever since Polly told me I can't go to the hospital yet. But every thirty minutes or so, a lump forms in my throat, and before I know it, the tears are flowing freely.

The latest thing that got me crying is a game of solitaire.

Polly fetched me a deck of cards and set up a tray in front of me. The television is all snow, so I needed something to occupy my attention instead of just concentrating on how intensely uncomfortable I feel. I dealt out the cards to play a game of solitaire, but it got me thinking about how Dennis was the one who taught me how to play solitaire when I was about five years old. He loved playing cards, and he taught me every game there is to know. From go fish to Texas Hold'em. He also tried to teach me to shuffle one-handed, but

I never quite got the hang of it no matter how many times he showed me.

And of course, that got me thinking about Dennis. About how he's probably pacing his apartment right now, sick with worry. I wish more than anything that I had my phone. Even if the cell service is spotty, eventually maybe a text would have gone through and I could let him know I'm okay.

I wonder what is going on with Simon Lamar. I wonder if he's worried that I'm going to the police to report him. I wish I could have heard what Jackson was trying to tell me right before I crashed.

Around noon, Polly comes down the stairs with a plate of food. Whatever it is smells incredible. I wipe the tears from my eyes and gather the cards into a pile so that I can eat.

"Lunchtime!" Polly calls out.

She deposits the plate on the tray in front of me. It looks like a barbecue chicken sandwich, with the bread perfectly toasted, and a side of french fries. She even cut the sandwich into quarters.

"Thank you," I say. "It smells great."

"You're very welcome!"

I glance from my sandwich to the snow-covered window. "Has the plow arrived yet?"

The smile drops off her face. "I'm so sorry, no. Not yet."

Polly picks up the deck of cards to get them out of my way, but I reach for her wrist to stop her. It's the same wrist with the purple bruise on it, and she winces when I touch her.

"Sorry," I say. "Could I keep the cards though? It's really boring here, you know?"

"Yes, of course." She pauses, still holding the deck of cards. "Would you like to play a game together while you eat?"

"Sure." Anything is better than more solitaire. "What do you like to play?"

Polly taps her finger against her chin. Her nail is bitten down to the quick. "I know gin rummy, old maid, crazy eights..."

In spite of the pain, I almost laugh. It sounds like the selection of games that somebody's grandmother would enjoy playing. But then again, there's something very old-fashioned about Polly, with her flower-print sweater and long braid. "Let's play gin rummy."

Polly deals ten cards each while I take a bite of the sandwich. It tastes just as good as it smells. I used to enjoy cooking, and I always imagined that when I got married, I would make fancy meals for me and my husband.

Of course, that will never happen now. I'll probably never get married. Why should I? From now on, it's just going to be me and Tuna.

"You're an amazing cook," I tell her as I pick up my cards. It's true—this barbecue sauce might be the best I've ever had.

Polly settles into a little wooden chair next to the bed. "I have to be. Hank is hopeless in the kitchen. We would starve!"

At the sound of her husband's name, I get a sour taste in my mouth, despite the delicious food in front of me. How can she talk about that monster with a smile on her face?

"Maybe Hank should learn how to make his own

food," I say as I pick up an ace from the deck. "You don't have to do everything for him."

"But I enjoy cooking for my husband," she says quickly. "He works hard, and he deserves a big, hearty meal when he gets home. There's nothing wrong with that, is there?"

"No. It's just that... Don't you work full-time as a nurse already?"

"Actually..." She looks down at her hands with their fingernails trimmed down to the quick. "I don't work full-time. Or...at all. Not at the moment anyway. Hank... He wanted me to stay home. He prefers it that way."

An alarm bell is sounding off in my head. Isn't that what abusive, controlling men do to their wives—force them to give up their jobs so they don't have their own source of income? Judging by the sad expression on her face, she clearly did not want to give up her job, but I'm sure he wouldn't have wanted Polly's coworkers to catch sight of the bruises he left on her.

Instead, she's all alone out here, in a dilapidated cabin in the middle of nowhere. She doesn't even have a cell phone to connect her to the outside world.

"I just think you shouldn't have to feel obligated to cook him every meal," I say. Polly is staring at me, so I joke, "That's what microwaves are for."

"Microwaves!" Polly looks affronted as she discards a card into the pile in front of us. "Oh no, Hank would never... I mean, I don't think microwaves are a good way to cook meals. Do you make dinner in the microwave for your husband?"

No, I don't. But to be fair, I don't have a husband.

"I'm joking," I finally say as I pick up an ace from the pile. "But... Hank is... I just think he's lucky to have you."

I study her face for her reaction to my statement. It's clear to me that Polly has been brainwashed into believing she must wait on her husband hand and foot. She even gave up a job she loves for him. She gets that sad look on her face again, and when she opens her mouth, I'm certain that she's going to confide in me, but then she shakes her head, almost to herself. Clearly, the time is not yet right.

I want to help Polly. Nobody was there for me, but I can be there for her at least.

"Hank and I are lucky to have each other," she finally says as she inspects the cards in her hand. "How about your husband? He must be excited about the baby."

I push back a surge of anxiety in the pit of my stomach. It's going to be so hard doing this on my own. Sometimes it feels completely overwhelming. At least before, I thought I was going to have money to help me out. But now it's going to be just me and Tuna—dead broke. "Yes, of course he's excited."

The words come out a touch more defensive than I intended.

"That's wonderful," she says. "Have you been married long?"

Little Tuna presses an elbow or a knee against my rib cage, and I squirm, which sets off that electric pain in my right leg. "About two years."

"And now a baby on the way." She discards a king, which I snatch up. "How perfect."

Once again, I am seized by the urge to tell her

everything. Like, everything. About meeting Simon in that bar, the positive pregnancy test, and then the gut-punch recollection of the way he drugged and raped me. The only people I have told are Simon himself and Jackson, who didn't believe me. But I'm certain Polly would believe me. She will get it.

Maybe I'll tell her after this game is over.

"Gin," I finally say as I lay the cards down on the table.

Polly frowns. She looks over at my cards on the table and shakes her head. "That's not gin."

"Yes, it is."

"No, it's not." She taps on the cards. It's like she's speaking to a child. "Ace is low only. Queen-king-ace is not a run."

"Ace can be high or low."

"No." She purses her lips. "Ace is low only. I've been playing this game my whole life, and I've never played it that ace can be high."

"Sorry—that's not how I play it."

"Well, that's just cheating." For a moment, her eyes flash. She seems quite upset over what is just a silly game of gin. But a second later, her shoulders relax. "Okay then. You're the guest, so we can play by your rules."

I nod, wondering how often she is forced to compromise in this house. She seems very used to it.

My left ankle throbs painfully within the boot, and I wince. Polly notices my reaction and follows my gaze to my left foot. "We really should get that boot off," she says in a worried voice. "If there's an injury under there..."

"No," I say before she can finish her thought. I don't want to see what's under the boot. It's like when I was a kid and I used to drop a heavy book on a spider to kill it, and then I was afraid to move the book for days after—I'd finally get Dennis to do it for me because he had no problem killing insects or wiping up their guts. But I couldn't help it. I knew whatever was under that book wasn't going to look good, and I was scared to see it.

I feel exactly the same way about my ankle. Considering how much it hurts, there's nothing good under that boot. Eventually, I will have to take it off, but for now, I want to postpone it as long as I possibly can.

"It's your decision," Polly says gently. "But I'm worried about it. At the very least, your leg is so swollen that the boot is putting pressure on your nerves and blood vessels. If it were me, I would want it off."

"It's fine. I'll be at the hospital tonight or tomorrow morning."

"Yes," she says slowly. "That's true." She clears her throat and nods. "Do you want to play again?"

"That's okay." I let out an exaggerated yawn. "I'm feeling pretty tired anyway. I might take a nap."

Really, I was trying to get rid of Polly. But as I let out another yawn, I realize that I actually am very tired. I suppose it makes sense, considering I hardly slept last night, and also, I'm growing another person inside me.

She flashes me a sympathetic look. "Of course. Go to sleep. I'll shut off the lights on my way upstairs."

"Actually," I say, "I'd rather keep the lights on."

She nods. "Of course. Whatever you want."

And then she collects my empty plate of food and climbs the stairs. Just before shutting the basement door, she forgets my request and flicks the lights off. I am plunged back into darkness.

"Polly!" I call out. "Polly!"

But she can't hear me. She's already gone, and I'm worried if I keep yelling, Hank might be the one who responds. And the truth is it's easier to sleep in the dark.

So I close my eyes and allow myself to drift off.

CHAPTER 19

I wake to the sound of a resounding thud coming from up above.

At some point between when I ate lunch and now, the sun dropped in the sky. All the windows are still completely obscured by snow. I look down at my watch and squint at the display in the dark. I can just barely make out the numbers.

It's eight o'clock. Oh my God. How could I have slept that long?

I often hear voices coming from upstairs but rarely that loud. Hank is shouting at his wife, and it's not for the first time. Even with a wall between us, he sounds *furious*.

Polly says something back. I can't make out her response, but there's a tremor of fear in her voice that makes me cringe.

And then the stomping of Hank's boots, which shakes the entire house down to its foundation. I hold my breath, waiting for the sound of the basement door opening. Will he come down here? That man terrifies me.

If he were to try to hurt me, what could I do? I can't get away from him. He can easily take his anger out on me. I'm trapped. Even if I weren't pregnant with a broken ankle, Hank could easily overpower me—I'm a sitting duck.

But no. The footsteps grow softer and then vanish completely.

It's only after the footsteps disappear that my heart rate slows back down to normal. I rub my eyes, trying to push away the fogginess in my brain. I don't think I've slept that many continuous hours since my third trimester started. And what's more, I still feel tired. I have a groggy, hungover feeling, and my mouth feels dry and disgusting.

I think back to the lunch Polly made for me. I had attributed the sour taste I had in my mouth to our conversation, but now I'm not so sure. Is it possible she slipped something into my lunch, and that's why I slept so long? Is she capable of doing something like that?

No, I doubt Polly would do that. After all, she was reluctant to even give me pain pills, for fear it might hurt the baby.

But Hank might.

Now that my eyes have adjusted to the dark, I can see a plate of food sitting on the tray next to my bed. It looks like spaghetti and meatballs, although it's obviously been sitting there for a long time, given that the sauce looks like it has congealed. Polly must have come down and left it for me while I was in my coma-like slumber.

The meal looks like it has seen better days, but I would devour it in seconds if my bladder weren't such a distraction. I need the bedpan—like, five minutes ago.

"Polly!" I call out. "Polly!"

I hope she's within earshot. I don't know how much longer I can hold it. I'm not sure what would be worse—the humiliation of wetting the bed or the agony of having to get out of bed for her to clean the sheets. But then again, I'll be on my way to the hospital soon anyway.

"Polly!" I shout one more time. I'm worried.

There were a lot of loud noises coming from upstairs, and Hank was shouting. What if Polly is injured? What if she can't get down to me because she's huddled in a corner, bruised and bleeding?

Finally, the basement door creaks open, and the light flicks on. I brace myself for the sound of Hank's thunderclap footsteps, but instead it's Polly's softer footfalls. She's okay.

"Good evening!" Polly sings out in a strained voice, her braid swinging behind her head as she descends the stairs. A second later, she comes to a halt at the foot of my bed.

And I gasp.

Polly has purple bruises under both her eyes. Hank's temper is truly out of control.

But then she comes closer, and I realize that she doesn't have bruises under her eyes after all. It was just a trick of the shadows in the room. Instead, she has dark circles under her eyes that appear even more prominent on her pale face. She looks exhausted. I don't detect any new bruises on her body either, but clothes can hide a lot.

"Did you have a nice rest?" she asks me. "I came to bring you dinner, but you were out like a light!"

"Yes, sorry about that," I mumble. "And…um… could I…use the bedpan? Right now?"

"Of course!"

She reaches over to pull my tray out of the way for me, and maybe it's my imagination, but she seems to wince with the movement, as if she has an injury to her arm or ribs. But I could be mistaken, because she's humming to herself as she goes into the bathroom to retrieve the bedpan. As she's rifling around in there, I feel a tickle in my throat. I give a little cough, and beyond my control, a trickle of urine comes out of me. It was inevitable, but it's still mortifying.

"Polly," I say when she emerges from the bathroom carrying the bedpan, "I…um…I think I wet the sheets a little."

"Oh!" She barely bats an eye. "No worries. I had put down a paper chuck on the sheet below you. I'll just swap it out."

And she does, without making a big thing of it. It's a damn shame Hank made her give up her job as a nurse. I feel guilty that she has to take care of me on top of everything and then I had the gall to yell at her for the snow not being plowed quickly enough. The poor woman is already dealing with enough.

"Thanks so much, Polly," I say after she's helped me off the bedpan.

Polly winks at me as she pulls the blankets off my bed, replacing them with fresh ones. "You're very welcome. Would you like me to heat up your food for you?"

"No, that's fine." I stick my fork into the cold spaghetti. "I don't want you to go to any trouble."

"It's no trouble at all."

"I'm sure you've heard this before," I tell her, "but you have this unbelievable nurturing nature. When you have children, you're going to be such an incredible mother."

She freezes in the middle of folding one of the blankets. Her face stiffens but then finally relaxes into a smile. "Thank you. That's very kind of you to say."

"I'll probably be an awful mother." I stuff a big bite of spaghetti into my mouth and take a moment to chew. "I have no idea what I'm doing. I don't know how to cook yet. I don't even know how to put on a diaper. To be honest, I'm terrified." And I won't have a husband or boyfriend around to help me, although I don't want to reveal that what I told her earlier was a lie.

"I'm sure you'll get the hang of it," Polly murmurs. "Everyone does."

"Maybe..." I let out a yawn. I really feel like I just got hit by a truck. To be fair though, that isn't far from the truth. "After I finish eating, could Hank drive me to the hospital?"

She shakes her head. "I'm afraid not. The plow must've gotten delayed—there was quite a lot of snow. Anyway, we're still stranded out here unfortunately."

My mouth falls open. It didn't even occur to me that I might not be able to leave tonight. "But what about the phone lines?"

"Still down."

She avoids my eyes when she says it, and I can't help but wonder if she's lying. What if the phone lines actually *are* working? What if the area around their cabin has already been plowed?

Yet they still won't let me go. *He* still won't let me go.

"I'm so sorry," Polly says anxiously. "I'm sure the plow will be here first thing in the morning."

I try to adjust myself in bed, which ends up being a huge mistake. Even just that slight movement sets off a white-hot blinding pain in my ankle that takes my breath away. There has got to be something seriously wrong—something even worse than just a fracture. For a second, I can't even think straight.

"Tegan?" Polly's voice sounds far away. "Are you okay?"

"Please..." My voice is hoarse. "I've got to get to a hospital. Please. There's got to be a way."

"There is," she says. "I swear, we'll get you there first thing in the morning."

"Please, no." Tears prick at my eyes. "I'll lose it before that happens. Please."

She flashes me a sympathetic look. "I know. I understand what it's like to...I understand. Really. I promise—we're doing all we can."

The tears spill over onto my cheeks, and now I'm ugly crying. I can't stop sobbing and sniffling. In seconds, there's snot all over my face, and my shoulders are heaving. I'm dimly aware of Polly holding out a tissue, and I take it to dry my eyes and dab my runny nose. Her brows are knitted together as she watches me.

"We will get you out of here," she assures me. "It's only one more night. You have my word."

But that's what she said last night.

"Don't worry," she adds. "The snowplow will be here soon."

Bullshit.

"Are we really trapped by the snow?" I lift my swollen eyes to meet hers. "Or is that just what Hank is making you say to me?"

She opens her mouth, and at first all that comes out is a surprised squeak. "It's the truth," she finally says, although her voice lacks conviction.

I wonder if I can appeal to her. She's in trouble, just like I am. Could the two of us escape here together? Will Hank let that happen? After all, he's more than a match for scrawny, undernourished Polly and me with my awkward belly and broken ankle. He could keep us here with one hand tied behind his back.

"Look," she says, "we'll get you out of here soon. But in the meantime, we really should get that boot off your ankle."

"No," I gasp. The idea of wrenching my ankle from the boot is unthinkable. "Please don't touch it."

"At least let me help you get your pants off. They're filthy."

She has a point. The bottoms of my leggings got a good dose of snow and mud, and they have dried stiff and crusty. But I can't imagine how she'll manage to get them off. "I don't know..."

"I've got a pair of shears in the bathroom," she says in that chipper voice of hers. "I'll just cut them off. Easy peasy."

"Fine."

Polly goes into the bathroom and returns with a pair of pink-handled scissors. She pulls back the covers to reveal my stylish (*not*) gray sweatpants that I had pulled on under my dress. With practiced efficiency, she slices through the fabric with her shears, making a final snap through the waistband. When she's cut the front completely open, she gently slides them out from under me.

The majority of the pain is centered on my left ankle, but my entire leg is swollen. I mean, both my legs were puffy even from before the accident, but the left is noticeably tighter and slightly pink. Between the weight of the boot and the swelling, it's hard to even move the leg. And when I try, the pain is excruciating.

My ankle is definitely broken. I can't even pretend it might not be. And instead of having it set in a cast or repaired surgically, I am lying in this bed while it heals completely wrong. This delay in getting medical treatment might cost me my ability to walk normally.

"Now isn't that better?" Polly says with a clearly forced smile.

"Uh-huh," I say dully.

Maybe Polly is telling the truth about everything. Maybe the plows are on their way and I'll get to the hospital tomorrow, and they will make this right. Modern medicine is an incredible thing. And I can still feel Tuna moving, so she must be fine. Tomorrow morning, I will go straight to the hospital.

After all, Hank can't keep me here forever.

Can he?

I lift my face to look up at Polly's eyes, staring down at me. Her eyes are bright green, but in the dim overhead light, they look much darker. And a sudden terrible certainty goes through my head:

I'm going to die here.

PART 2

THE DAY BEFORE THE CRASH

CHAPTER 20

POLLY

As I chop carrots on the kitchen counter, I sense I am being watched.

There aren't many people out here. Hank and I own a home well off the beaten path—the seller advertised it as a house, but I'd really call it a large cabin. We live in a rural part of Maine, and there's only one other house within a mile of ours. Even our postboxes are all the way down the road, since the postman won't drive down the one narrow, unpaved road to our home, which tends to get overgrown with trees and branches that Hank cuts down himself when they get out of control. We don't get many visitors—not these days.

Now more than ever, I appreciate the solitude. But when Hank is at the shop, I get nervous. This is the kind of place where if you screamed, nobody would hear you.

I lay down the knife on my red cutting board. I've now peeled and chopped three large carrots, which will be added to the stew Hank and I will eat for dinner. I turn around, and two blue eyes are staring at me through the window on the back door. Then I hear it. Three soft raps in succession.

I cross the room and flip open the single lock on the back door. I pull the door open, and there's a little girl standing there, her dark-blond hair gathered into two messy pigtails. Her giant eyes stare up at me.

"Sadie," I say. "What are you doing here?"

She shifts between her gray sneakers, which look like they were once white. There's a little hole over her big toe on the right sneaker, although really, she should be wearing boots in this weather. "Daddy isn't home yet. Can I help you make dinner?"

I hesitate, even though I know I'm ultimately going to let her in. Sadie's father specifically told me he didn't want her to come here after school, but I've been letting her do it anyway. Sadie is seven years old, and in my opinion, she's far too little to be making the half-mile trek back from the bus stop on her own, but her father doesn't seem to care, and her mother cares so little that she doesn't live here at all. I told Mitch I would pick Sadie up every day—God knows I don't have anything better to do these days, ever since The Incident—but he didn't like that idea. Actually, his exact words were *Mind your own goddamn business, Polly.*

I've never been good at that.

"Sure," I say to Sadie. "Come on in!"

As she skips into my kitchen, I mentally tick off in my head whether I have all the ingredients to make oatmeal chocolate chip cookies, because those are Sadie's favorite. But I'll feed her some stew as well before I send her on her way. The girl is far too skinny. As she slips off her winter coat, which is frayed at the sleeves, I can see all the bones jutting out in her arms. That girl is all sharp angles.

"What are you making?" Sadie asks me.

"I'm making beef stew," I say. "That's Hank's favorite."

Hank loves my beef stew, but to be fair, anything I put in front of him gets demolished and the plate practically licked clean. My husband sure can eat.

I put Sadie to work dropping the stew ingredients that I chop into the simmering pot. When she's a little older, I'll teach her to chop vegetables herself, but she's too young now. Still, she likes to watch me. She crinkles her tiny nose as I light a candle on the kitchen table.

"Why are you doing that?" she asks me.

"I'm chopping onions," I explain. "If you light a candle before you chop onions, it burns off the toxins so your eyes don't water."

That's a tip my mother taught me when I was a girl, and we've got a ton of candles lying around since the power always goes out whenever there's a storm. It's always good to be prepared.

I've got the radio tuned in to the news. The two big stories are the snowstorm coming tomorrow—which is hardly news, since it seems like there's a snowstorm every week—and also some big merger from a businessman I've never heard of. Neither story interests me, but I like the background noise.

As I chop the onions, the flame on the candle grows brighter the way it always does. I always imagine that the toxins from the onion are feeding the flame. Sadie watches with wide eyes as the fire grows, her chin balanced on the ball of her palm. I can't help but notice the dirt caked deep into her fingernails.

When was the last time this little girl had a bath? If I had to guess, I'd say it's been a few days at least.

I instruct Sadie to scoop up the onions and drop them in the pot. I chew on my lip, watching her. "Sadie?"

"Yes?"

"How would you like a bubble bath? It'll be like a spa."

Sadie's blue eyes light up. Hank is going to kill me, but I can't let this girl leave my house without making sure she's at least achieved the minimal level of hygiene.

I turn down the heat under the pot so the stew can simmer, and I head to the bathroom to run a bath for Sadie. I don't have a real bubble bath solution, but I have a bottle of baby shampoo that bubbles up nicely when I pour it in with the warm running water. While the water is filling the tub, I allow Sadie some privacy to undress and climb in. I stand outside the door, listening to the sound of her struggling to peel off her shirt and pants.

"You can come in now, Polly!" she calls out.

I gently push open the bathroom door and find Sadie in the tub, the bubbles nearly up to her neck. The water is the perfect temperature, and she's smiling ear to ear. I pick up the clothes she abandoned on the toilet; they are stiff with old dirt. I'll throw them in the washing machine now for a quick cycle, and they'll be clean and toasty warm when she's ready to go home.

The tub is nearly full now. I reach over to shut off the water, and that's when I notice the angry purple bruise encircling her upper arm. It's the exact shape and size of a man's hand.

My cheeks burn. I used to be a nurse before The Incident, and I recognize what this must be. Mitch got a little too rough with his daughter. It's not the first time I've seen a mark like that on Sadie. I even called Child Protective Services once, but nothing came of it. Except Mitch suspected I was the one who did it, which gave him reason to hate me even more.

"How did this happen, Sadie?" I ask her.

She looks down at the bruise on her arm. "I fell."

I can't imagine how falling would cause a bruise that looks like that, but I'm not about to interrogate this little girl. I did what I could. I called Child Protective Services. It's not like I could take Sadie and rescue her from that awful man all by myself.

Could I?

No, I can't.

Sadie spends the next half hour in the bathtub. The formerly clear water turns gray, and I have to unplug the drain and turn on the faucet to let the dirty water leave the tub. I shampoo her hair for her, trying to comb through the knots with my fingers. I use a cup from the kitchen, and I have her lean her head all the way back so I can rinse out the shampoo without getting any soap in her eyes. It's the way my mother did it for me.

"Will you braid my hair like yours, Polly?" Sadie asks me.

I touch the braid at the back of my head. Over the last couple of years, especially since I stopped working, I've been wearing my hair in one long braid hanging down my back. It's not stylish, but it keeps it out of my way. "Sure. I can even French braid it for you."

"What's a French braid?"

I don't entirely know how to answer that question. "It's like a regular braid, only fancy."

Sadie's eyes light up. She definitely wants a French braid.

Just as I'm straightening up to help Sadie climb out of the bathtub, a large fist pounds on the bathroom door. My heart is in my throat as I brace myself for what's about to happen. I crack open the door, and my hulking husband is standing there, a deep crease between his eyebrows. He attempts to push the bathroom door open, but I hold my ground for once, keeping it open only a sliver.

I force my lips into a smile. "You're home early."

Hank looks down at me, his own lips turned down. I always felt too tall and gawky at five foot ten and used to envy women who were smaller in stature. But that all changed when I met my husband, who is an impressive six foot four. He's built like a lumberjack, and half his face is obscured by a thick brown beard that has gotten bushier every year over the past decade, although he swears he trims it once a week.

Hank is the sort of man who if you saw him in a dark alley, you'd run the other way.

"What are you doing in there?" he demands to know.

I slip out the door, keeping it cracked slightly. "I'm giving Sadie a bath."

Hank doesn't talk much. He doesn't like to say something if he doesn't feel like it's worth saying, and in his opinion, not much is worth saying. Before him, I dated a lot of men who liked to talk just to hear the sound of their own voice. Hank isn't like that. On our first date, I talked and talked to fill the silence, and Hank just sat across from me at the restaurant, nodding like he was hearing every word. It was the first time I ever felt like anyone was really listening.

And now all he says is "*Polly*."

"I *know*," I hiss at him. "But she was filthy, Hank."

This time, he doesn't say a word. His own shirt under his coat is stained with oil. And like Sadie, he has dirt ground into his fingernails, from his work at the auto shop we own. But he's going to go upstairs and take a shower now, like he does every day when he gets home from work. Sadie can't do that.

"She came here to find me." I fold my arms across my chest. "I'm going to have her clothes cleaned, and then I'll send her home. Mitch won't even know."

Hank lets out a long sigh, but he doesn't say anything else. After ten years of marriage, I know exactly what he's thinking anyway. *You're asking for trouble, Polly.*

And he's right.

But I don't care.

CHAPTER 21

As I pass the door to our basement, a chill goes through me.

I've never been a spiritual person. I have always believed all that stuff about ghosts and the afterlife was a bunch of hooey. But I am like 90 percent sure that my mother's spirit is contained in our basement.

The one silver lining to The Incident that caused me to lose my job is that when my mother was diagnosed with an aggressive breast cancer two years ago, I was able to be there for her. And when she got very sick near the end, Hank and I converted our basement into a hospital room for her. We stuck in a hospital bed, a commode, a television set, and a bookcase filled with magazines and all her favorite books. She loved horror novels best of all. *There's nothing like a good scare,* she used to say.

I took care of her until the very end, and she died holding my hand.

I don't think the ghost of my mother is floating

around the basement. I haven't *completely* lost my mind. But I do feel her presence every time I walk by the basement door. And when I press my fingers against it, I swear I can feel her fingertips touch mine.

But that's the extent of my spiritual belief. I don't hold séances. I don't attempt to communicate with her spirit in any way. But I do keep the basement door closed, because I feel like that might keep her with us longer.

I miss her an awful lot. I love Hank, but there is nobody like your mother. She was a receptionist at a medical clinic, and she was the one who encouraged me to apply to get a bachelor's in nursing, even when I wasn't sure I could make it through. She believed in me in a way that nobody else did. She told me I was capable of anything.

While I'm lingering by the basement door, the sound of my cell phone echoes through the first floor. I left it on the coffee table when I was watching television, so I race over to the living room to see who's calling. I smile when I see Angela's name on the screen. Angela is my closest friend and the only other nurse from the hospital who still speaks to me regularly anymore.

"Hi, Angela," I say, grateful for a break in the perpetual silence of our home.

"Hi, Polly. How are you doing?"

It used to be that Angela was the only person who could ask me how I'm doing without it sounding like she's speaking to a mental patient. But something about the inflection in her voice right now makes me uneasy.

"I'm fine," I say. "How are things at the hospital?"

Angela and I both worked at Roosevelt Memorial since nursing school. She was the first person I met on my first day as a nurse getting oriented on the job. On my very last day at the hospital, she was the one who called Hank and told him he needed to come get me ASAP.

"Carol is retiring," Angela says.

"She isn't!"

"She is." I can feel Angela smiling on the other line. Carol trained both of us, and we always joked that she would still be working there when both of us were retired. She outlasted me at least. "I can't believe it. She's only about a hundred years old."

"Well, good for her." I consider asking if she's having a retirement party and if I should come, but I decide against it. Who am I kidding? I'm not going to any parties at the hospital. It would be far too painful. "You ready for the storm coming tonight?"

The weather forecast is calling for a blizzard, although right now, there are only a few snowflakes dusting the ground. It's coming though.

"Got a whole closet full of canned food and water," she reports.

"Same here. And Hank chopped a big pile of firewood."

Blizzards can sometimes trap us here for days, so I've learned to always be prepared. The last thing you want is to deal with the supermarket when a storm is on the way.

"There's something else, Polly." Angela's voice drops, and instantly I know what she's going to say. And all I want to do is stick my fingers in my ears. "I…I'm pregnant. I'm due in August."

I should never have picked up the phone. I should've

known this moment was coming. It's happened so many times, I've lost count—and every time is equally painful. But Angela is the last friend I have from my old life, and somehow it still hurts. "Oh..."

"I wanted you to hear it from me," she says.

I push all my dark emotions down into a pit in my stomach. "Angela, that's fantastic!" I cry. "Congratulations! I'm so happy for you!"

"Well...thank you."

"Are you having a little girl or a little boy?"

"It's a girl."

"How wonderful!" I don't know how I'm able to make my voice sound so cheerful while my eyes are tearing up. "Congratulations! Really!"

"Are...are you sure you're okay?"

"Of course!" My voice nearly breaks on the words. I've got to get off the phone quickly, because I am not going to let Angela hear me cry. "I'm just really happy for you! How wonderful. I mean, what a blessing. I didn't even know you were trying..."

"Well, I just figured with everything going on with you, I didn't want to bother you with—"

A fist raps against our front door three times, pulling my attention from Angela and her news. I jerk my head up, confused. The sun has already gone down, which means it's too late for Sadie to be stopping by. And she usually doesn't come every day, so the fact that she came yesterday means I won't see her again until at least tomorrow or the next day.

But I don't care. It's an excuse to get off the phone.

"Angela," I say, "I better get off the phone. There's somebody at the front door."

"Oh, no problem. But we'll have to talk again soon, okay? Maybe we can get together for coffee?"

"Absolutely! Just give me a call."

I press the red button on my phone to end the call. I stare at the screen of my phone, and then I bring up the list of my contacts. I click on Angela's name—her contact information has been in every phone I've had for the last thirteen years. My index finger hovers over the words "block this contact."

Then I press it. I'm not interested in talking to Angela again.

Knock, knock, knock.

Who could that be? I'm certainly not expecting anyone, and we're so far from town that it's unlikely somebody wandered here by accident. We *never* get solicitors. Hank is still at the shop, although he usually comes home around now to grab some dinner before heading back to work for another couple of hours. He often stays later when a storm is moving in to help stray motorists who get stuck. I worry about him driving in the heavy snow, but he's got his truck, and he's a careful driver.

Anyway, it's not Hank at the door. He wouldn't knock.

I walk over to the front door and check the peephole. It's Mitch Hambly from up the road—Sadie's father. He's never shown up at my door before. Is Sadie okay? I haven't used my nursing skills since my mother passed on, and I hope to God they're not needed today.

I unlock the door and crack it open. The whoosh of frigid air from outside smacks me in the face, and along with the ever-present scent of damp wood, I am hit with a strong whiff of whiskey. From the looks of Mitch's bloodshot eyes, he had a drink or two before he stopped by. His receding hair is wild, sticking up in all directions.

"Hello, Mitch." I squeeze my hands together, both because the doorway is cold and because I'm anxious. "Is everything okay with Sadie?"

"*No*." He throws his weight into the front door, shoving it all the way open so he can step inside. I can see the web of blue veins on the sides of his nostrils. The snowflakes have started to fall from the sky, and little white dots speckle his hair and shoulders like dandruff. "It's *not* okay."

I instantly realize my mistake. Mitch didn't come over here because he's worried about Sadie or wants to borrow some supplies for the storm. He's here because he's *furious*.

And he's drunk.

I should never have opened the door for him in the first place. But now it's too late. He's already stepped across the threshold of the doorframe. He's inside my house.

"Mitch." I smile as placatingly as I can. "What's wrong?"

"*You* are what's wrong." He takes a step toward me. "What gives you the right to invite my daughter into your house? I told you to stay the hell away from her!"

"Now, Mitch." I wrap my shaking hands across my chest. "There's no need to get in a tizzy. Sadie just stopped off for a short while after school. That's all."

"You gave her a bath! You washed her clothes!" He sneers at me. "Are you saying I don't take care of my daughter?"

I take a few steps back, and Mitch follows me, backing me into the living room. I nearly stumble over my own feet as I try to create distance between the two of us. Mitch's right hand is balled into a fist, his white hairy knuckles jutting out. I've already seen what he did to a defenseless seven-year-old girl. I don't want to know what he'd do to me. He's the same height as me, but he's got at least fifty pounds on me—probably more—and a lot of muscle.

"I'm not saying you don't take care of her," I say quickly, even though it's a lie. "She just wanted to try out the bubble bath. That's all."

"You're a real piece of work, Polly." His lips twist into a grimace. "You think I don't know how you went to the crazy house two years ago? I know. *Everyone* knows. You're the last person I want around my kid!"

I flinch. "Mitch, please understand..."

"I don't want to hear your goddamn excuses!" His scratchy voice echoes through my empty house. "I told you a bunch of times to stay away from my kid. And this time, you're going to learn your lesson."

As I take another step back, I search wildly for a weapon. Hank keeps a gun up in the closet in our bedroom, but I'll never make it that far, and anyway, it's not loaded—he keeps the bullets hidden in an entirely different place. I wouldn't even make it to the kitchen, where I've got a whole block of knives. My best bet might be the paperweight on the coffee table. It's surprisingly heavy, and if I clock Mitch a good one on the head, it will slow him down until I can find a better weapon.

But before I can reach for it, he grabs me by the wrist, his thick fingers biting into my skin. I try to pull free, but his grip is like a vise.

I'm trapped.

CHAPTER 22

"Let me go!"

I scream as loud as I can, even though I know full well the only house besides Mitch's is miles away. Nobody will hear me. Nobody is coming.

Like I said, nobody can hear you scream around here.

Mitch laughs. His breath stinks of alcohol even worse than his clothes. I should never have let him in. What was I thinking? I thought it would be okay because he's my neighbor, and I was worried about Sadie. And even now, as he tightens his grip and the bones of my forearm grind together, I'm worried about Sadie. What did he do to her when he found out she came to our house? I've got to make sure she's okay.

But I don't know how I'm going to do that when this man is about to break my arm in two. And that's all he'll do to me if I'm lucky.

"What the hell is going on here?"

Instantly, the pressure on my wrist eases up. I hadn't

even noticed the sound of my husband's heavy boots on the carpeting in our foyer. He's tracked mud all over our carpet, but I couldn't care less, because I've never been happier to see Hank. He's standing over Mitch, towering over the other man by several inches, looking like he wants to smash his face in.

Even in his drunken haze, Mitch knows enough to be afraid of my husband. He retreats by a few steps. "Your wife is nosing around in our business. I just came over to tell her to stay the hell away."

Hank cracks his knuckles, and the sound resonates through the living room. Mitch looks like he's about to tinkle in his pants, and I can't say I don't enjoy it.

"You listen to me," Hank says in the low growl of a pit bull about to pounce. "I don't want to *ever* see you in my house again. I don't want to *ever* see you within ten feet of my wife again. Do you understand?"

Mitch opens his mouth, but no sound comes out.

Hank's eyes darken, and he steps in front of Mitch, blocking any chance of escape. "*Do you understand?* Because if you don't, we've got a big problem here, Mitch."

My husband is not a violent man by nature, but that rule doesn't apply when it comes to protecting me. When we were married barely a year, he smashed a man's nose at a bar for getting fresh with me, and he ended up spending two months in prison for assault. It was a miserable two months for him—something he's not eager to ever repeat—but he still means business right now. He would still break every bone in Mitch's body if he did anything to truly hurt me.

"Yes." Mitch's voice is now a wheeze. "Yeah, I got it."

"Good. Now say you're sorry for scaring Polly."

"Sorry, Polly," he mumbles. "Sorry, Hank."

Hank steps away from the door, allowing Mitch to scramble back outside. I doubt Mitch will cause any trouble for us again. Unfortunately, I don't know if the same is true for Sadie. If Mitch couldn't hurt me, will he take it out on her? I make a mental note to find a way to check on her tomorrow.

Hank slams the door shut behind Mitch. He throws the lock and then turns to look at me. Not surprisingly, there's a deep groove between his thick brown eyebrows.

"Polly," he says, "didn't I tell you to stay away from them?"

"Yes." I rub at my wrist. Tomorrow, there will be bruises on it, as dark as the ones on Sadie's arm. "But she came here to see me. What was I supposed to do?"

He shakes his head slowly. "You tell her to go home. That's what you do."

"But—"

"You tell her to go home, Polly." His tone leaves no room for argument. "From now on, that's what you do."

"But he's hurting her!" Tears leap into my eyes at the thought of what he does to that little girl. What kind of justice is there in the world if a man like that has a beautiful, wonderful daughter who he doesn't even care about? "He's hurting her, and we're not even going to do anything about it?"

Hank looks at me for a long time, and I can tell he's choosing his words carefully. "Polly, we called Child Protective Services. They investigated. It's none of our business."

"But—"

"*It's none of our business.*"

"But, Hank, how could you turn away a little girl who needs our help?"

My husband heaves a sigh. He brushes past me and sinks into the living room sofa, which grunts under his weight. He always sits in the same spot, and now there's a permanent Hank-shaped indentation in the cushion.

"Polly." He looks up at me. "What if I hadn't come home now? What if I had been working late? What would have happened to you?"

Hank is staring up at me, and it hits me at this moment that my six-foot-four, two-hundred-and-fifty-pound husband is scared. He's scared of what would've happened if he hadn't come home when he did. He's scared of what might happen the next time.

"Okay," I finally say. "I'll stay away from them."

Hank holds out his arms, and I fall into his lap, wrapping my arms around his thick neck. Hank means well. He's the best man I've ever met—there's nobody better. And he would have been a great father. It's all my fault he'll never get to experience that.

"I'm sorry," I murmur into his neck.

He squeezes me tight to his warm body—he radiates heat better than any furnace. "Just stay away from them. That's all."

He doesn't even know what I'm saying sorry for.

CHAPTER 23

I wish my husband wouldn't stay out so late in a blizzard.

Despite the fact that I begged him not to, Hank went back to the auto shop after dinner. He often goes back in the evenings, because we need the money from the extra business. Plus, the shop is right off a main road, so he gets a lot of motorists filling up their tanks just as the storm is starting.

I made him cross his heart he'd be back before the snow started coming down heavy, but when I peer out the window, there's got to be close to a foot of white powder on the ground. The power went out half an hour ago, and I've been walking around the house lighting candles. Yet there's no sign of Hank's truck.

Where is he? What if he got in an accident?

Or worse, what if Mitch went after him? Without a weapon, Mitch isn't any sort of match for my husband. But Mitch seems like the sort of man who might have an arsenal of rifles stashed away somewhere. If Mitch went after Hank with a gun…

My stomach clenches at the thought. Without Hank, there wouldn't be any reason at all to go on.

Just as I'm starting to panic, Hank's green truck appears in the distance. He's driving slowly and carefully like he always does when there's a storm, but even so, his tires are struggling. He pulls up in front of the house, but instead of getting out right away, he lingers behind in the cab of the truck.

What's he doing in there?

I squint into the darkness, trying to see through the windshield of his truck. It almost looks like…

Is there someone with him?

After a good minute, Hank climbs out. He stuffs his black beanie on over his short hair and tromps through the foot-high snow to get to our front door. Before he can reach the door, I've thrown it open for him.

"Where have you been?" I blurt out.

Hank glances back at his truck behind him. "Found a woman on the road. Told me her name is Megan—no wait, *Tegan*. She got in a bad accident—hit a tree. I had to pull her out, and I think she's hurt. Something with her ankle."

"Oh!" I clutch my chest, but I shouldn't be surprised. Hank is always stopping for stranded motorists on the road, even though it doesn't mean getting paid. On any given road trip, he ends up changing at least one tire for a perfect stranger. "That's terrible."

"Are the phones working? We can try to call an ambulance."

I shake my head. "The phones and the power are both out. And there's no cell service."

"Then she'll have to spend the night." He glances over his shoulder again. "Will you help me get her out of the car?"

I frown at the foot of snow covering the front of our house. "What do you need me for?"

"Well, she's hurt, and you're a nurse."

I don't bother to point out that I *was* a nurse. I doubt I'll ever get hired again.

"Also..." He shoves his hands into his coat pockets. "I think she's scared of me."

I nearly laugh out loud at that one. I admit it must have been scary to be stranded in a busted car in a snow-storm and then catch a glimpse of my yeti of a husband coming toward her.

I obligingly put on my coat and white puffball hat, then follow Hank out to the car. The woman in the passenger's seat is in bad shape. Although she's not quite a woman—more like a girl. The skin of her cheeks and her forehead is perfectly smooth and unlined. She looks like she could be in high school.

Hank carries her out to our sofa and sets her down as gingerly as he can. She's clearly in quite a lot of pain—he said her ankle is injured, and she's got quite an egg on her forehead. But one thing he didn't warn me about is that she's very pregnant. I don't notice it until her coat falls open. Her abdomen bulges out in the flickering lights of the candles I lit around the living room.

And despite how absolutely miserable she looks, I feel a sharp jab of envy.

I can't let that bother me though. This girl is injured and will be spending the night here, and I will be her host. If I can't handle that, I've got serious problems.

CHAPTER 24

Stepping into the basement of our house always gives me a wave of déjà vu. I've been down there only once since my mother died, and that was to change the sheets on the hospital bed. I expected the basement to smell like death, but it just smelled vaguely of sanitizer. Even the scent of her perfume has left the room.

Everything was just how I left it a year ago. The hospital bed is still reclining thirty degrees from an upright position. And the commode is still next to the bed, although she wasn't even strong enough to use that at the end, and I used to have to bring her the bedpan. Even the bookcase is still filled with my mother's magazines and her favorite paperbacks. Her favorite book was *The Shining*, and the one copy is so creased and dog-eared, I'm afraid if I picked it up, all the pages would simply fall out.

As Hank lowers Tegan into the hospital bed, I feel a jab of sadness in my chest. The last time I stood by this bed, I was holding my mother's hand as she slipped away. She had been in hospice for months, but somehow we'd both known this would be the day.

Hank and I were both sitting with her that morning. She looked at my husband with bleary eyes and said to him, *You'll take good care of my Polly, won't you?*

For the rest of my life, he promised. He'd said those same words at our wedding, but somehow it meant more now, at my mother's deathbed.

He eventually had to run to the auto shop because we were in no financial shape to keep it closed. And then it was just my mother and me, her cold, fragile hand clutching mine.

Don't worry, Polly, she said to me. *Someday, your family will be complete.*

She knew about my infertility problems, of course. Aside from Hank, she was the only person who knew all the sordid details. But unlike Hank, she believed that someday, I would get my baby.

Just shows she didn't know everything.

As Tegan gets adjusted on the bed, the subject of her pregnancy comes up. I'm an old hat at plastering a smile on my face and pretending to be delighted about someone else having a baby, but it gets harder every time. One of these days, I will open my mouth to congratulate someone on their baby, and I will simply be mute.

Her ankle is badly injured. It's hard to say how bad it is since she won't allow me to take off her boot, which is immensely frustrating. Imagine being a full-grown woman, on the verge of motherhood, and not even allowing a trained nurse to assess your injuries! But despite the fact that I can't get a good look at her ankle, the amount of pain she's in indicates it's likely fractured. I'd bet the farm on it.

Then Tegan starts begging for pain medication.

All my mother's narcotics are still in the medicine cabinet of the bathroom upstairs. I've got enough pills in that cabinet to kill a horse. Or even more easily, a five-foot-ten woman who weighs approximately 130 pounds whose entire life has fallen apart.

Not that I thought about it. Not *recently* anyway.

"I can give you Tylenol," I tell her. "Nothing else is safe to take in pregnancy."

She does *not* look happy about this. I would give my right arm to have a baby on the way, and she couldn't care less what she puts in her body. But there's no point in scolding her. I'm just trying to keep her comfortable for the night, so I'll be as pleasant as I can manage.

"Fine," she grumbles. "I'll take the Tylenol."

"I'll go get it for you."

Tegan asks me to leave the flashlight behind, and I give it to her, even though I hate to give up my only source of light. I have to hold on to the railing of the stairwell leading out of the basement to keep from tripping over my feet, and I climb the steps very, very carefully to get to the top. The last third of the stairwell is pitch-black. I have to wave my hand in front of me to keep from bumping into the door.

But when I get the door open, my vision returns thanks to the light of all the candles on the first floor. And I get another piece of good luck: Hank already pulled Tegan's purse and luggage out of the car and set them down next to the basement door.

She may have requested her purse, but the luggage

will come in handy too. The blankets will only do so much, and she'll be grateful to have an extra sweater instead of lying in bed with her coat on. I decide to crack that one open first.

Unfortunately, she didn't bring much clothing. Just a few shirts, underwear, a pair of pants. Wherever she was going, she hadn't planned to stay long. As I sift through the clothing, I wince slightly at a flash of pain in my right wrist. Not surprisingly, it's still smarting from where Mitch grabbed me earlier, and there's even a dark red bruise forming that will be purple by tomorrow. I've been keeping my sleeves down because Hank will be furious when he sees the bruise.

And then I set my sights on Tegan's purse. I should probably bring it down to her, but I can't resist opening it up and looking inside. The second I get it open, the stench of whiskey hits me, and I nearly have to close it up again. But I breathe through my mouth and plow forward.

Her driver's license lists her name as Tegan Werner. And when I check her date of birth, I get a surprise. I thought for sure she was no older than twenty, but she is in fact twenty-three years old.

Hank goes down to bring Tegan the extra blankets while I continue rifling around in her purse. I put back her wallet, which contains only two dollar bills. Who walks around with only two dollars? I wonder what her story is. Hank will yell at me again for not minding my own business, but I have a feeling that Tegan Werner has an interesting history.

The next thing I find in her purse is her cell phone. I swipe at the screen, but it's locked. I start to drop the phone back in her bag, but at the last second, for reasons I don't quite understand, I power it down and slip it into my own pocket.

The next thing I pull out of her purse is a flask. I unscrew the cap and take a whiff, as if there was any doubt where the smell of whiskey was coming from. It's strong stuff too—high octane.

She's chugging whiskey. While she's heavily pregnant. No wonder she was so quick to request pain medications—she clearly does not give a hoot what she puts in her body. We've got the mother of the year in our basement apparently.

I drop the flask back in her purse, my face burning with anger. Some of us would give absolutely anything to get pregnant. And other women get pregnant without hardly trying, then poison the baby before it even has a chance at life.

It makes me furious.

The next thing I find in there is a gold lighter. I don't see any crumpled boxes of cigarettes in the bottom of her purse, but I'm sure that's only because she ran out. If she's not going to stop drinking while she's pregnant, why quit smoking?

I rummage around in her purse one last time. I discover one more item that makes me very glad I took one final look.

It's pepper spray.

I slip the pepper spray into my pocket as well, nestled next to the cell phone. Not that I think that girl would hurt us, but I don't like the idea of a guest in our home having a weapon.

CHAPTER 25

Tegan has requested a tuna sandwich to eat.

I mix the canned tuna with a little bit of mayonnaise by candlelight. Tuna has mercury that could be harmful to a developing fetus, but I suppose a small amount would be okay. Not that she cares very much if she's shooting whiskey while driving.

Tegan Werner claimed she was married, but I suspect she lied. She doesn't have a wedding band after all. And when I asked her, she hesitated a bit too long. And she's so *young*.

I don't think she's married. I think she's one month away from becoming a single mother. A single mother who carries around a full flask in her purse. Who drives recklessly into a blizzard. A liar.

I flinch at the memory of her complaint about being "ridiculously fertile." Every time a woman complains to me about how fertile she is, a blood vessel in my temple comes closer to popping. *Poor me—I'm too fertile, I've got too much money in the bank, and every time I eat a slice of chocolate cake, I lose two pounds!*

Lucky me—I don't have a problem with being too fertile. In fact, Hank and I have spent every penny we had to have a child, and what do we have to show for it? Absolutely nothing.

It all took me by surprise. My mother warned me that it took her a long time to conceive me. More than ten years, and she couldn't get pregnant again after. But even with my irregular periods, I couldn't imagine that I would have trouble. So much so that I was shocked when my first pregnancy test came back negative.

Now it's eight years, three bank-shattering IVF cycles, and one failed adoption later. And it's still just Hank and me and an empty spare bedroom upstairs.

I go back to the pantry, candle in hand, to grab some crackers to supplement the sandwich, and I notice something I stuffed in the back, behind the cans of Spam and creamed corn and a useless container of prenatal vitamins. Something I hadn't thought about in a long time—not since I stuck it back there in the first place.

It's a teddy bear.

It's a brown bear with his lips sewn into a perpetual smile, clutching a heart in his hands. Hank bought it for me. Or I should say he bought it for our baby. There was one month early on when my period was late and I thought I was pregnant, and in his excitement, he jumped the gun. I left it in the bookcase in the living room, but then when it became increasingly clear that a baby wouldn't be in our future, I stuck it in the back of the pantry. I couldn't quite bring myself to throw it away.

I stare at the bear for a moment, my heart pounding.

Then I give my head a shake to clear it. There's no point in dwelling on that now.

After the tuna and mayonnaise mixture is complete, I spread it over two slices of whole wheat bread and stick them together to make a sandwich. As an afterthought, I pick up a knife and slice the sandwich into halves.

I hear a crash from the living room, then the sound of Hank swearing. He must have stumbled on a table or chair, like he often does when the power goes out. He's too large for most spaces, and our living space is small to begin with. My fingers linger on the handle of the knife, still thinking about that teddy bear in the pantry that Hank bought me all those years ago. Someday, Tegan will probably give a teddy bear like that one to her baby. And the baby will smile and gurgle happily. She might suck on one of the bear's soft ears. The way I always imagined my child would.

"Polly?"

I spin around, instinctively raising the blade of the knife. My husband is standing behind me, and when he sees the knife in my hand, he takes a step back and raises both hands in the air. "Whoa, Polly! Jesus."

I lower the knife and drop it on the kitchen table. Thankfully, it's too dark for him to see how much my hands are shaking. "You startled me."

"Sorry."

"I heard a crash in the living room."

"Oh." He rubs his elbow and winces. "Bashed myself knocking over the end table. Really smarts."

"Do you want some ice?"

"The whole house feels like it's made of ice," he

points out. He looks down at the sandwich on the counter. "What are you doing?"

"I'm making a sandwich for Tegan."

"Okay." That crease is between his eyebrows again. He's worried about me being around a pregnant woman. He doesn't say so, but ever since The Incident, he's been waiting for me to crack again. "Do you want me to bring it down to her?"

I shake my head. "No, you were right. She's terrified of you."

Hank clutches his chest like he's offended, but if he had any interest in being less scary, he could shave off the beard for starters—or at least trim it. He wasn't nearly as frightening when I first met him, back when he was in his early twenties and the beard was short and neatly groomed. He was working at an auto shop, and I was a nursing student with a shot transmission and no money in the bank.

I frantically explained the car situation to Hank, pleading with him to see if he would charge me on some sort of payment plan, although it wasn't his auto shop back then. He told me he would see what he could do, and when I returned a couple of days later to get my car, he told me he had fixed it free of charge. I tried to at least offer him something for the parts, but he wouldn't take it.

When I first met him, I had thought he was cute, and I expected him to ask for my phone number, but he didn't. I didn't know back then how shy he was around women—I couldn't fathom that a guy that big could be intimidated by the likes of *me*. But I couldn't walk out of there without showing him how grateful I was, so I offered to take him out to dinner as a thank-you. I still remember the way his eyes lit up.

There's a lot that I regret in my life. But I don't regret asking Hank to dinner that night.

Although sometimes I wonder if he regrets saying yes.

CHAPTER 26

Tegan refused the two pills I offered her for pain.

In actuality, they were *not* Dilaudid like I claimed they were. They weren't pain medications at all. I looked in our medicine cabinet for things safe to take during pregnancy, and I ended up fishing out two tablets of Benadryl. I figured at the least, it would give her a good night's sleep. And I'm sure there would be some placebo effect for her pain.

Then she ended up not even taking them. I'm glad she did the right thing for her baby—eventually. Fractured ankle or not, she shouldn't be popping narcotics.

When I come back up to the bedroom, Hank is already in bed. His short, dark hair is damp, and so is his beard.

"Did you take a shower?" I ask him. "In the dark?"

"I brought a flashlight with me. You know I can't fall asleep if I'm covered in grease from the shop."

I glance at our bathroom. "Is there hot water?"

"Nah. I took a cold shower."

I crawl into bed next to my husband and lay a hand on his abdomen. His arms and shoulders are tight with muscles from the work he does at the shop, but his belly is soft. "A cold shower, huh? That's a shame."

Hank's eyebrows shoot up. "Polly?"

He looks stunned, which makes me feel a flash of guilt. Hank and I don't have sex much anymore, and when we do, I am rarely the one to initiate. Fine—I am *never* the one to initiate. And ever since The Incident, Hank treats me like I'm made of glass, and he's so gentle most of the time. Too gentle. We are basically abstinent.

It wasn't always like that. When we were first dating, it felt like we were going for some sort of world's record. Our sex life slowed down a bit after we were together for a couple of years, but then after we got married and decided to try to have a baby, we got back in the running for the world's record.

Back then, it was *fun*. But eventually "trying for a baby" morphed into "struggling with infertility." Sex became something we had to time perfectly when the ovulation kit said we were supposed to do it.

It all turned out to be for nothing anyway.

"It's so cold in here." I run my fingers down Hank's chest. "You up for something to warm us up?"

"Of course I am," he says like it's a stupid question, and I suppose it is.

He leans in to kiss me. Hank was always a really good kisser—he's very gentle for a man his size. I try to lose myself in sex by candlelight, grateful that we made it through that rough patch. I'm glad I didn't completely destroy our relationship, although I did my best.

I'll never forget the look on my husband's face when he picked me up from work two years ago. That was after the failed IVF treatments that emptied out our bank accounts. And it was after the failed adoption, when the teenage mother changed her mind after she held her little baby girl in her arms and decided she couldn't give her up after all.

Hank was a rock through the whole thing. *We'll try again, Polly. Our child is still out there somewhere.*

No, I had sobbed to him, *I can't go through this again. I can't.*

So it'll just be you and me. Nothing wrong with that.

His words were echoing in my ears the next day when I had to work an overnight shift in the newborn nursery at the hospital. I should have refused, given how I was feeling. But I thought I was stronger than my feelings. I thought it might lift my spirits to be around all those new babies.

I was wrong.

After what happened that day, I lost my job at the hospital. I'm lucky they didn't lock me up. I loved that job, and as hard as it was leaving, it was even harder to admit *why* I had to leave. I usually tell people that Hank wanted me to stay home to focus on our family. Unfortunately, The Incident meant there would be no family—we had to withdraw our name from the waiting list for adoptions and foster children. We would never become parents.

We don't need a child, Polly, Hank kept telling me. *We've got each other.*

And then my mother got sick, and I threw myself into her care—it gave me a purpose and a reason for living again. But since she's been gone, there's been little else to occupy my time. Bookkeeping for the auto shop is hardly a full-time job. Hank may be satisfied without a child, but I'm not.

I never will be.

It's been a long time since we've had sex, and it's been even longer since we've had really good sex. Tonight, we have really good sex. And when it's over and I collapse against him, Hank whispers in my ear, "I love you so much, Polly."

I get a flashback to him kneeling beside my bed in the inpatient psychiatric ward, gripping my frail hand in his much larger one. The desperate look in his eyes. *Please talk to me, Polly. Please. I love you so much.*

"I love you too," I say.

He squeezes me close to him, our bodies stuck together with sweat. "That was so great. I didn't expect...I mean, I thought you might be upset tonight...with that woman downstairs being..."

"I'm not upset."

He beams at me. "I'm glad you're doing so much better."

"Me too."

He kisses me one more time. "And I'm glad you're my wife. I'm glad that it's just the two of us."

I don't answer him this time. I won't lie to him. I'm *not* glad that it's just the two of us. I will *never* be happy with our situation the way he apparently can be.

But that's okay. Because I made up my mind tonight. Very soon, we will have a child of our own. We will finally get to use that teddy bear with the heart that I've had stuffed in the pantry all these years. He just doesn't know it yet.

My mother was right after all. Very soon, our family will be complete.

CHAPTER 27

I feel good this morning.

I'm humming to myself as I spread butter over Tegan's toast. I don't even know exactly what I'm humming. It's just generic music. It just seems like *such* a nice day. Despite all the snow on the ground, the sun is shining, and I'm glad we got our electricity back.

Tegan was lying about having a husband. I saw the look on her face when I repeated the name she gave me. I don't know if any Jackson exists, but he's definitely not her husband. There's no husband. There probably isn't even a boyfriend. It's just her, all alone. And soon it will be her and a baby she didn't even *want*, who she won't even look at once it's born.

A set of muscular arms encircles my shoulders, and then the warmth of Hank's body radiates against mine. "Hey," he breathes in my ear.

I lean back to rest my head against his chest. "Hey yourself."

He squeezes me close to him. He's got on nothing but boxers and a white undershirt. "Last night was great."

I feel a twinge of guilt that my husband is so excited about the fact that we had sex last night. He's been so unbelievably patient with me—I haven't exactly been easy to deal with for the last couple of years.

"It *was* great." I squirm out of his grasp so that I can turn around and plant a kiss on his lips. I have to tilt up my head and stand on my tiptoes to do it. "*You're* great."

He beams at me, and it reminds me of that day at the shop all those years ago—before we were married, before we were even dating—when I invited him out to dinner and he looked so happy. He runs his fingertips along the side of my face. "Maybe I can keep the shop closed today and we can do something together. Whatever you want."

I laugh. "I'm not sure what I feel comfortable doing with that woman down in the basement."

"Well, after she goes to the hospital, I mean."

The smile I've had on my lips the entire morning drops off my face. "How can she go to the hospital? The phones are out."

He lifts a shoulder. "That's okay. I'll drive her."

"You'll do no such thing! The roads are still covered in snow!"

"Yeah, but I got that plow attachment in the garage," he reminds me. "I'll just get it hooked up, and that should get us to the main road."

Oh right. I forgot all about the plow attachment he bought last winter. He said he was sick of waiting for the plow to come and that we would save money in the long run. That means nobody's coming to plow our driveway.

"I just…" I wring my hands together. "I don't think it's a good idea to move her right now. She's in a whole lot of pain. It's better to wait till we get our phones back and we can call for the paramedics."

"I'm sure she wants to leave though."

"Oh no." I shake my head. "I told her it might be a little while longer, and she was fine with it. She's anxious about going to the hospital."

Hank scratches at his beard, and I hold my breath, waiting to see if he'll buy it. Finally, he shrugs. "If she's okay with it."

I nod eagerly. "Oh yes. And I'm sure the phone lines will be back up soon. You should go on to the shop and let me take care of everything."

He looks hesitant, but he goes back upstairs to get dressed. He is going along with this, but when tonight comes and Tegan is still in the basement, he's going to start asking a lot more questions. When that happens, he may not like the answers quite as much, but when it comes down to it, he's going to do exactly what I tell him to do.

He doesn't have a choice.

CHAPTER 28

Tegan sleeps all afternoon.

It's no surprise since I crushed twenty-five milligrams of Benadryl into the sauce I cooked her chicken in for lunch. Benadryl is perfectly safe during pregnancy. I'm sure she could use the sleep, and it's better than her lying awake all afternoon wondering when we're going to take her to the hospital. It's easier if she's groggy and pliable.

Especially since I have no intention of taking her to the hospital today or tomorrow.

Or ever.

Now that our internet is back up, I run a search on Tegan Werner. I find a social media page, and it's ripe with pictures of the girl in our basement. She's not pregnant in any of them. There's no mention of a husband, that's for sure. She looks pretty in a young and fresh sort of way, with her heart-shaped face and silky blond hair. In every photo, she's holding some sort of alcoholic beverage, which isn't any surprise based on the fact that her purse reeked of it.

Yes, I'm sure she'll be a fine mother.

She told me that story about wanting to be a nurse, and I'm sure that was also a crock of lies. She's trying to suck up to me. But even if it is true, that doesn't change anything. She's still a girl who made an irresponsible decision and will now be saddled with a baby she can't take care of. Tegan won't give that baby the life she deserves.

I will.

After staring at far too many photos of Tegan looking young and irresponsible, I get up and walk to the kitchen to plan dinner. I can just barely make out the Hambly house from the window in my kitchen. Before he left, Hank cleared a path around our house, and he also cleared out a path to our neighbor's house. Even though neither of us cares for Mitch Hambly, Hank does it to be a good neighbor and to give Sadie a path to walk to school.

Mitch's truck isn't in the driveway, which means he must've gone to work today. Since the schools are almost certainly closed for snow, that means Sadie is home all by herself.

I hope she's okay. I hope I didn't get her in too much trouble.

I look down at my own wrist, which has turned a dark purple color, as I predicted. Mitch Hambly is *not* a good man. I don't care what Child Protective Services decided—he should not be taking care of that little girl. In all the times that she's come over here, I've never once seen her well groomed. And the poor thing looks positively malnourished—it's not normal to have collarbones that stick out so much.

If I had a child, they wouldn't know the meaning of the word. They would be positively chubby.

I wonder if Mitch even left some food for Sadie when he went to work. I imagine her opening the refrigerator and finding only a six-pack of beer, five of which are mostly empty.

On an impulse, I open the refrigerator and pull out some bread and turkey. I'm going to make Sadie a sandwich. I start adding ingredients, and I slather the bread with lots of mayonnaise, just the way my mother used to make it. I wrap it carefully in tinfoil, and then I grab a couple of Oreos from the pantry and drop them into a Ziploc bag.

I pull on my boots and pea-green coat, and I make the trek over to the Hambly house to check on Sadie. Our own house is nothing to write home about, but Hank is good about fixing anything that needs to be repaired, and the two of us put a fresh coat of paint on it every few years. But the Hambly house looks like it's one broken shingle away from being condemned. As I put my foot on the first step of the porch, the wood crumbles slightly under my weight. The screen door is hanging off by the top hinge—I'm amazed it didn't blow away during the storm.

I gently nudge open the screen door, hoping it doesn't fall off in my hand. Then I rap on the front door. And I wait.

Please be okay, Sadie. Please.

After what feels like an eternity, little footsteps approach the door. I wait for the lock to turn, but nothing happens.

“Sadie?” I say.

Another long silence. “Daddy says I’m not s’posed to let anyone in.”

“It’s okay. He meant strangers. He didn’t mean me.”

“He *said* you.”

I get an ache in my chest. If Sadie can’t come over to my house after school, then she’ll be returning home to an empty house every day. Mitch doesn’t get back from work until late.

“Have you eaten lunch?” I ask her.

“Yes. I had crackers.”

Crackers are *not* a well-balanced meal for a seven-year-old girl. “Sadie, I made you a sandwich. I’m going to leave it at the door. You don’t have to let me in, but if you’re hungry, you can eat the sandwich.” I notice her hesitation, and I add, “I also have some cookies for you.”

Sadie doesn’t say anything. I bend down and leave the cookies and sandwich on the doormat. I back away from the door, and when nothing happens, I start walking in the direction of my house.

When I’m about halfway back, I hear a noise from behind me. I turn around just as the front door to the Hambly house cracks open. A little hand reaches out and picks up the sandwich and the cookies I left behind. Then before I can even lift my hand to wave, the door slams shut again.

CHAPTER 29

Tegan is still asleep when the sun goes down.

I crack open the basement door to check on her, and I can make out her heavy breathing. Actually, it's more like snoring. Anyway, she is still out like a light. That Benadryl really did the trick.

When my mother was still alive and staying in our basement, I sometimes used to crack open the door to the basement and listen to the sounds of her breathing. I knew we didn't have much time left together, so every inhale and exhale felt like a gift. My mother was a great mother. She taught me everything: how to tie my shoes, how to read, how to cook a perfect turkey for the holidays with all the trimmings. Every time I think of these memories, I can't help but smile. I always dreamed of passing on that knowledge someday to a child of my own.

There's some irony in the fact that the woman occupying my mother's death bed will be the one to make my dream come true.

Someday, your family will be complete.

Hank comes home at seven o'clock, greasy and hungry like he always is at the end of the workday. He catches me at the stove, cooking some meatballs. Hank loves my meatballs. I use 80 percent lean ground beef, with lots of seasoning and breadcrumbs and a pinch of Parmesan cheese, and I let them simmer in tomato sauce for about half an hour. Hank could devour an entire pot of them all on his own.

"Smells like meatballs," Hank notes as he leans in to give me a kiss and gently brushes the hair from my face, the way he always does when he greets me in the kitchen after work. "My favorite."

I laugh. "What *isn't* your favorite?"

"Hey, it's not my fault my wife is such a good cook." He swipes at a dot of oil on his forehead but just manages to spread it. "Seems like the phones are working again. That lady get picked up by the paramedics?"

"Yes," I lie, giving the sauce a stir.

"Good. Hope she's okay."

He's going to find out sooner rather than later that Tegan is still in our basement. It isn't the sort of thing I could hide from him. But it'll be easier to talk to him about it after he's had a shower and there's some food in his belly.

Hank goes upstairs to shower while I throw some spaghetti in a pot of boiling water. I always dreamed of getting my own pasta machine and making fresh pasta, but it didn't seem worth it for just the two of us. I always figured when we had children, that would be something I could do with them. I could show them how to make pasta, their little chubby hands covered with flour. We would cook together every night.

Hank was whistling in the shower, and he's still whistling when he comes downstairs, dressed in a fresh T-shirt and jeans, his hair still damp. He flashes me a smile, wider than any I've seen in the last few years—even the fine lines around his eyes crinkle. When he smiles at me like that, it suddenly hits me how unhappy we've been. He used to smile all the time, but now it's a rare occurrence. I had almost forgotten what it looked like.

I serve Hank a plate of spaghetti and meatballs, piled about three times as high as my own plate. He flashes me that smile again, and he digs into the food. I twirl some spaghetti around my fork, my stomach filled with butterflies. This is not going to be an easy conversation.

"Hank," I say.

"Uh-huh."

"There's something I need to tell you."

He pauses mid-chew, his brown eyes wide. "Are you pregnant?"

How could he ask me that? How could he think I could *possibly* be pregnant? Why would he even *say* it? And the worst part is the hopefulness in his eyes. Even after all these years, he's still hoping.

"*No*," I say tightly. "I'm not pregnant."

"Oh." He does his best to mask his disappointment. "Sorry, I..."

"Never mind." I wave a hand. "Anyway, what I wanted to tell you is that...Tegan is still here. She's sleeping in the basement."

A look of confusion floods my husband's features. "What? Why?"

"Because she's tired. I didn't want to make her run to the hospital right now."

"Okay, that's fair," he says slowly. "So we can call for the paramedics as soon as she wakes up."

This is the hard part. I've got to play this exactly right. "That's the thing. I don't think we should. She's better off recovering here."

Hank wipes at a glob of tomato sauce on the side of his mouth with the back of his hand, even though there's a perfectly good napkin right in front of him. "She's hurt, Polly. She needs to go to the hospital."

"Does she?" I reach out with my own napkin and dab at his lips, which still have a little sauce clinging to them. "She's fine. She just needs a few days of TLC, then we can send her on her way. Hospitals aren't always best—I know after working at one for so many years. Don't you remember when we brought my mother to the hospital for a urinary tract infection, and then she got pneumonia?"

"Tegan is hurt. She needs the hospital."

Hank's logic is so black-and-white sometimes. It's maddening. "I *am* a nurse, you know. I can take care of her."

"With a broken ankle?"

I wave a hand in dismissal. "It's not broken," I lie. "It's barely a sprain."

"It looked pretty bad."

"You didn't even get a good look," I point out. "And she doesn't have insurance. She can't pay for the hospital. It would bankrupt her."

That crease between his eyebrows is back again. The smile is a distant memory. "And Tegan wants to stay here?"

"She… Yes, more or less."

Hank inhales sharply. "Polly..."

"Look, she's just a girl. She's in no state of mind to know what's best for her. She's confused, and she's looking to me to tell her what to do."

He pushes his plate of spaghetti and meatballs away, even though he's only eaten half of it. "I'm calling 911. Now."

"Hank, no." I push back my chair, and it topples to the floor. "You don't understand. I'm trying to do the right thing here."

"Polly, I'm not holding a pregnant woman hostage in my basement, okay?"

"God, we're not holding her *hostage*. Don't be so *dramatic*."

He isn't listening anymore though. He gets up out of his chair and stomps over to the telephone right by our sofa. I try to grab his arm, but he easily shakes me off. I sprint after him, and before he's able to start dialing, I yank the phone cord out of the wall. The entire phone goes clattering to the floor with a loud thump that breaks it into four pieces and echoes throughout the room.

"Polly!" He rarely raises his voice, but now it's as loud as I've ever heard it. "What the hell do you think you're doing?"

I hug my arms to my chest. "Wait. Just wait, okay?"

"My cell phone is charging upstairs. I'll just call on that."

I contemplate running up the stairs and tossing his phone out the window before he can get to it. But I'll never make it. My eyes fill with tears. "Can you please just listen to me for five seconds?"

Hank turns to me, his shoulders sagging. "Look,

Polly, I know you've been feeling kind of lost since your mom passed. And all this baby stuff…it's been hard on me too. I understand that. But there's something not right about all this. I'm going upstairs, and I'm going to call 911 for Tegan, and then we'll talk about… Maybe you need to get some help again. We should give Dr. Salinsky a call. Okay, Polly?"

He looks at me, waiting for me to nod in agreement, to tell him it's a great idea to call for an ambulance and then give my former shrink a jingle. When I don't, he lets out a loud sigh. "Okay, then," he says.

He turns around, heading for the stairwell. Just as he places one large hand on the banister, I call out, "Hank!"

He climbs the first step, showing no signs of stopping.

"Hank, wait! Will you please wait!"

He's not listening to me. He doesn't want to talk about this anymore. All he wants to do is call the police and get Tegan out of our house.

I can't let him do that. I can't let him ruin everything.

"Hank!" I cross the living room until I'm at the base of the stairs, where I'm sure he can hear me. "Hank, if you do this, I'm going to call the police."

He freezes midway up the stairs, his hulking frame rigid.

"And," I add, "I'm going to tell them what you did."

CHAPTER 30

I've got Hank's attention now.

He turns around so slowly, it's like watching a boulder move. The sad expression he wore a few moments ago has been replaced by a wary look in his eyes.

"You wouldn't," he says.

I arch an eyebrow at him. "Wouldn't I?"

His breaths are ragged as his shoulders heave. "That wasn't my fault."

"Oh, and I'm sure the police will see it that way." I fold my arms across my chest, looking up at him still halfway up the stairs. "Remember those two months you spent in prison for breaking that guy's nose? Remember how much fun it was for you? What did you say when you got home?" He doesn't answer, so I remind him: "You said, 'I'd rather jump in a bathtub of battery acid than ever go back there.'"

The parts of Hank's face I can see above his beard turn pink. "The whole thing was your idea!"

"Yes, but it's *your* signature."

"Yours too, Polly."

"I'm aware."

The wariness in his eyes is morphing into anger. He's right—it *was* my idea. But he went along with it, and that's all that matters.

He stomps down the stairs, his footfalls so heavy that I fear he might crack one of the steps. When he gets to the bottom, he glares at me. "What do you want?"

"I just want to let her stay here a few more days—that's all. I want to make sure she's okay, and then she'll go home. I'm trying to *help* her to avoid the hospital."

"A few days," he repeats.

"Yes."

"So two days?"

"A few means *three*, Hank."

"And what if she says she wants to leave?"

"We won't keep her against her will, of course. If she says she wants to leave, we'll let her leave." And to be fair, it's not like she's going anywhere under her own steam, although Hank doesn't know that.

"You swear you'll let her leave?"

"Of course. I'm not mentally ill."

He shoots me a look. I suppose there are a few psychiatrists out there who might disagree with that statement. And several staff members who were working in the newborn nursery on that morning two years ago.

"Three days." Hank holds up three fingers, one of which contains his gold wedding band. "Three days, and she either goes home or to the hospital. I mean it, Polly."

"Of course."

Except in three days, nothing will have changed.

Hank still won't want to end up in prison. Tegan will still be an irresponsible child who doesn't deserve to raise a beautiful daughter. And I'll still be barren.

In three days, I'll make Hank see reason. I'm sure of it.

PART 3

TWO DAYS AFTER THE CRASH

CHAPTER 31

POLLY

Hank is already in the shower when I wake up the next morning. Yesterday, he woke me up by kissing me on the neck, his beard hairs tickling me awake. But he's not feeling quite as amorous this morning, which I suppose is no surprise.

While he is showering, I put on my slippers and housecoat and go down to check on Tegan. Today is going to be difficult. She looked frantic when I told her she'd need to stay another day, and if I don't report the arrival of the plow very soon, she's going to get agitated. She may even start to suspect that I'm not being entirely honest with her.

Like with Hank, I've got to play this exactly right. Because Tegan can't leave here until she has that baby.

When I get down to the basement, the lights are out, but Tegan's eyes are cracked open. For one terrifying second, I'm scared she's dead. That she passed away during the night and now I'm going to have to cut her open to get the baby out and then dispose of her dead body. But then she moves, and I let out a sigh of relief.

"Good morning!" I say in my most chipper voice. "How are you doing?"

Tegan opens her mouth, and for a moment, no sound comes out. She looks terrible—even worse than the first night she came. There are dark circles under both her eyes, and her hair is matted. She looks simultaneously ancient and painfully young. "Bedpan," she croaks.

I fetch it for her and help her empty her bladder. Her urine looks a little dark, which isn't a surprise since she hasn't been drinking as much as she should. She's going to be prone to urinary tract infections, given that she's lying on dirty sheets and she's pregnant, so I'll have to make sure she drinks enough today. She certainly won't do it for the sake of the baby. It's unclear to me how much she cares about or even wants this child.

When I come out of the bathroom after emptying the bedpan, I bring her a glass of water. I place it on the tray in front of her. "Drink up."

She stares at it for a moment, not moving. "Is the plow here yet?"

"Yes, it is."

That listless look vanishes from her eyes, and there's a spark of the girl she used to be. "Really?"

"Yes, really. They need a little time to get all the snow cleared away, but we should be able to get you going by the end of the morning."

"Oh, thank God." Her eyes fill with tears. "I'm sorry. You've been very kind to me, but..."

"I understand." I clear my throat. "What would you like for breakfast?"

A tiny smile touches her lips. "I'm sort of in the mood for eggs and bacon. Is that okay?"

"Of course." That's Hank's favorite breakfast. It won't be any trouble to make extra for Tegan. And I would do anything to keep her happy right now. "I'll have it ready for you in a jiffy."

"Thank you, Polly." Her smile is lopsided but genuine. "I just want you to know that I really appreciate everything you've done for me the last couple of days. I had a really tough time lately… I don't want to get into it, but my life has really gone down the toilet lately. Anyway, it helps to know there are good people like you out there."

My face burns. I'm sure she considers getting pregnant out of wedlock to be an example of her life going down the toilet. She probably wishes every night that this hadn't happened to her. She's the kind of mother who will let her baby cry all night rather than comforting her.

I climb back up the stairs to make some breakfast. I have to buy two dozen eggs a week just to have enough to make my husband eggs in the morning. I should try to get him to eat healthier, but he keeps in good physical condition, and he's only thirty-nine. At some point in the next five years, I'll attempt to transition him to oatmeal and fruit in the morning, but right now, I can't deprive him of his favorite breakfast.

I leave a plate heaped with eggs and bacon on the kitchen table, and I bring Tegan a plate of breakfast as well. I've never been able to eat a big breakfast—usually, all I can manage is a little toast. The truth is just the smell of the eggs in the morning sometimes gets me queasy. I never told Hank that, because he would tell me not to make them if he knew. And he deserves to have a breakfast of eggs and bacon.

I'm sitting at the kitchen table, nibbling on my toast, when Hank's loud footsteps on the stairs echo through the house. A moment later, he appears in the doorway to the kitchen.

"Good morning," I say.

He grunts something inaudible and drops into the seat in front of the heaping plate of food.

"Did you sleep well?" I ask him.

He shoots me a look, which I suppose is deserved, because I know very well that he was tossing and turning all night long. We both were.

I'm trying to think of something to say that will get him to stop glaring at me when I am saved by the sound of the doorbell ringing. "I'll get that," I say.

I'm so glad for the interruption that it doesn't even occur to me how strange it is for somebody to be knocking on my door at this hour of the morning. And it doesn't occur to me to wonder who it is until I look through the peephole and my stomach sinks.

It's the police.

CHAPTER 32

POLLY

A police officer is standing on our doorstep, and I am freaking out.

It should have occurred to me that this would happen. I am, after all, keeping a missing woman against her will in my basement. It's not surprising that the police would show up here. I just have to handle this correctly, like everything else. I can't let myself panic.

It's just one officer. If they really thought she was here, they wouldn't send one guy. The whole cavalry would be outside.

"Just a moment!" I call out. "I'm not decent!"

I hurry back to the kitchen, nearly tripping over my fuzzy slippers. Hank is still sitting at the kitchen table, pushing the eggs around his plate with his fork. He's barely made a dent in them.

"Hank," I say, "there's a police officer at the door."

His eyes fly open. "What?"

"I'm sure it's no big deal," I say quickly. "You just stay here and eat your breakfast—"

Hank rises from his seat. "Stay here? But—"

"Stay here unless he calls for you." My voice is firm. "And if he does ask, you can't tell him she's here."

Panic fills his eyes. "What? Why not? You said she's fine with being here."

"Well, it's *mostly* true."

"Polly…"

"Look," I hiss at him, "if they find that girl down in our basement, we're both leaving here in handcuffs, okay? So just keep your fool mouth shut. You're good at that."

Hank glares at me. My husband is the most honest person I've ever met. It's something he's always prided himself on. It's only because of me that he's ever bent the rules, when he was on the brink of losing his auto shop.

That was my fault too, of course. He had to shut the shop down for a while after The Incident, and sinking all our cash into infertility treatments and that failed adoption didn't help matters. We were going to lose the shop, and once that was closed and neither of us had a steady source of income, we would likely lose our house too. We were about to lose everything he had worked for in the blink of an eye. Because of me.

Since I couldn't work as a nurse anymore, I was doing his bookkeeping, and I was the one who hit on the simple solution to his problems.

So I fudged the tax return—a bit. I was careful. I didn't do anything that would raise a red flag. I didn't tell Hank about it, because I knew he'd refuse to do it and lose the shop before he risked doing anything that would send him back to prison. I simply handed him the tax return, and he signed it, because he trusted me. I figured if we ever got caught, I would take the fall.

But then he found out. He was frantic when he saw what I did, but it was too late by then, and if he tried to correct the mistake, it would have been admitting wrongdoing. Not to mention we still didn't have the money to make it right. So he kept his mouth shut.

It's been almost a year since I handed in the tax documents. Nobody has come pounding down our door. We got away with it.

I never thought this was something I would ever use against my husband. To blackmail him. After all, I had planned to fall on the sword if we ever got caught. But I won't have to ever turn him in. Hank will do what I want. He'll do anything for me.

I'm sure of it.

Finally, he drops back down into his chair so heavily, I'm scared it might break under his weight. "Fine," he says.

I knew it.

I wrap my pink terry-cloth housecoat more tightly around my body and rush back out to the door. I turn the lock and crack it open. "Hello there, Officer," I say. "How can I help you? Is everything all right?"

The policeman standing at our door is in a navy-blue uniform. Like Tegan, he's painfully young—looks like he can't even be that far out of high school. He smiles politely at me. "Hello, Mrs. Thompson. My name is Officer Malloy. I was wondering if I could ask you a couple of questions."

"Of course." I crack the door open slightly more. I don't like the fact that he called me by my name, but

I suppose the owners of this house are public record. "What's wrong?"

"Any chance I could come inside? I'd hate for you to lose all your heat out the door."

I read once that a policeman can't come inside your home without a warrant unless you invite him in. Once he's inside, he has a lot more leeway in what he is allowed to do. And what if Tegan calls up to me from the basement? There's no way I'm letting him inside.

"I just had the carpet cleaned." I look pointedly at his snow-caked boots. "I'd appreciate it if you stay on the porch."

"No problem, ma'am." He nods at me. "Anyway, this shouldn't take long. We're looking for a woman who disappeared two nights ago. Her name is Tegan Werner."

I tap my finger against my chin. "The name sounds a bit familiar."

"You may have heard about her disappearance on the news this morning," he says. "She was traveling in this direction to visit a family member, and we found her car not far from here. It looks like she had been in some kind of accident, but she's not in the vehicle."

"Oh, dear!" I clasp a hand over my mouth. "Do you think she got thrown from the car during the accident?"

"No, ma'am." He shakes his head. "Her purse and her luggage were missing from the car, and we haven't been able to locate her. We think she took off on foot, but the snow covered her trail. We've been searching the area, and I was just wondering if you may have seen her."

"Sorry, Officer. I'm afraid I haven't seen anyone here for the last two days. We've mostly been buried by the storm."

He doesn't look surprised, but even so, he digs a photograph out of his pocket. "Can you take a look at this? This is what she looks like."

I peer down at the color photograph of Tegan Werner—it's one of the photos from her social media page, where she looks very young and pretty, her round cheeks flushed from alcohol. If he saw her now, he would barely recognize her. I hand the photo back to him. "Sorry, no."

He starts to put the photograph back in his pocket. Did I just get away with this? Is he just going to walk away? But then he hesitates. "Does anyone else live here?"

I want to say no and put an end to this, but I shouldn't lie about something so easily disproved. "My husband. But he hasn't seen her either."

"Would you mind if I asked him myself?"

I look over my shoulder. "He's in the middle of breakfast. Is it really necessary?"

"I wouldn't ask if it wasn't important, ma'am. We've been looking everywhere for this lady."

Hank is a terrible liar. The last thing I want is to drag him out here and force him to talk to this police officer. But I can't very well say no. That would look very suspicious.

"Of course," I say. "Let me get him."

I apologetically close the door in the officer's face, explaining about keeping the heat in. I have to trudge back to the kitchen and get Hank. He's not going to be happy.

Sure enough, when I get to the kitchen, Hank is still sitting at the table, listlessly staring down at his plate.

He's not even pretending to eat anymore. This isn't good. When Hank loses his appetite, it basically means the world is coming to an end.

"Hank," I say, "the policeman wants to talk to you."

He doesn't say anything. He keeps staring down at his eggs.

"It's not a big deal," I say. "They just want to know if you've seen Tegan. All you have to do is tell him no and then we're done."

He raises his head to look at me. The circles under his eyes look a lot like Tegan's. "Yeah? Is that all I have to do?"

"Hank…"

His chair scrapes against the floor as he gets up. He walks slowly toward the front door, like he's being led to his execution. He puts his hand on the lock, and just before he turns it, he shoots me one last pained look.

Over Hank's shoulder, the policeman gives Hank the same friendly and apologetic smile he offered me. "Hello, sir. I don't know if your wife told you, but we're looking for a missing woman."

Hank just grunts.

The officer reaches into his pocket and pulls out the same photograph he showed me. "Have you seen her in the last two days? Her name is Tegan Werner."

Hank stares at the photo for a long time. Too long. Oh *no*, he's going to crack. He's going to tell the policeman everything. He's going to lead him right down to Tegan in the basement. My husband is not cut out for this. Why did I ever think he was?

"No," Hank finally says. "Didn't see her."

"You sure?"

"I'm sure."

My shoulders relax. I knew Hank would do anything for me. After all, he smashed a man's face in for me. This is nothing.

I look at the officer's face, but there's no suspicion there. He shoves the photograph back in his pocket and nods at us. "Well, thank you both for your time. Please don't hesitate to contact the police if you do happen to see her anywhere."

"Will do, Officer!" I say.

He starts to turn around. My knees almost collapse with relief. Did I really just get away with this? But just before he reaches the door, he stops short.

"Mrs. Thompson," he says, "would you mind if I take a look around the house? Just make sure she isn't hiding out somewhere in your backyard or something along those lines?"

It's within my rights to say no, but what possible reason could I have for telling him he can't do a lap around my house?

"Absolutely!" I say. "Gosh, I really hope you find her and that she's okay."

"Me too, ma'am," he says in a subdued voice that indicates he doesn't think it's likely he's going to find her and that she's going to be okay.

It isn't until the door is locked again and the policeman is making his way down our front steps that I hazard a look at my husband.

"Thank you," I say to Hank.

He gives me a look that I can't quite decipher. I'm used to Hank looking at me like I'm out of my mind or like he's worried about me. Or, back when we were dating or first married, he used to look at me like I hung the moon. But this is something different. Something worse, but I can't quite figure it out. We've been together so long, I thought I could always tell what he was thinking, but maybe not.

But I can't worry about him right now.

I hurry over to the kitchen to see what the police officer is doing in our backyard. From the kitchen, I've got a view of the yard from the window on the back door. The officer is walking around, knee-deep in snow, circling the giant oak tree that Hank once mused was "perfect" to hang a swing from for a future child. I don't know what exactly the cop is looking for, but he won't find anything in our backyard.

At least I don't think he will.

The officer is just standing there. He seems to be looking at something on the ground, although I can't see what. He pulls his radio out of his pocket, and he starts talking into it as my heart thumps loudly in my chest.

There's nothing in the backyard, of course, but it hits me that there is one window into the basement that is visible from where he's standing. But the snow should be high enough to conceal it. He can't possibly see through that window into my basement.

Can he?

He looks up, and for a moment, his eyes meet mine through the window. He knows I've been watching him. I freeze, waiting for him to march back into the house and demand to search my basement.

But instead, he raises a hand. He's waving hello.

I raise my own hand. And I force a smile.

I make myself busy cleaning the kitchen, but all the

while, I've got one eye on the policeman in the backyard. After a few more minutes, he puts away his radio and vanishes from sight. I hurry back to the living room, just in time to see him get back in his patrol car and drive away.

I let out a sigh of relief. The police are gone, and there's no reason to think they'll ever come back. We got away with it.

Tegan's baby will be mine.

CHAPTER 33

TEGAN

Little Tuna hasn't moved in a while.

Usually, she's a super active baby. So the fact that an hour has gone by and she hasn't moved once is cause for concern. It could be that I'm not drinking enough. Polly mentioned this morning that it was important for me to drink more water. I know she's right, but if I drink a lot of water, it means I'm going to need the bedpan more frequently. And that is not a pleasant experience.

And not only that, but I wonder if it's possible Hank might slip something into my drink before Polly brings it down. It wouldn't be the first time such a thing has happened to me.

I massage my abdomen, trying to wake her up. "Come on, Tuna. Give Mama a kick."

Finally, I get a little poke in my rib cage. *I'm still here, Mama. But I don't feel very good.*

"Me either, Tuna," I whisper.

By the time Polly comes back down to the basement

close to noon, I'm ready to leap out of bed, if only that were possible. I recognize Hank will have to help me out of bed and into the car, and the last thing I want is that terrible man touching me again, but it's my only choice if the phone lines really are down.

"Is the road all cleared?" I ask Polly.

She hesitates, clutching a bowl of food in her right hand—my lunch, I assume. "Yes. Mostly."

I almost can't believe the stupid plows finally cleared the road and I'll be able to get out of here. It seems too good to be true.

"Okay." I sit up straighter in bed, which sets off another white-hot jolt of pain in my left ankle. "When can we go?"

"Well, Hank had to go to work," she explains. "And I can't possibly manage to get you up the stairs all by myself."

"I could do the stairs," I protest. "I'll just hold on to the railing."

Her eyebrows shoot up. "Can you? Every time I move you the slightest bit, you cry out in pain."

That is not untrue. I would have hoped the pain in my ankle would have subsided by now, but if anything, it's getting worse by the day. Getting up those stairs, even with Polly helping, would be a challenge. But I'm so eager to get out of here, I'm willing to try.

Just as I'm about to suggest this, a loud groan echoes from the ceiling above us. "What was that?"

"That?" Polly fluffs a pillow at the foot of the bed. "Oh, nothing. Just the house settling."

The house settling? Really? "It sounded like footsteps."

"How could it be? Nobody is upstairs."

Is that really true though? It occurs to me that Hank might not really be at work and that this is just a lie he forced her to tell me. What if he's right upstairs and just doesn't want me to leave?

I knew it was too easy.

"I want to try the stairs," I insist.

"I can't support your weight on the stairs," she retorts, her voice frustratingly calm. "And the banister isn't very stable either. If you were to take a fall down those stairs… Well, you don't want to risk your baby's life." She pauses meaningfully. "Do you?"

I look over her shoulder at the steep staircase to the main level of the house. If I fell down those stairs, that might be the end of me and Tuna. I'm still itching to try, but I reluctantly admit that she's right.

"What about the phones?" I say desperately.

"Sorry. The phone service is never very good out here, and I still can't get a dial tone."

Of course she can't.

"Don't worry," she says. "We'll leave as soon as Hank gets back."

"And when will that be?"

Polly puts down the bowl of what looks like rice and vegetables on my tray. "Six or seven?"

"*Six or seven?*" I want to cry all over again. "That's hours from now!"

"Well, you've been here two nights. What's a few more hours?"

"No." My right hand clenches into a fist. "If the road is clear, maybe you can drive to a store that has a phone that works. I can't stay here another six or seven *hours*. I just can't."

She's quiet for a moment, as if considering it. "I don't know if that's a good idea. You're better off staying put for now."

Is she kidding me? "I'm sorry, but I really need to get to a hospital. I appreciate all you've done for me, but I need hospital-level care right now."

"If you'd just drink a little more water, you'd be fine."

"Don't tell me what to do!" I shoot back. "I need to get to a hospital! *Now*. You're a nurse, for God's sake. Shouldn't you know better?"

Polly stands there, her body rigid. I'm sorry I yelled at her, but I'm also not sorry. She needs to know that I'm not just going to lie down here in the basement, twiddling my thumbs.

"You can get out of bed if you want," Polly offers. "We have a wheelchair that my mother used to use. I'm happy to help you get into it."

She gestures at the corner of the room, where there is indeed a wheelchair tucked away in the shadows. It looks like it's been sitting there a long time. A string of cobwebs decorates the gap between the armrest and the wall. The footplates at the bottom are brown with rust.

I don't want to get into that wheelchair. Polly claims she's trying to do what she can to help me since Hank won't let me leave, but it's not enough—all I want is to leave this house. "I just want to go to the hospital."

"But you know what they'll do at the hospital, don't you?" she says. "They'll pump you up with the drugs, especially if they're going to do surgery. That's the worst possible thing for your baby."

She keeps saying that. But I'm the one in pain. She has no clue how awful this is. And anyway, it's not her decision to make. "So what am I supposed to do? Lie around with a broken ankle?"

"What do you care more about—walking or your own child?"

She says it like I would be selfish to even consider the former. But she's wrong. The hospital won't do anything to hurt me or Tuna. I care about my baby more than anything in the world, but I can't believe that going to a hospital is the wrong thing to do. And it's hard to imagine that as a nurse, she would think so either.

I think she's telling me exactly what Hank told her to tell me.

"I want to go to the hospital," I say firmly.

She nods slowly. "Okay, I think you're making the wrong decision, but I understand where you're coming from. Why don't you finish your lunch, and then we'll talk about it more. But I truly think it's best for you to stay put until Hank gets back."

I start to protest, but Polly has already turned away from me and is walking up the stairs.

As soon as she's gone, I grab my purse. I rifle through it one more time, making good and sure that my phone isn't inside. It's not. It's definitely not.

I can accept that I might have forgotten to put my phone back in my purse. But I am feeling more uneasy about the fact that my pepper spray isn't in my purse anymore. That was definitely in my purse when I started my trip. And now it isn't.

Where did it go?

One thing I do locate in my purse is a gold lighter. This lighter was a present from Jackson on my birthday last month, even though I hadn't even told him it was my birthday. He must have figured it out from the paperwork.

Dennis was starting to get into the busy season at the ski resort, and I had grown apart from my friends since I was working around the clock to save money for when the baby came. I resigned myself to spending my twenty-third birthday alone. And then Jackson showed up with a chocolate cake—my favorite. *A little birdie told me it was your birthday.*

We left the cake at my house, and he took me out to dinner rather than chowing down from Chinese food cartons in my living room. We went to a nice restaurant a thirty-minute drive away, and we had a great time. The waitress in the restaurant didn't give me the stink eye for being a pregnant girl without a wedding band. In fact, when speaking to Jackson, she referred to me as "your wife," and he didn't correct her. For a moment, it felt like I was in a parallel universe where Jackson really was the father of my baby and the two of us were going to raise her together and live happily ever after.

When we got back to my apartment, Jackson whipped out some candles to put on the cake, although thankfully not twenty-three of them. He teased me when I didn't have a lighter to light the candles.

How do you not own a lighter?

Well, I don't smoke, I explained.

Everyone should own a lighter. You never know when you'll need it.

When he said good night, the two of us lingered in front of my door, and for a split second, I was sure he was going to kiss me. But then the moment passed, and instead, he reached out and squeezed my hand in his.

Happy birthday, Tegan. This time next year, you'll be celebrating with your daughter.

I thought that was the end of it. But then two weeks later, he showed up with a cupcake, a single candle, and a lighter engraved with my name on it. *Now we can do this properly,* he said. And I laughed as he lit the candle on the cake and told me to make a wish and blow it out.

My wish was that when he said good night that night, he would kiss me.

It didn't come true.

The lighter is beautiful. He had it engraved. You don't just pick up an engraved cigarette lighter on your way home from work. He ordered it in advance just for me.

My eyes fill with tears at the memory. I don't think I realized until now how deeply I had been falling in love with Jackson. I was such an idiot. I had no idea who he really was. I didn't realize that all he was doing was "handling me" for his boss. I was hurt that he didn't believe me when I told him what Simon really did to me, but maybe he knew it all along. Maybe Simon told him what happened, and he was pretending to be my friend to keep me from going to the police.

I have no idea what the truth is. All I know is that Simon assaulted me and Jackson betrayed me.

But whatever his motivation was, thanks to Jackson, even though I don't have my pepper spray, I do have a cigarette lighter. I still have a chance.

CHAPTER 34

POLLY

My conversation with Tegan did not go the way I hoped it would. She's so young, I thought it would be easy to bully her into staying with us. But she's more stubborn than I thought.

Of course, the truly smart thing would be for her to give her baby to somebody who could take care of it. Somebody like me. And in exchange, I would help her out with her medical bills. We don't have a lot of money, but I would scrimp and save to give her whatever she needed if she was willing to give me what I have been craving for years.

Perhaps she could stay here. She could stay in our basement permanently, and we could raise her baby together—mostly me. She doesn't even need drugs or surgery for her injuries. Yes, her ankle is almost certainly fractured, but I could splint it for her, and she's young enough that eventually it would probably heal on its own—more or less. I could even buy some material to make casts. And we've got that wheelchair—I would let her have it. Even if she couldn't ever walk again without crutches, it wouldn't be the worst thing in the world. Someone who isn't even mature enough to allow me to take off that boot and administer first aid couldn't possibly care that much about her health and certainly does not have the maturity to be a single parent.

I'll also need to buy some supplies for the birth. It's been quite a long time since I assisted in a delivery, but I'm sure it'll all come back to me.

Before I go down to talk to Tegan again, I make a sandwich and wrap it in foil. I also grab a few more Oreos and put them in a Ziploc bag. Just like yesterday, I walk over to the Hambly residence across the way. Mitch's truck is gone again, but there's a light on inside. That means Sadie is home.

This time when I ring the doorbell, I walk away without waiting for a response. I don't want to get her in trouble, but the girl needs to eat.

After I've taken care of feeding Sadie, I make my way down to the basement. When I reach the bottom of the stairs, Tegan has practically cleaned her plate. Usually she eats only about half of what I give her. Now that I know she isn't keen on staying here, I wish I had spiked her food with a little bit of Benadryl. Next time.

"Somebody's got a healthy appetite!" I say.

She offers me a watery smile. "I have to eat—for the baby."

"Of course you do. Everything you do is for her from now on."

Tegan nods tentatively. "Yes, I know. And that's why

I've decided. I have to go to the hospital—now. You're not going to talk me out of it."

I raise my eyebrows. "You really think this is what's best for your baby?"

"Yes." Her voice is unwavering. "It is."

"You know, the first thing they're going to do when you roll in the door is stick an IV in you and give you a bunch of drugs."

Her eyes grow shiny with tears. "Please, Polly."

Just as I suspected. She doesn't care about her baby at all.

"Okay then," I say. "Hank isn't back yet, but I'll find a working phone and call for an ambulance."

Her shoulders sag. "Thank you, Polly."

Of course, I have no intention of calling for an ambulance. She's not leaving her basement anytime soon. But the longer I can keep Tegan happy, the easier this will be.

CHAPTER 35

POLLY

For dinner, I'm making Hank his favorite: country-fried steak.

Show me a man who doesn't like fried steak, and I'll show you a man who doesn't know what he's missing. I use my mother's recipe, which was passed down from her mother. Mom convinced me to make it the first time I had Hank over for dinner, back when we were still dating. *From what you've told me about Hank, he sounds like a man who would appreciate a good country-fried steak.* She was right. I think Hank fell in love with me the day he tried my fried steak.

She was right about Hank too. The first time she met him, she told me that he was the one I would marry. I had already been thinking as much, but I trusted her opinion more than my own. Since she's died, I've been feeling a little lost. How do you know what's right or wrong without your mother telling you so?

But when I'm at my lowest, I still search for comfort in her final words to me.

Someday, your family will be complete.

And now I'm going to make it true.

I coat the steaks in eggs, then dredge them in a mixture of flour, saltines, and lots of seasoning. Then I fry them in the skillet until the coating is brown and crispy. I've made country-fried steak so many times, I could make it in my sleep.

To entertain myself, I turn on the little television we keep in the kitchen. The screen is about the size of my hand, and we don't use it too often, but I'm curious about any updates about Tegan's disappearance, so I tune in to the local news. There's a brief mention about her, and I can't help but note there's no mention of a husband. It doesn't surprise me to get confirmation that she was lying.

As the steak sizzles in the frying pan, I mash some potatoes in a bowl. I pour in lots of butter and cream and salt. The mashed potatoes are just getting to the right consistency when the front door slams—Hank is home.

There's a moment of silence while he takes off his boots; then his heavy footsteps echo through the hall until he stops at the doorway to the kitchen. I smile up at him from the stove. "I'm making your favorite," I say. "Can you smell it?"

Hank stares at me. "Is she still here?"

"Of course she is. I told you she'd be staying a few days. She's fine with it."

He doesn't say anything. He just turns around and leaves the kitchen, his footsteps straining the wood on the stairs. A few minutes later, the shower turns on.

Clearly, Hank still isn't happy about Tegan staying

with us. Fine. He'll get used to the idea. It's a means to an end.

The steak is sufficiently brown, so I pull it off the stove. Hank will be a few more minutes in the shower, so I make a plate for Tegan. I've been down to the basement once since lunch to help her with the bedpan, and I assured her that the ambulance is on its way. That seemed to placate her, but it won't work for long. So I grind up a tablet of Benadryl and mix it into her mashed potatoes. That will keep her quiet tonight.

I also slice her steak into pieces for her. No good will come out of giving that girl a knife.

When I open the door to the basement, Tegan is quiet. I know she is still down there, because where else could she have gone? But it makes me uneasy when she's so silent.

"I brought you some dinner!" I announce.

Her eyes look almost hollow as she stares at me. She doesn't look good. Even if she didn't have a broken ankle, she'd struggle to leave the bed. "Where is the ambulance? Why isn't it here yet?"

I lift a shoulder. "Who knows? This isn't a big city like you're used to. People move at a slower pace here. It can take a while for things to happen."

"It's been *hours*."

I deposit the plate on the tray in front of her. She barely looks at it. She's angry with me. "Maybe they went to the wrong address?" I suggest.

She stares up at me, her eyes bloodshot. "Did you actually even call for an ambulance?"

She's young, but she's not an idiot.

"Of course I did."

"Because I feel like if you had called," she says, "then the ambulance would definitely be here by now. I don't think we would still be waiting."

"Like I said, maybe they got the wrong address."

"Well, maybe you should call again."

I nod slowly. "I could do that. But first, let's have some dinner."

I look down at the mashed potatoes heaped on her plate. If she finishes that, she won't be thinking about leaving anymore. But Tegan doesn't seem interested in the mashed potatoes. She just keeps staring up at me with her red-rimmed eyes.

"I don't think you called for an ambulance at all," she says.

"Don't be silly."

"You didn't, did you?"

I place my hands on my hips. "Even if I didn't, it was for your own good. Do you think you would be better off under a surgeon's knife than here?"

"It's not your decision! It's *my* decision!"

I push her plate slightly closer to her on the tray table. "Maybe you should make better decisions then."

What happens next happens so quickly that if I had blinked, I would have missed the whole thing. She picks up her fork off the plate I brought her, and for a moment, I'm relieved. She's going to drop it and eat her dinner. But that's not what she does at all. She raises the fork over her head, and before I can process what's happening, she has plunged the prongs deep into the flesh of my hand.

CHAPTER 36

POLLY

I scream.

Of course I do. The woman *stabbed me with a fork*. I'm sure glad I never gave her a knife!

I yank my hand off the tray table, the fork still jutting out of the skin between my thumb and forefinger. Thankfully, a second later, it falls out, because I would definitely have not enjoyed pulling that out of my skin.

"What's wrong with you?" I cry.

"You need to call an ambulance," Tegan says through her teeth. "You need to call *right now*."

I've had enough of this tomfoolery. I race up the steps of the basement, clutching my right hand, which is oozing quite a bit of blood by now. Can you get tetanus from a fork? I'll have to look that up, although I do think I'm up-to-date with my tetanus booster.

"Polly!" Tegan screams after me. "Call an ambulance!"

I slam the door to the basement behind me, breathing hard. I certainly didn't need to run, since there was no way she could follow me. But it seemed like there was some chance she might summon superhuman strength and chase after me with her broken ankle. After all, I never expected that she would stab me with a fork, for goodness' sake. That girl has more spunk than I thought she did.

Hank is coming down from the bedroom. He passes me on his way to the kitchen but then stops and does a double take. "Polly?"

That's when I notice there's blood all over my shirt.

"Polly," he gasps. "What did you do to her?"

I glare at him. "I didn't do anything. This is *my* blood. She stabbed me with a fork."

I show him my wounded hand as evidence. He winces. "Jesus Christ."

"It's fine. Could you just… Could you bring me the first aid kit? I need to get it disinfected."

Hank obediently marches over to the hall closet where we keep the first aid kit. I follow him into the living room, and he opens up the kit for me on the coffee table. I sink onto the sofa and sift through the kit with my left hand, searching for the Betadine swabs while he watches me.

"Why did she stab you?" he asks.

"She's a little confused."

"Maybe it's time for her to go."

"Hank…"

"I just don't understand what you're trying to accomplish here." He peers at me from the other side of the sofa. "The roads are clear now. She needs to go to the hospital."

"You never trust me," I grumble. "I'm doing this for her own good."

Hank is quiet for a moment, watching me fumble with the bandage. Finally, he scooches over and helps me get it secured on my hand.

"Next time," he says, "I'll go down there."

I shake my head emphatically. "I don't think it's a good idea. She doesn't like you."

"Well, she can't do anything worse to me than what she did to you." He raises his eyebrows. "Anyway, if she's mad at you, you should give her a chance to calm down."

I'm not thrilled about this idea, but then I remember about the Benadryl in the mashed potatoes. If she eats that, she'll be groggy by the time Hank comes down to collect her dirty dishes. It's not like they're going to have a big conversation, which is something I would rather avoid.

And right now, I'm really not excited to go down there again.

"Fine," I say.

I hope this isn't a mistake.

CHAPTER 37

TEGAN

I'm not sorry I stabbed Polly with a fork.

She was asking for it. She told me she called for an ambulance, but she never did. She's lying on Hank's behalf. It's fine if she can't stand up to him herself, but she can't expect me to swallow this bullshit. The second I saw her hand lying vulnerable on the tray table, within my reach, I couldn't help myself. I was so angry.

After she screamed and then ran upstairs bleeding all over her shirt, I did feel a twinge of regret though. She still has that dark bruise on her wrist, and even though she is the one who always comes down to the basement, I don't believe she's the one pulling the strings.

Hank is the one who wants me to stay here. I'm sure of it. He's the one keeping me captive, and she's just doing his bidding. And if that's the case, she isn't the one who deserved to get stabbed with the fork. She's a victim too.

I wonder what Hank's plan is for me. The thought sends a chill down my spine.

I eat the meal that Polly brought for me, despite my lack of appetite. The fried steak is pretty amazing, although I have to eat it with my hands since my fork is still on the floor. The mashed potatoes are good too, but after I've taken a few spoonfuls, I start to notice that chalky aftertaste that was in the barbecue chicken, so I push it to the side. I'm almost 100 percent sure that whatever was in that barbecue sauce was what made me sleep half the day away. Hank has been drugging me to keep me subdued, and I'm not going to go along with it anymore.

At around eight o'clock, the basement creaks open. I expect to hear Polly's light footsteps on the stairs, but my stomach sinks when the footsteps are much louder and heavier. It's not Polly coming down the stairs.

It's Hank.

My heart thuds painfully as the footsteps grow louder. When he gets to the bottom of the stairs, he just stands there for a moment. Even if I could stand, he would tower over me—he looks like he's a foot taller than me and twice as heavy. With me captive in this hospital bed, I am completely at his mercy. He's wearing a well-worn pair of blue jeans and a red-and-black-plaid shirt, and like that first night I saw him, a thick beard conceals half his face.

He's even larger and more frightening than I remember him. Especially when he just stands there at the foot of the stairs, watching me silently. I can't stop trembling.

This man is why I'm here. He beats up on his wife, and now he won't let me leave.

"I'm here to get your plate," he says quietly.

"Okay," I mumble.

"You're not going to try to stab me, are you?"

I jerk my head at the floor, where the slightly bloody fork is still lying there. "I can't."

Hank picks it up off the floor, examining the prongs, then shoves it in his shirt pocket. He takes a step forward, and I cringe.

"Please," I whisper. "Please don't..."

He sighs and grabs the plate in front of me. I squirm, trying to get as far from him as I can, even though I'm clearly not going anywhere, between my belly and my legs. But he doesn't do anything creepy like reach for me or try to stroke my hair or my face. He just takes my plate like he's a busboy.

"Good night," he mumbles as he turns to leave.

"Wait!" I cry. Maybe I can't trust him, but I can't stop myself from trying to get out. "Please! Don't go! I'll do anything you say. Just please call for an ambulance. Please!"

Hank doesn't say anything as he walks toward the stairs.

"Please!" I cry again. "I'll do anything you want! Anything! Just please... Let me go..."

And now he's climbing the stairs like he didn't even hear me.

Okay, begging has not gotten me anywhere. People like him—they get off on watching others suffer. He probably loves to see me beg.

No, the first thing that's really gotten their attention was stabbing Polly with that fork. Maybe I was on the right track with that. Maybe they'll decide I'm too much trouble if I try to fight back. I've heard men target women who seem submissive like Polly is—women who won't put up a fight.

I've got to show him I'm not weak.

"Hey!" I call out. "Hey, Hank?"

He keeps walking up the steps, ignoring me.

"Hey!" I call out again. "You need to tell Polly that the next time she comes down here, she's getting stabbed in the *eye*."

Hank freezes on the steps. He rotates his head to look at me. "Excuse me?"

Well, I finally got his attention. "You heard me. And if you don't give me a fork, I'll find something else to do it with. Maybe my fingernails."

A dark look comes over Hank's face. It seemed like a good idea to say all those things, but now I'm not so sure. He stomps down the stairs, tossing my plate at the foot of the bed so that it hits my leg and sets off an eye-watering wave of pain. I can't tell if that was his intention or not, but it does the job.

And then he walks right up to me so I can look him right in his dark-brown eyes.

"You listen here." He leans in closer to me so that I can smell fried steak and sour beer on his breath. "We'll get you out of here in a couple of days, Miss Werner. I promise you that." His voice becomes a low growl. "But if you lay another finger on my wife—just one little finger—you're going to regret it."

I haven't used the bedpan in a few hours, and the contents of my bladder spontaneously release onto the paper pad beneath me. I don't think I've ever felt quite this terrified in my life. I had judged Polly for not standing up to him, but now that I see what she's up against, I get it. This man looks like he would happily rip me limb from limb.

"*Do you understand me?*" he says in that horrible growl.

I nod, because I can't get my voice to work.

He lingers there for a moment while my body trembles. Finally, he straightens up. He picks the plate back up from the bed and dusts it off. Then without another word, he walks back up the stairs and slams the basement door behind him.

CHAPTER 38

POLLY

Hank is lying awake beside me in bed.

I know he's awake because he's not snoring. He snores like a chain saw, but I always manage to sleep through it. But right now, it's one in the morning, and he's not snoring. His eyes are wide open, and he's staring up at the ceiling. I can feel my hand throbbing beneath the bandage.

Hank and I have been through a lot. He's been through a lot because of me. And this is one more thing.

I hope I didn't break him.

I didn't make him go down there to the basement again after he collected her plate. Tegan had to use the bedpan, and I couldn't ask him to help her do that. It wouldn't be right. When I went down there, her hair was matted and clinging to her scalp, and she looked like she needed a good shower. She could barely look at me, and she didn't answer when I asked her how she was doing. *Trust me,* I told her. *This won't be the worst thing that happens to you in your life.*

Really, I'm doing her a huge favor. I'm giving her her life back. She won't have to be a mother to a needy baby she doesn't even want. And I'm giving Hank and me a chance at happiness.

Someday, your family will be complete.

Before, I used to hope and pray that my mother was right. But I'm tired of waiting for the universe to give me what I want. I'm going to *make sure* my mother's words come true.

"Hey." I run a hand over Hank's bare chest, which is covered in a healthy layer of dark hair. "Are you okay?"

He rolls his head in my direction. "We need to talk."

Uh-oh. No good conversation has ever started with those four words. "Okay…"

He turns the rest of his body so he's facing me. It's hard to see his eyes clearly in the dark room. "Why are you doing this?"

"Doing what?"

He grunts. "Stop it, Polly. Just tell me why."

"I already told you. I'm trying to help her. They're not going to take good care of her in the hospital."

"Bullshit. Tell me the truth."

He knows me too well. He can see through all my lies—well, most of them. "Tegan is so young, and she's not even married. I'm not even sure if she knows who the baby's father is. We would be so much better parents for that child."

"Oh, Polly." He brushes a strand of hair behind my ear. I take it down from the braid when I'm in bed—Hank is the only person who gets to see me with my hair down these days. "That's never going to happen, you know."

"You don't know that," I say stubbornly. "If you give me enough time, I can talk her into it. She and I can come to an understanding. We can help her."

"Polly, she stabbed you with a fork today. She's not giving you her baby."

Tegan did stab me with a fork. That is true. But she was much nicer when I came down later to help her with the bedpan. That is to say she didn't try to attack me. She even mumbled an embarrassed apology to me for having soiled her sheets.

"I want to try to convince her," I say. "You agreed to give me three days. And if you don't…"

"Don't you threaten me." He grits his teeth. "I told you I would give you three days, and I'm not going back on that. Besides, we already lied to the police. If you don't make nice with that woman, she'll have us both arrested for kidnapping."

"I'll make this right. You have to trust me."

"How do you think this is going to work? You think you're going to deliver that baby in our basement? Just show up at the pediatrician for a checkup with a random baby?"

I could deliver her baby—I'm sure of it. As for the pediatrician, I'll figure out some story to tell her. "Let me worry about all that."

Even in the dark, I can see the doubt on Hank's face. He doesn't trust me. He doesn't think this is going to work out.

"Listen," Hank says. "I think you should give Dr. Salinsky a call."

I hate it when he says that. Why should I call my shrink? I'm *happy* for the first time in a while. I'm excited for our future together. All three of us. "I don't need Dr. Salinsky," I say through my teeth.

"You don't have to tell her what's going on. Just… I think you should call her."

"Hank." I trace the curve of his collarbone with the tip of my finger. "Don't you get it? This girl could give us everything we've ever wanted. This girl could make our lives complete. Isn't it worth taking a chance for that?"

"But I've already got everything I ever wanted."

My husband can be so maddening sometimes. "Well, I don't. And if you don't think it's worth trying to make our family complete, then I don't even know what."

"Polly…"

I'm done with this conversation though. If Hank is pretending he doesn't want a child as badly as I do, then there's no point in even talking to him. I grab the covers, pull them up to my chin, and roll over so that I'm turned away from him. His fingers are on my shoulder, but I don't turn around.

"I need you to make this right, Polly," he says.

I don't answer him. I am going to make this right, but it's not going to happen like he wants it to happen.

One way or another, I'm getting Tegan's baby.

CHAPTER 39

TEGAN

Pleading with them hasn't worked.

Trying to bond with Polly hasn't worked.

Stabbing her with a fork hasn't worked.

If I'm going to get out of here, I have to do something else. I've got to get on my feet, because it's clear that's the only way I'm leaving.

I wait until the house is completely silent. Even though I can't make out any conversations, I'm able to hear the sounds of footsteps on the floor above me. Hank's boots are particularly distinctive—they sound like bolts of thunder. When those sounds vanish, I assume Hank and Polly have gone upstairs. I then wait another hour, just to be sure.

I'm taking a huge risk, but I have to do this to save myself and save my daughter. I'll have to be extremely quiet. Even if Polly and Hank are asleep, any sounds from the first floor could wake them up. The thought of Hank catching me on the first floor of the house, trying to leave, is nothing short of terrifying. And I'm in no shape to run from him. I can only imagine what he'll do to me if he catches me.

If he catches me.

My eyes have adjusted to the dark, which is a good thing, because I'm too scared to turn on the lights. In the shadows, I can make out the stairs leading to the first floor. I listened carefully when Polly went back upstairs, and I didn't hear any locks turning, but that doesn't mean there isn't one. Even if I make it all the way up the stairs, I may not be able to leave.

But they might not have locked the basement door because they don't think I'm capable of climbing the stairs. And if I get out of this basement, I'm going straight for the keys to Hank's truck. My right leg is fine, more or less, so I should be able to drive. I'm not going to stop till I get to a hospital.

Okay, here I go.

I am lying in the very center of the bed. I work the controls to lift the head of the bed all the way up to try to give me some leverage. And…

Why do I feel so dizzy?

Mommy, I don't feel so good.

This is the most vertical I've been since I arrived here. My forehead breaks out in a cold sweat, and for a split second, it almost feels like I'm going to pass out. I take a few deep breaths, and the lightheaded sensation eventually subsides.

I'm okay. I can do this. I'm okay.

Now that my head is no longer swimming, I look around the room, which is poorly lit and mostly shrouded in shadows. I squint into the darkness, trying to assess the dimensions of the basement. It's relatively small, like the rest of the house, and the distance to the foot of the stairs from the foot of my bed is only about ten feet. It's not far at all.

While I'm contemplating my next move, something catches my eye in the corner of the room. The far right corner, which is farther from any windows and darker than all the other corners. It almost looks like…

Something is moving.

My breath catches in my throat at the flash of movement. Something is there—I'm sure of it. I had thought I was alone here in the basement. But what if I'm not alone? What if Hank has been here the whole time, watching me? Watching me sleep. Watching me panic. And watching me suffer. What if he's been listening to every conversation Polly and I have had, and he's making sure that she doesn't allow me any chance to escape? What if…

Wait.

Oh, thank God. It's just a rat.

I can't say I'm not a little disgusted that I'm sharing my living space with a rodent that likely slipped inside to avoid the cold, but it's still far better than the alternative. A rat isn't going to do anything to hurt me. It's just disgusting.

I push the balls of my hands against the bed to shift my considerable body weight to the right, figuring I'll be able to get out of bed on the right side more easily, with my non-injured leg. I get a flash of that electric pain down my right leg, which isn't pleasant, but I'm able to breathe through it.

You can do this, Tegan.

I manage to swing my right leg partially out of the bed. The electric pain is bad but nothing I haven't dealt with before. Now it's time to move my left leg. I take a deep breath and grab my left thigh with my hands to shift it over.

But the second my left leg moves on the mattress, a shock of pain goes through my entire body that makes my sciatica pain pale by comparison. It's eye-watering pain. It's enough to make me gasp and stop me in my tracks.

Oh. My. God.

I didn't think the pain would be that bad. I haven't tried to put weight on it yet. I haven't even swung it out of bed yet, but the pain is blinding. There's no chance of powering through this pain—it is all-encompassing.

And it's getting worse.

I stare down at the boot that is still covering my left foot. I refused to allow Polly to remove it because it hurt too much and I thought I'd be at a hospital soon, but now I wish I had. There's nothing good happening under that boot. The worst part is that although the pain is overwhelming, I can barely feel my foot. The entire leg is just a mass of pain but without any footlike sensations.

Wiggle your toes.

I attempt to wiggle the toes of my left foot. I can't tell if they're moving since I've got that stupid boot on, but I definitely can't feel them. This is not a good sign.

My eyes fill with frustrated tears. I can't get out of this bed. I can't save myself and Tuna. We are all at the mercy of that terrible man.

CHAPTER 40

TEGAN

THREE DAYS AFTER THE CRASH

After my failed attempt to get out of bed, I spent the rest of the night racking my brain, trying to figure out what to do next. Unfortunately, when Polly comes down the stairs first thing in the morning, I still don't have any bright ideas. She's got her hair in a perfect braid behind her head again, but I can't help but notice that she has circles under her eyes and her skin looks splotchy.

"Good morning!" Her usually cheerful voice sounds strained. "Do you want the bedpan?"

"Yes," I say.

As Polly helps me, I notice her right hand is bandaged where I stabbed her, and I feel a jab of guilt. Hank is the one forcing her to keep me here. God knows what he does to her when they're upstairs. Sometimes I hear thumps or crashes up there, and I always cringe. Hank is an incredibly terrifying man; I've seen it myself. I can't imagine what would happen if she ever defied him.

But maybe that's the key. Maybe Polly and I can help each other.

"How long have you and Hank been married?" I ask when Polly emerges from the bathroom after emptying the bedpan.

She freezes, taken aback by my question. "Just over ten years."

"How did you meet?"

"He fixed my car." She usually seems so chatty and friendly, but now there's a wariness to her tone. "And then we went out to dinner."

"Ten years is a long time," I muse. "And marriage isn't always easy."

Polly looks at me for a long time before finally answering, "No, it's not easy."

This is my chance. She's not happy in her marriage. I can help her. Even though she's older than me, maybe I can give her advice. Maybe we can both have a happy ending here. "Sometimes husbands can do things to hurt you."

She nods slowly. "Yes…"

"But that doesn't make it right, Polly."

"No," she agrees, "it's never right. A husband should never hurt you."

I give myself a little pat on the back. I'm actually getting through to her. I can work on this woman. I can convince her to call the police when her husband goes to work. Maybe even today.

"Polly," I say slowly, "you don't have to do what Hank tells you to do just because you're afraid he'll hurt you."

Her head snaps up. I should not have said that—it was too soon. I can almost see the walls crashing down. "What are you talking about? How dare you! Hank would never hurt me. *Never.* He's a good man."

"Yes, but..." I gesture at the fading purple on her wrist. "Obviously, sometimes he gets out of control."

She looks down at her wrist, and her face turns pink. She yanks down the sleeve of her sweater. "Hank didn't do that. That was... It was an accident."

"An accident?"

"That's right," she snaps, but she doesn't elaborate, and I can't imagine any "accident" that could cause bruising like that. "Anyway, you should worry about yourself. You're going to get bedsores if you spend much more time in that bed. And you don't want your muscles to atrophy."

It isn't an idle threat. There's a dull ache in my bottom from lying in the bed for so long, and I am getting weaker every day. I desperately want to move around more, but my ankle isn't even the tiniest bit better. I can't even imagine attempting to walk. "What can I do?"

She points at the wheelchair in the corner. "Let me get you up. It'll be better than lying in bed all day."

As much as I hate lying in this bed, the thought of moving my left ankle makes me nauseated. But she does have a good point. It doesn't look like I'm getting out of here today, and it would be a good idea to move around a bit.

Maybe I can figure out a way out of here.

"Maybe after lunch," I say.

Polly brightens. "That's a great idea. I think it will be really good for you."

As Polly walks back up the steps to fetch my breakfast, I run my hand over my belly. I feel a reassuring kick from Little Tuna. She's okay. That's all that matters.

Don't worry, Tuna. Mama is getting you out of here, one way or another.

CHAPTER 41

POLLY

I don't know what on earth Tegan was talking about.

She started babbling some nonsense about Hank, who wouldn't hurt me even if there were a gun to his head. But of course, she saw the bruises Mitch gave me, and now she's made assumptions.

It's not like Tegan is a saint. She lied about having a husband, and she clearly got knocked up by accident. She doesn't want this baby or even care enough not to chug whiskey from a flask during her pregnancy—while driving, no less! I'm not surprised she wrapped her car around a tree. She's lucky she didn't lose the baby.

I want her to admit she's lying about having a husband. I want her to admit she's all alone and that she doesn't want this baby. Because if she does that, then I'll feel certain this is the right thing to do.

Either way, this baby needs to come out ASAP. She told me she was eight months along, which means it could be a while before she goes into labor on her own.

I have no doubt that the accident will speed things up, but not enough.

I spent some time working as a nurse in Labor and Delivery, and I feel confident that I could deliver her baby. I remember the doctors used to prescribe magnesium to speed the labor along, but I can't do that here. So I start researching ways to induce labor at home.

A lot of the websites suggest sex and long walks. Well, she's not doing either of *those* things. She can't take long walks. And as for sex, I suppose I could ask Hank to…

No. No way. He'd never even agree to it.

I've been trying to encourage her to get out of bed into the shower, thinking maybe that will help. But it's still not much of an athletic challenge. No, there's no physical activity that she's capable of right now. It's got to be something taken orally.

After scouring the web, I eventually discover a recipe for something called Midwives Brew. The website boasts an 85 percent success rate for inducing labor within twenty-four hours. The ingredients include castor oil, apricot juice, lemon tea, and almond butter.

I check the cabinets to see what I've got in stock. I've got tea, but it's not lemon tea. I have peanut butter but not almond butter. Orange juice but not apricot juice. Looks like I'm going to need to make a trip to the supermarket. Which means I'll have to leave the house with Tegan alone in the basement.

It's risky. But it's worth it if this drink induces labor as promised. Hank is not going to let me keep that woman in the basement much longer.

When I go downstairs to serve Tegan her breakfast,

she is lying in bed quietly. She seems strangely subdued compared to earlier. Maybe some of the fight has left her.

"Here you go." I place the plate of eggs and bacon on the tray in front of her, along with a big glass of orange juice. I was careful not to include a fork—she can eat with her hands. "A nutritious breakfast."

"Thank you."

"You know," I say, "when you have a child, you'll have to make her three meals a day, every day."

She looks at me irritably. "I know."

"You can't skip just because you're tired or hurt or hungover."

She shoots me a look but doesn't say anything. She picks up a piece of crispy bacon and takes a bite.

"I'm just saying," I continue, "being a mother is hard work. And you're so young. There must be a lot of other things you want to do with your time."

"I can handle it," she insists, although there's a quaver in her voice.

"Well, I hope so. But motherhood isn't for everyone."

I wait for her to blurt out that she's dreading having to take care of a screaming infant. I can see in the eyes that it's the truth. But she's stubborn and obviously refusing to admit the truth.

Fine.

When I get back upstairs, Hank has already left for the auto shop without saying goodbye. He always says goodbye in the morning. He always kisses me, tells me he wishes he didn't have to leave me, and then wraps me in a hug that reminds me how much he loves me. Today, he didn't do any of that.

But the truth is I'm just glad he's gone. I need to dash over to the supermarket, and I don't want him to know what I'm buying.

I climb into my Bronco and drive down to the strip mall that contains the supermarket. I do a lot of my grocery shopping at the small family-owned store five minutes away, but I'm not sure if that place will have all the right ingredients. Plus, the cashier at Benny's knows me and will wonder why I am buying such strange ingredients. Better to shop at a grocery store where I can stay anonymous.

I find all four ingredients pretty easily, and then I drop a few other items in my cart to serve as a buffer. A carton of milk. Some hamburger meat. I almost grab a can of formula, but then I wonder if it would be suspicious and decide against it. I'll send Hank out to get some when the time comes.

I've got about a dozen items by the time I get to check out, where a gray-haired woman is taking her sweet time ringing up all the orders. I look down at my watch. I've been gone for less than an hour. It's not that long, but it feels like an eternity when there's a ticking time bomb in the basement.

While I'm standing in the checkout line, I can see through the sliding doors to the parking lot. There's a cop car in the lot, and my heart sinks. Is that the same officer who was at my house yesterday? Like the other day, he's speaking into a radio. I force myself to look away.

Is it possible he could be here for me? Did Tegan somehow get free during the short time I've been gone and alert the police? But no, that's not possible. How would they know I'm at the supermarket? It's got to be a coincidence.

Either way, I've got to get home as soon as possible. I need to check on Tegan.

"Well, hello there, hon," the cashier says when it's finally my turn. "Cold day out there, isn't it?"

"Yes," I say. Usually I enjoy making chitchat with cashiers. I've got nothing but time on my hands these days. But today I'm irritated by this chatty cashier.

She picks up the bottle of castor oil, then looks down at the apricot juice. "You past due, sweetie?"

"Excuse me?"

The cashier looks pointedly at my stomach. I'm wearing a very bulky winter coat, so you can't see much. I could be forty weeks pregnant for all she knows. "You've got all the ingredients for a German labor cocktail. I thought maybe you're hoping to get things moving on the baby front. How many weeks are you?"

I place a hand on my belly. I consider denying it, but maybe I shouldn't. After all, if I come back here in the future with a baby, it won't hurt for people to think I was pregnant. "Forty-one weeks."

"Ouch." She winces. "Well, I'm sure you're eager to get that little one out of you. Good luck with the cocktail! It really works."

That's what I'm counting on.

When I get out to the parking lot with my brown paper bag of groceries, I half expect that police officer to point a gun at me and tell me I'm under arrest. But that doesn't happen. In fact, the police car is completely gone. I'm just being paranoid.

As I navigate back to the house, I feel increasingly

uneasy about my interaction with the cashier. I should have just told her they were random ingredients. Now she's going to remember me. What if the police start asking around about a pregnant woman? Maybe she'll remember me and tell them I was buying ingredients to induce labor. The cashier couldn't tell I wasn't pregnant, but the police will know by looking at me.

Why didn't I just keep my fool mouth shut?

But as I come to the end of the dead-end road containing my house, I forget all about the cashier. Because there's something else to worry about.

There's an unfamiliar car in my driveway. And a man standing on my porch, at my front door.

And he's waiting for me.

CHAPTER 42

TEGAN

I don't have my pepper spray. But I have the lighter Jackson gave me.

I'm not exactly sure what to do, but I can't walk out of here—that much is clear. If I want to get out of here, I'm going to need help to come to me. And while I may not have a weapon, I do have a way to make fire.

I'm sure when Jackson bought me this lighter, he had no idea that it would save my life.

There's a smoke detector in the corner of the room, not far from the bed. The red light in the detector indicates that it's functional. So if there's a fire down here, it will go off.

I have to be very careful though. The last thing I want to do is set the basement on fire and burn myself to a crisp. But if there's a small fire, the alarms will go off, and Polly will be forced to call 911 for help.

I am admittedly a bit worried it won't be enough. Polly may feel capable of putting out a fire on her own. But it's the only chance I've got.

First, I need something to burn.

That part is easy. There are plenty of magazines stacked up on the nightstand next to the bed. I pick one of them up and rip out a picture of Jennifer Aniston's face. Nothing against Jennifer Aniston. I've got to burn something though.

My hand is shaking slightly as I press my thumb against the spark wheel and into the ignition button. There's a little spark but no fire. I try again, and this time, it ignites. A steady orange flame rises from the lighter. This is a very high-quality lighter.

Thank you, Jackson.

Why did you have to turn out to be such a jerk?

I hold out the pages from the magazine and touch the flame to the edge. Almost instantly, they catch fire.

Bingo.

As the flame grows, I hold the papers up in the air and fan them around. I keep my eyes on the smoke detector.

Start ringing.

Please, for the love of God, start ringing.

CHAPTER 43

POLLY

I don't recognize this man.

Part of me wants to drive away, but that would be the worst thing I could do, given what's hidden in my basement. Anyway, he's already seen me. At the sound of my Bronco's engine, the man swivels his head and squints at my car, his eyes making contact with mine.

On the plus side, he doesn't look angry. He doesn't look drunk. And he's not in a police uniform. He's wearing a woolen hat with a ski jacket over blue jeans and boots. He certainly doesn't seem like a detective. Maybe he's just a salesman. Maybe this is nothing to worry about.

So I kill the engine of my Bronco and step out of the car, clutching the bag of ingredients in my right hand. At least *he* won't recognize what I'm trying to do with them.

"Hello," I say with forced pleasantness. "How can I help you?"

The man fixes his bloodshot blue eyes on me as I join him on the front porch. He pulls a hand out of his coat pocket and thrusts it in my direction. "Hi. My name is Dennis Werner. Could I talk to you for a moment?"

Werner. That's not a name I want to hear right now.

"Yes…" I hover on the porch, the cold air biting at my cheeks. But I'm not going to let him in. "What is this about?"

Dennis Werner shoves both hands back into his coat pockets. "It's actually… It's about my sister, Tegan. She's been missing for the last three days."

"Oh." I fix a confused frown on my face. "I…I'm sorry to hear that…"

"She was…she was on her way to see me." His Adam's apple bobs slightly. "But I guess she got caught in the storm. Anyway, her car was found wrapped around a tree not too far from here. But the police haven't been able to find her. And they've been looking hard."

"Gosh," I say. "How terrible. Yes, they were around here asking about her yesterday, now that you mention it. But I haven't seen her."

"Right…" Dennis looks back over his shoulder at the white landscape with snowcapped trees as far as the eye can see. "But it wasn't like she was thrown from the vehicle. There weren't any broken windows, and all the doors were closed. Her purse and her luggage weren't in the car, and… My sister wouldn't leave on a trip without those things, so she definitely had them with her when she left."

"How strange!"

He presses his lips together. "My sister is a fighter. She's eight months pregnant, and she would have done everything she could to find help. And these houses here... They're the closest ones to where her car was found."

I lift a shoulder. "I really wish I could help, but like I said, I didn't see her."

"This was a few nights ago—the night of the storm. Are you sure there weren't any sounds? Knocks on your door that you thought might have been something else? If we know she came by this way, maybe we could find her..."

Desperation is in his eyes. I could tell him that his sister is right in our basement. I could put an end to this right now. "I'm afraid not."

"I see." His shoulders sag. "What about the other house? I knocked on the door, and nobody answered."

"Mitch Hambly and his daughter live there," I say. "He's usually gone during the day." I lower my voice a notch. "He's kind of a drunk, so I doubt he would take kindly to a woman coming by looking for help. But you never know."

Dennis Werner nods slowly. He takes a shaky breath, blinking rapidly. He's fighting back tears. "I'm sorry," he manages. "I...I'm worried sick about my baby sister. I just keep imagining all these terrible things that could have happened to her and..."

Send him on his way, Polly. Tell the nice man you can't help him, and then send him on his way.

But instead I say, "Would you like to come in for a cup of coffee? You can warm up for a minute."

He hesitates for a moment, then nods. "Thank you. Just for a minute."

As Dennis follows me into the house, the epic

stupidity of what I am doing hits me like a ton of bricks. Our basement is not soundproof. If Tegan calls out for me or makes any loud noises, the jig is up. And Hank and I will get a one-way ticket to jail. And more importantly, we won't have our baby.

"Cozy house you have here." Dennis pulls off his cap, revealing a head full of sun-kissed light-brown hair. He looks a bit like Tegan. "Really nice."

"Thank you. The kitchen is this way."

I hold my breath as we pass the basement door. It also strikes me that there is a very real chance that Tegan could hear her brother's voice from the basement. I quickly steer him into the kitchen.

"Please have a seat." I gesture at the kitchen table. "How do you take your coffee? Milk? Sugar?"

"Just a little of each." He slides off his ski jacket and hangs it on the back of his chair. He's slim and muscular, but he would be no match for my husband. Unfortunately, Hank isn't here to protect me at the moment. "Thank you so much…"

"Polly."

"Polly." He manages a smile. "Good to meet you. Sorry I lost it a bit out there."

I start the coffee brewing, hoping to get him out of here as quickly as possible. My hands shake a little as I scoop the grounds. "Completely understandable."

"And I keep blaming myself," he goes on. "She was coming out to visit me. I thought she had time before the storm, but she didn't leave when I told her to. I should've come out to see her instead. I didn't want to miss work, but… Christ, she's my sister, and she's pregnant. I should have…"

"You can't think that way." I glance nervously at the gurgling coffee pot, willing it to brew faster. "And if they didn't find her in the car, I bet she found help somewhere. I bet she's fine."

"Then why hasn't she contacted anyone?"

"Maybe she lost her memory?"

"Yes, but she has her purse." He shoots me a perplexed look. "Her wallet is in there with all her information."

I don't have an answer for that one that doesn't involve telling him that his sister is trapped in my basement without access to a phone. "I usually try to think positive. I'm sure she'll turn up safe and sound."

He manages a tiny smile. "You sound like Tegan. She always tries to be positive about stuff."

"It's the key to happiness."

He shakes his head. "I…I'm just scared they're going to find her buried under a snowdrift, frozen to death."

The coffee machine buzzes, signifying the coffee is ready. Thank goodness. I grab one of the white mugs from the cabinet over the sink and I pour him about two-thirds of a cup. I add a dollop of milk and a pinch of sugar, and then I present him with the steaming cup.

"Thanks so much," he says. "You're not having any?"

If I drink a cup of coffee, I'll be ready to jump out of my skin. "That's okay. I had some earlier."

Dennis sips on the cup of coffee while I join him at the kitchen table, willing him to drink faster. I absently start drumming my fingers against the table.

"Sorry," he says. "You must be busy. I should get going."

"I just have a few errands to take care of." I force

a smile. "But I wish you the best of luck finding your sister."

He slides the half-drunk cup of coffee across the table and starts pulling on his coat. I let out a sigh of relief. He's leaving. I made a stupid mistake, but nothing terrible will come of it.

And then there's a loud crash from downstairs.

Dennis jerks his head up. "What was that?"

"That?" My laugh sounds horribly fake to my own ears. "That's our cat. She's always knocking things over. I've gotten up in the middle of the night thinking we had a burglar in the house!"

"Oh."

For a moment, Dennis Werner studies my face. My cheeks grow warm—he's going to see right through me. He's going to burst into the basement and find his sister down there, and it will all be over.

Of course, if I'm really quick about it, maybe I can push him down the basement stairs. A fall like that would surely knock him unconscious. I can get him tied up before he comes to—*if* he comes to. But then there is the matter of his car. I'd have to find a way to get rid of that too. But he's got the keys in his pocket.

I can get rid of this man if I need to.

"I used to have a cat growing up," Dennis says. "She was always knocking things over. You couldn't leave a glass of water on the table."

"You know what I mean then!"

He smiles at me. Hallelujah—I've gotten away with it. I don't have to knock him out and dispose of his body after all. Good thing, because I'm honestly not sure I could do it.

I follow him back to the front door. He thanks me one more time for my hospitality and scribbles down his phone number on a piece of paper. He tells me to call him if I hear anything at all. I promise that I surely will. And just like that, he's gone.

The second the front door slams shut, I hurry to the basement door. I throw the door open and call out, "Tegan? Everything okay?"

There's no answer.

I open my mouth to call her name again, but before I can get the word out, I get a powerful whiff of smoke. And not just a little smoke—it's strong enough that I'm shocked I couldn't smell it upstairs.

Our house is on fire.

CHAPTER 44

TEGAN

I have ignited three sets of magazine pages without any luck.

I finally grabbed the entire magazine—I have to risk making a larger fire. In my hurry, I knocked several magazines to the floor, and the entire tray table tipped over, which I'm worried might have alerted Polly that something is going on down here. That means I might not have much time.

Just as the tip of the magazine catches fire, a voice floats down the stairs. "Tegan? Everything okay?"

Polly is coming. This is my last chance.

I hold up the flaming magazine in the direction of the smoke detector. I wave it around, hoping I will set off the alarm. Nothing happens. I don't have much time, and the fire is starting to scorch my fingertips, so instead, I toss the magazine into the pile I dropped on the floor. Quicker than I thought, the whole pile goes up in flames.

Now we're talking.

I hold my breath, waiting for the fire alarm to sound off. But before that can happen, Polly bursts into the basement. She must see the smoke from the top of the stairs, and she hurries down as fast as she can.

"Tegan!" she cries. "What on earth are you doing?"

The pile of magazines beside my bed is quickly disappearing beneath the growing flames. In a flash, Polly yanks one of the blankets off my bed and throws it on top of the fire to smother it. And then, before I realize what she was doing, she snatches the gold lighter off the nightstand where I left it.

"What is wrong with you?" she cries. "You could have burned the whole house down with you in it!"

"I'm sorry. I thought the fire alarm would—"

"There's no fire alarm in the basement," she says.

So it was all for nothing. And even if there had been a fire alarm, who knows if anyone would have heard it?

"How could you be so stupid?" She shakes her head at me. "If you can't act responsibly for your own sake, at least think about your baby!"

It hits me how right she is. As far as I know, Polly has not done anything to hurt me or Little Tuna. But if I had set fire to this room, I could have died here. Polly isn't capable of getting me up the stairs. And considering how far we are from civilization, it would take the fire department a while to get here. The house would have burned to the ground with me in it.

I wouldn't have done it if I hadn't been desperate.

My eyes well with tears. "I just want to go to the hospital. Can't you please just call 911?"

Polly is quiet for a moment, looking at me. "I'm afraid I can't. Not right now anyway." She closes her fingers into a fist around the lighter. "But I'm going to hold on to this for you so you don't do anything else stupid with it."

"It was a gift..."

"I'm not *stealing* it." She looks affronted. "I'll give it back to you when you leave here. And trust me, you will." She gives me a pointed look. "Just make sure it isn't in a body bag."

Polly slips the lighter into her jeans pocket. And that's that—my one potential weapon is now gone.

I'm worried that no matter what, I'm leaving here in a body bag.

CHAPTER 45

POLLY

At around one o'clock in the afternoon, while I am cleaning the dishes from lunch, I hear the knock on my front door.

I'm still feeling on edge from finding that fire in the basement. I didn't even realize she had a lighter. I vaguely remember seeing it in her purse, and I was too stupid to take it away like I did with the phone and pepper spray. She could've killed us both with that little stunt. Well, I would have gotten out all right. But she and the baby likely would have perished.

And what if she had succeeded in setting off the fire alarm while her brother was here? That would have been extremely bad. She doesn't know how close she came to making some serious trouble for me.

I've got to keep a closer eye on Tegan. It's obvious she can't be trusted alone for very long. Even stuck in the bed, she's a troublemaker.

And now there's someone at the door again.

Immediately, my heart skips in my chest. This can't be anything good. Has Dennis Werner returned, having decided to investigate the noises coming from the basement? Is the police officer from yesterday back again?

I'd like to pretend I'm not home, but my Bronco is right out in the driveway. And anyway, whoever it is will certainly come back later.

I wipe my hands on my blue jeans and hurry out to the front door. I don't see any flashing red and blue lights from my window, so that's a good sign. Nobody's here to arrest me for kidnapping. I check the peephole, and my heart slows down.

It's Sadie.

I pull the door open, and she's standing there in her threadbare coat, her dark-blond hair still in the braids that I tied for her days earlier, although mostly coming loose. I want more than anything to get this girl a decent coat. And boots. And scrub her face a bit.

"Hi, Sadie," I say. "What's wrong, honey?"

"Hi, Polly." She scratches at the stretch pants she's wearing, which have a hole in the left knee. "Um, we're out of crackers."

It takes me a second to realize what she's telling me. Two days ago, she said she had crackers for lunch. And today, there are no more crackers. Which means the crackers are all she's had to eat the last two days, aside from the sandwiches I made her, and now she's finished them.

"Come in," I tell her. I had vowed not to let anyone else into our house, but Sadie doesn't fall into that category. There's no way I'm not letting this little girl inside.

Sadie follows me into the living room, a flush coming into her cheeks. "It's so warm in here!"

It's not *that* warm in our house. It's just warm enough to be comfortable, which makes me wonder if Mitch Hambly is paying the heating bill.

I lead her straight into the kitchen, where I pour her a brimming glass of orange juice and get to work making her some lunch. I'd love to make her a nice home-cooked meal, but the poor thing is probably starving, so faster is better. I reach for the cold cuts again. Sadie likes bologna.

"Is school canceled because of the snow?" I ask.

"No," she says. "But when there's too much snow piled at the school bus stop, the bus doesn't come."

Anger surges in my chest. The school bus is obligated to pick her up one way or another—they aren't supposed to forget about her just because of a little extra snow. And anyway, Mitch could have shoveled the area around the bus stop. I'll have to ask Hank to do it when he gets home. I would do it myself, but I'm very reluctant to leave Tegan alone again.

I lay the sandwich down in front of Sadie, and before I can even sit down to join her at the kitchen table, she has demolished the sandwich in, like, three bites. I watch her, wondering when she last had a decent meal. I don't even give her a chance to ask me—I grab her plate and set about making her a second sandwich.

"Do you have any more Oreo cookies?" she asks hopefully.

"But of course!" I say.

I keep the cookies in the pantry, just so I won't be too tempted to snack on them during the day. It's hard being home all day, and the temptation to eat my way through the boredom is strong. I finish making Sadie's second sandwich, and then I leave the kitchen to check the pantry closet.

I don't even really like Oreos that much, but Sadie likes them, so I always keep them stocked. I find a nearly full package of them on the third shelf, and just before I close the door to the pantry, I catch sight of that brown teddy bear again. The one clutching the red heart.

Hank was so excited when he brought home that teddy bear. His face was practically glowing when he pressed the stuffed animal into my arms. *It's for both of you.* I had laughed, *It's her...or* his...*first gift.*

Then the next day, I got my period.

I reach out and stroke the soft fur of the bear. It's still in perfect condition—it's never been played with, never drooled on, never had a toddler nibble on its ear. I had started to believe we'd never give that teddy bear to a child of our own.

But now it's so close, I can taste it.

I close the pantry door, armed with the package of Oreos. I return to the kitchen to see if Sadie finished her second sandwich. I'm tempted to let her take as many cookies as she wants, but I probably shouldn't. Two or three will be enough.

Except when I get back inside the kitchen, the seat Sadie had occupied is empty.

"Sadie?" I call out.

I step outside the kitchen, figuring she went to use the bathroom. And that's when I notice it.

The basement door is wide open.

CHAPTER 46

POLLY

Sadie went into the basement.

This is not good.

If she sees Tegan down there… Well, I'm not sure what she'll do. She may be seven years old, but she's a smart kid. She's got to realize what's going on.

I need to deal with this situation.

I approach the basement door, my heart pounding. The lights are on inside, and as I get closer, I can see Sadie standing there, on the third step from the top. It's like she's frozen, afraid to go any deeper into the basement.

"Hello?" Tegan's voice calls out. "Polly?"

Oh no.

"Sadie!" I hiss at the little girl. "Sadie, you shouldn't go down there!"

Sadie swivels her head to look back at me, her big blue eyes luminous. Her mouth is open, but no words are coming out.

"Who's there?" Tegan calls out from her hospital bed. Her voice cracks. "Is there someone there? I need help! Please help me!"

I make a split-second decision. I wrap my fingers around Sadie's skinny wrist, and I tug her in the direction of the basement door. Obediently, she follows me, stumbling on the top step. When we're out of the basement, I shut the door behind us. Sadie is staring at me.

"What were you doing down there?" I snap at her.

"I heard a noise," she says in a small voice, which makes me immediately regret my harsh tone. "I thought you were down there looking for cookies, and I wanted to tell you that Fig Newtons would be okay too. If you were out of Oreos."

I can't get my heart to slow down. My hands are shaking badly, and I have to wrap them around my chest. "You shouldn't have gone down there."

Sadie's chin wobbles. "I'm sorry."

"That woman down there," I say, "that's…that's my cousin. She's been very sick. Really, really sick. And I've been taking care of her." I pause. "And nobody can go down there because you'll catch her sickness." I pause again. "Do you understand?"

"You're taking care of her?" Sadie asks slowly.

"That's right."

"Because you're a nurse?"

"You got it." I manage a tiny smile. "She's going to get all better, but I don't want you or anyone else to get sick like she is." I ask again, "Do you understand?"

She nods solemnly.

"Also," I add, "don't tell anyone about this. Because if people knew, they would want to visit her, and they might get sick. So let's keep this just between you and me. Okay?"

"Okay," Sadie says quietly. And I believe her. She's going to keep my secret.

"Good girl." I lay a hand on her delicate shoulder. "Now I'm going to pack you some Oreos to go home with. And if you ever want food again, just come by, and I'll make you whatever you like. You don't have to wait until you're really hungry."

Except next time, I'm going to have some food ready in advance so I can give it to her and send her on her way. I can't risk having anyone in the house while Tegan is down in the basement. Even Sadie.

CHAPTER 47

TEGAN

I'm going out of my mind with boredom.

There isn't much to do down here. I've been doing the puzzle books Polly gave me and flipping through the magazines, which are largely out of date. I tried reading a couple of books, but I couldn't focus on anything. I'm actually starting to miss my job at the grocery store.

At around lunchtime, I was certain I heard someone come into the basement. I didn't know who it was, but it didn't sound like Polly. The footsteps sounded different from hers—softer and more hesitant. I could almost make out the sound of breathing, and then—I was almost certain—a tiny sniffle. But when I called out for help, there was no answer.

And then I wondered if I had imagined the whole thing.

So when Polly comes downstairs midafternoon and offers me the opportunity to get out of bed, I decide to take it.

"Do you think you can manage to get me up on your own?" I ask her as she wheels the chair over to the bed and locks the wheels.

"Of course," she laughs.

I don't doubt her. Polly is several inches taller than I would be if I could stand, and she is thin but wiry. I have no doubt based on her knowledge and efficiency with the equipment in this room that she really is a nurse, and I'm sure during her career, she has transferred a fair number of patients into wheelchairs. But at the same time, I'm terrified of anyone even touching my leg at this point.

She sponges off the chair before attempting to get me into it. There's a fine layer of dust over the seat, and when she's done, the metal in the chair reflects the light overhead.

"You ready?" she asks.

No. But I need to do this. If I have any hope of getting out of this basement, I need to first get out of bed.

Polly is very gentle, and she has an air of confidence that makes me trust she won't drop me. I can't help but think that if I ever do get to live out my dream of going to nursing school, she is exactly the sort of capable nurse I'd like to be. We take it extremely slowly, and when she shifts my legs for me, the pain isn't quite as excruciating as last night when I tried to do it myself. When she sits me up, I get that wave of lightheadedness that takes even longer to pass than last night.

"Are you okay?" Polly asks me.

"Uh-huh," I manage.

She waits for close to a minute before I give her the go-ahead to proceed. Then she very, very slowly moves my legs off the bed. It's going okay, but the second my left boot hits the floor, I scream in pain.

"Tegan." She straightens up to look me in the eyes. "I'm really worried about that leg. Will you please let me take off the boot?"

She's right. I'm sure she's right that the boot needs to come off. Except at this point, it's been long enough that I am overwhelmed with fear about what is under there. I've got this idea in my head that the boot is holding my entire leg together like a splint. And if she takes it off, my foot will just disintegrate.

"No," I say. "Leave it."

She gives me a look, but she doesn't push me harder.

Polly brought a belt, presumably from her own closet. She ties it around my waist, just below the bulge of my belly, and she holds on to it as she shifts me from the bed to the chair in one controlled movement. Even though she's being careful, the pain from my left leg from moving is enough to make my eyes water. But then we've done it. I'm in the chair.

"Look at you!" Polly says, her voice bright. "You got out of bed!"

Objectively, it's not that stunning of an achievement, but right now, it feels like it is. Polly gets my legs positioned in the footrests, another agonizing adventure, but then I'm okay. I'm secure in the chair, and for the first time, I can move around the room.

"Thank you," I say. "This is great."

She smiles at me. "You're very welcome!"

"So how do you use it?"

"Oh, it's not rocket science." She touches the push rim of the chair. "You just push them forward to move forward, back to move backward. If you want to turn right, turn the right wheel... You get the idea."

I test it out, pushing myself the length of the room. It's harder work than I thought, given my abdominal girth. But Polly is cheering me on.

"This is great exercise," she tells me. "You should do a few laps across the basement."

"Yes." I run my fingers along the push rim. "I...I just wish I could leave this room."

Instantly, the smile vanishes from her face. I shouldn't have said that. We were bonding, and maybe this was an opportunity to talk to her about her husband's abuse. But I can see those walls crashing down once again.

"I'll give you some privacy," she says. "I need to get started on dinner anyway."

She disappears back up the stairs, but that's not a bad thing. After all, I couldn't really explore this room with her here with me. If she's here, I have no chance of getting out of here.

Once the basement door slams overhead, I start exploring the room. Thankfully, Polly has kept the floor relatively clean. Aside from a small amount of furniture, I have a clear path to wheel myself around.

Some basements have doors inside that lead directly to the outdoors. Presumably, Polly wouldn't leave me alone if I could get out through the basement, but maybe she doesn't know about the door. It's a bit of a long shot, but it could be my only hope.

I do a lap around the basement, but there's no sign of a secret door. Figures. And as for the windows, they're far too high for me to reach even if I could stand, which

I can't. But if I could get to my feet, I could stack some of the boxes in the corner and climb up there…

It's stupid to contemplate that. I can't stand. I could barely get from the bed to the chair with Polly doing all the work. And even if I could get up there, I doubt my belly would fit.

Yes, my number one priority is survival. I've got to get myself out of here, and I've got to save Little Tuna. But I'm selfishly worried about the damage that's happening to my ankle every day without medical care. If it's broken, the bones are surely setting improperly. And I'm still not entirely sure if I can wiggle my toes, because I can't see them.

What if my leg has permanent damage? What if I somehow manage to get free but it's too late for the doctors to repair the damage? What if I need crutches for the rest of my life? What if the pain never gets better?

Okay, there are worse things. I can't think about that right now anyway. I need to focus on getting out of this room. I need to do this for my daughter.

Please save us, Mama! I'm counting on you!

I can't let her down.

I wheel over to the stairwell. The front wheels of the chair bounce uselessly against the first step. I'm not going up a flight of stairs in a wheelchair, that's for sure. But now that I'm up, maybe there's a way to climb the stairs. If I could lower myself out of the chair, I could use the strength of my arms to pull myself up the steps one by one. And maybe I could reach up and open the door at the top.

I grab the push rims, testing my weight. Can I do this?

No. No, I can't. It's just as hopeless as it was last night.

I can't lower myself safely onto the stairs. Even if I could do it under the best circumstances, I can't do it with this basketball on my belly. There's too much weight. I'll fall on the floor, which might hurt the baby, and then Polly will figure out what I was trying to do. She won't let me out of bed ever again.

If I can't get out of here on my own, there's only one other thing I can do.

I've got to find myself a weapon.

CHAPTER 48

TEGAN

There's got to be something in this basement that I can use as a weapon.

Unfortunately, the basement was used as a hospital room for Polly's mother, and it's correspondingly clean and sanitary. It's not going to be easy to find something I could use as a weapon. But there must be *something*.

I wheel myself over to the hospital bed. I feel along the plastic sideboard, seeing if there's anything that I could pry loose that has a sharp edge. But the bed is well made. Nothing dangerous about it.

Polly left me a glass of water on the nightstand. If I smash it, the shards of glass will be extremely sharp. But then I pick it up and instantly realize that it's made of plastic. Not a weapon.

This is harder than I thought.

I sift through the drawers of the nightstand. There's got to be something in there. Even a paper clip could be fashioned into a weapon. But the only thing in the entire nightstand that even comes close is a couple of pencils. And their points are frustratingly dull.

Damn it.

I can't give up though. I have to do this for Tuna. I have to get her out of here. Because I have a bad feeling that if I don't do something, neither of us is getting out of here alive.

My next stop is the bathroom, which thankfully has a wide enough door for the wheelchair to fit through. There's got to be *something* in there that I can use as a weapon. Even a pair of tweezers might do the trick.

The medicine cabinet is out of my reach. Even when I hold on to the armrest of the chair and stretch as far as I can, I can't reach it. It might be a good thing, because if I found pain medications in there, I would almost certainly be tempted to take way too many of them. Similarly, there are a couple of shelves mounted on the wall that are far out of my reach.

I lean back into the chair with a huff. The sink has a small drawer underneath it. I have searched everywhere in this basement, so this drawer is my last chance to find something I can use to potentially get out of here. I yank it open, craning my neck to see what's inside.

The contents are utterly unexciting. A hairbrush with a few strands of gray hair laced between the bristles. A comb. A container of toothpaste advertising a whiter smile. Dental floss.

With growing frustration, I stick my hand into the drawer, feeling around, hoping my fingers will hit something sharp. But they don't. It's just extra toothbrushes, more dental floss, and then a plastic baggie that feels sort of sticky. I pull out the plastic baggie, and that's when my heart stops.

It contains two syringes. And one needle.

Considering I had been planning to use a pencil as a weapon, the needle feels like a gift from God. This is going to get me out of here.

I open the plastic baggie. I pull out the syringe and peel off the packaging. It's obviously been in this drawer for a while, but it still seems functional. Anyway, I don't need it to dispense medication. I just need it to hold the needle.

I pick up the needle next and peel away the plastic covering. It looks like it screws into the syringe. I pick up the syringe, preparing to screw it on, and…

I drop the needle.

Oh no.

This wouldn't be a big deal under ordinary circumstances. Even a week ago, I could have taken my time bending down to pick it up. But right now, that needle lying on the floor feels like it is miles away. Like I'd have to run an entire marathon to get to it. And I'm sure any minute now, Polly will come down to check on me. How can I possibly get to it in time?

You can do it, Mama!

I have to try. For my daughter.

I position my chair just to the side of the needle. I figure there's no way I'm reaching over the basketball on my stomach, but maybe I can get to it from the side. I reach down as far as I can, and my back spasms, followed by a white-hot jolt of pain in my ankle. But I'm still several inches short.

Damn it.

I need to figure out a way to get closer. I look down at my right foot, positioned in the foot rest. If it weren't in that foot rest, I could get closer to the needle.

I take a deep breath. I gently raise my right leg from the footrest, ignoring the way it sets off a jolt of excruciating pain in my other leg. I then reach down and flip the plate up. I've now given myself a couple more inches of reach. And when my fingers close around the needle, it's worth all the pain.

When Polly comes back down here, I'm going to be ready for her.

CHAPTER 49

POLLY

While Tegan is wheeling herself around downstairs in the basement, I make her a batch of Midwives Brew.

I still feel shaken about Tegan's brother showing up this morning, Sadie almost discovering our secret, and, to top it all, Tegan nearly burning the cabin down with her inside. All this underscores the fact that I can't keep Tegan here forever. It's too risky. I need to move things along, which means speeding up her labor.

I start out by boiling some water, and then I brew the tea. I let the tea bag sit for ten whole minutes in the ceramic mug, because the directions said that it needs to be "pretty strong." When the tea has turned a dark-brown color, I pour it into the blender. Then I add two tablespoons of castor oil, two tablespoons of almond butter, and half a cup of apricot juice. And I hit blend.

I watch the liquid morph into a homogeneous mocha color. Admittedly, it does not look appealing. It's going to be a challenge to get Tegan to drink it.

But maybe she will. She seems to be more cooperative, especially now that I've helped her get out of bed. It was a risk to give her more mobility in the basement, but I worry about the possibility of her developing a blood clot from lying in bed all the time. While this isn't the same as walking, it's better than nothing.

The wheelchair used to belong to my mother. We bought it when she became too weak to walk, and I used to encourage her to get into it at least once every day. I remember transferring her with the same care that I used with Tegan and her broken ankle. My mother was so fragile near the end that it felt like I could break her bones if I lifted her too roughly. But she always trusted me.

Tegan needs to trust me the same way. She seems to have accepted that she's stuck here for the foreseeable future at least, and Hank is...well, he doesn't seem to be actively doing anything to get her to leave. Hopefully, if this drink does what it's supposed to do, she won't have to be here much longer.

I pour the mixture back into the mug. I dip a spoon into it and take a sample. It tastes like almond butter. It's not quite as bad as it looks, but it's not something I'd drink for enjoyment.

"What's that?"

I'm so startled I practically drop the mug. Hank is standing at the entrance to the kitchen, that deep groove between his eyebrows. After the last couple of days, he will never, ever get rid of that crease.

"It's for Tegan," I say. "It's to help with nausea."

"Oh," Hank says.

"What are you doing home so early?"

"I just wanted to check on things." He frowns at me. "Is she doing okay?"

"She's fine," I assure him. "She's doing really well. I got her into my mother's wheelchair, and she's moving around great. She's very grateful."

"I'm sure," he mumbles.

"She told me she thinks we would give her baby a good home," I say. "She's thinking about her options."

Hank just stares at me.

"Maybe by tomorrow, she'll have decided," I add.

Again, Hank is silent. He scratches the back of his neck with his oil-stained fingertips. "I'm going to take a shower."

He doesn't believe me. He doesn't think this is going to work out the way I want it to. I wish he would trust me the way he used to.

As soon as Hank disappears upstairs, I climb down the basement steps with my mug of Midwives Brew. I find Tegan in my mother's wheelchair, sitting by the bookcase, inspecting the selection.

"Hello," I say.

She looks up at me. "Hi."

"Those books were my mother's."

She nods. "Is Hank home?"

She keeps asking me about him, as if that's going to change anything. "Yes."

She looks like she's going to say something else, but then her eyes drop to the cup I'm holding in my right hand. "What's that?"

"Oh." I swish the concoction around in the mug. "It's a natural remedy for pain. I looked it up on the internet. I thought it would be better than pain medications."

"What's in it?"

"Lemon tea," I say. "Also, apricot juice and almond butter." I don't mention the castor oil. I'm worried that might scare her off drinking it.

She crinkles her nose. "How does that work to relieve pain?"

"The combination of lemon and apricot dulls the nerve fibers," I explain, making it up as I go along. "And the almond butter keeps it in your digestive system longer, so it works for a longer period of time."

That sounds like it could be true, doesn't it?

"Try it," I urge her.

She narrows her eyes at me. "You drink it first."

Ah, it seems that she has figured out I've been spiking her food with Benadryl. Thankfully, there's nothing in this concoction that I'd be reluctant to ingest. I obediently take a drink, letting her watch my throat bob as the liquid travels down my esophagus.

"It's good!" I say.

Tegan gives me a side-eye as she accepts the mug. She sniffs at it like she's still not sure if it's been poisoned. But she must really be in agony, because she eventually takes a sip. I can barely suppress the smile on my face.

Soon our family will be complete.

"Wow," she comments. "I can taste the almond butter."

"I don't know if it will work, but it can't hurt, right?"

"I guess." She hesitates and then takes another sip. "Actually, it doesn't taste too bad."

"I'm glad," I say. "I hope it works."

I really, really do.

She takes another long sip. "I want you to know that if

I do go to the hospital, I won't let them give me any pain medications. You're right—it's not good for the baby."

"I don't think it works that way. They're not going to be able to set your fractures without medications."

"Then I'll wait until I deliver before I let them set the bones."

I frown. "I thought you were worried about your legs not healing right."

"I was." She takes another sip. Almost half the drink is gone. Eighty-five percent chance of labor in the next twenty-four hours. "But you were right. She's more important. If I can't walk again, that's not as important as having a healthy baby."

"Yes," I say. "I'm glad you agree."

"So..." She swallows another sip. "Do you think you could call the hospital?"

Ah, so that's what this is all about. All this stuff about not letting the doctors give her pain medication is a crock of lies. She's just trying to convince me to take her to the hospital.

"Tegan..."

"Please, Polly." Her blue eyes beseech me. "I need to go to the hospital. You know I do."

"Tegan..."

"I know of a women's shelter." Her eyes fill with tears. She's not drinking from the mug anymore. "If you need to get away from Hank, I'll help you."

I stare at her.

"I can help you get away from him, Polly," she says. "You can start a new life. And then you won't have to worry about him hurting you ever again. You'll be safe. I promise."

"I should go," I mumble.

"Polly, no!" Panic floods her features. "It can't go on like this. You know that. Sooner or later, somebody is going to figure out you're keeping me hostage here."

"Not necessarily. Your brother was searching for you here this morning, and he didn't know you were here."

I shouldn't have told her that. I was trying to make some sort of point, but it seems to infuriate her. Before I know it, she's hurling her drink straight at me. The brown liquid stains my shirt, and the mug falls to the ground and shatters. And then her hand closes around my arm with surprising strength, dragging me close to her.

"If you move," she says, "I'll jam this right into your neck."

It takes me a second to realize what she's talking about. Then I see it.

She's holding a syringe in her right hand with a needle, millimeters away from my neck.

CHAPTER 50

POLLY

How could I have been so stupid?

At the end of her life, my mother required more and more pain meds just to get through the day. It felt like I was constantly running to the pharmacy for more pills. But sometimes the pills weren't enough, and sometimes it was hard for her to swallow, so I also had injectable pain medications for the really bad times. Thankfully, since I am a nurse, it wasn't a big deal to inject them for her. And I used to keep the syringes and the needles in the bathroom.

I guess I never got rid of them.

"Tegan," I manage, "don't do this. You're making a terrible mistake."

She lets out a harsh laugh. "You're joking, right? I'm actually doing something to get out of here, and you're telling me it's a mistake? I don't think so."

I look at the syringe in her right hand. She's got a good grip on my right wrist, but my left hand is free. I could try to take a swing at her, or I could try to grab the syringe. In a fight, it's hard to imagine I wouldn't win. She has a lot going against her right now.

Then again, Tegan is desperate. Who knows what she's capable of? I don't want to get stabbed in the jugular with a needle.

"What do you want?" I ask as calmly as I can.

She grits her teeth. "I want you to call 911 and tell them I'm here. I want you to do it right this minute."

I make a show of patting my pocket. "Tegan, I would help you, but I left my phone upstairs. I can't call anyone."

"I don't believe you."

"I'm sorry, but it's true."

She's itching to check my pockets herself, but with the syringe in one hand and holding on to me with the other, she can't do it.

"So we'll wait," she says decidedly. "When your husband comes home, I'll tell him he has to call 911 or else you get stabbed."

"He won't be home for another hour or two," I lie. "You really think you can hold my wrist effectively for hours on end?"

"I absolutely can."

"Really?"

Her chin wobbles. She knows she can't. She took a gamble here, and she lost. It's a good thing I really did leave my phone upstairs. And it's also a lucky thing she wasn't able to hear Hank's voice earlier.

"Let go of my wrist, Tegan," I say as calmly as I can. Thankfully, I have a lot of experience talking to pregnant women in the throes of labor, so I know what to say to talk someone down.

She shakes her head even as the grip on my wrist loosens just a bit.

"You're going to get out of here," I say, "but it's not going to be good for either of us if you try to hurt me. This is not the right way."

"It's the *only* way," she chokes out.

Tegan's grip on my arm loosens just a tiny bit more, and that's all I need. I yank my arm out of her grasp and take several steps back, away from that syringe she is still clutching. Her face collapses.

"You should drop that syringe," I tell her, "before you hurt yourself with it."

She doesn't drop it though. She tightens her grip on it, her knuckles turning white. "No."

"Tegan," I say patiently, "I'm going to leave now, and I won't come back unless you drop that syringe. If it's not me, it's going to be Hank coming down here. You don't want that, do you?"

I might not be her favorite person right now, but the dread on her face when I say my husband's name is unmistakable. She's terrified of him, which is a bit ironic since he's the one who wants to bring her to the hospital. But she doesn't know that.

She glares at me, her eyes burning with hatred. We stand there for a moment, staring at each other, before the syringe clatters to the floor.

I don't waste a second scooping it up off the floor. My next stop is the bathroom to make sure there aren't any other syringes left in there, but I don't find any. I do a quick sweep of all the dressers to make sure she didn't stash any away. I come up empty.

This is getting to be quite a hassle. I hope that

Midwives Brew is effective, and by tomorrow, she's in labor. Then I can finally be done with this.

"You better not try that again," I admonish her.

She looks away from me, her cheeks scarlet. She hates me right about now, but I can't let that bother me. Real soon, she's going to give me exactly what I want. I can't let anything get in the way.

CHAPTER 51

POLLY

Hank returned to work soon after showering, but not before he caught me covered in the drink Tegan threw at me. Thankfully, he didn't make too much of a fuss over it and let me change my clothes in peace. Then he left again without another word.

Now it's nearly seven, and he's back home for dinner. He looks exhausted. Even though that beard conceals much of his face, I can see it in his bloodshot eyes. He looks ten years older than he did a few days ago. And as he pulls off his black beanie, he doesn't say "Hello, Polly" or "How was your day?" The first thing he blurts out is "She still here?"

"Hello to you too," I retort, wiping my hands—still damp from washing them in the kitchen sink—on my jeans. "Did you have a good day at work?"

Hank stares at me.

"Tegan is fine," I tell him. "She's sleeping, so don't bother her."

That's not true. She's still in that wheelchair I gave her, because I was afraid to get close enough to help her back into bed. It makes me uneasy to know she can move around the basement, but it wasn't worth the risk of getting within biting or scratching distance of that girl.

"Did you call 911 to get her?" he asks me.

"Why should I? Like I said, she's doing fine."

"She's not fine," Hank says stubbornly. "I saw the way her leg was swollen last night. It's not just a sprain, is it?"

"It's possible she has a small hairline fracture."

His jaw tightens. "She needs to go to the hospital, Polly."

"Nonsense."

He pulls his phone out of his pocket. "I'm calling 911. Now."

"Why are you doing this?" My chest fills with panic. "Hank, you promised me you'd give me three days."

"That was before she stabbed you with a fork and threw her drink at you. She clearly wants to leave. This isn't right. I'm calling 911."

Our reception isn't the greatest out here, but it's good enough to place a call to 911. I watch in horror as he punches the first number into the screen, and before he can type in all three, I snatch the phone out of his hand and hurl it to the floor with all my might.

The screen shatters and goes dark. Hank's mouth drops open as he stares at the remains of his phone. And he can't call on our landline since I smashed that phone the other day.

"Fine," he says tightly. "I'll take her to the hospital myself."

He marches purposefully in the direction of the basement door. I race after him, stumbling over the living room rug. He wraps his fingers around the basement door and yanks it open, and I get there just in time to jump in front of him and shove it closed again.

"Polly." He glares at me now. "Get out of my way."

I block the basement door with my body so that he can't get past me. He eyes me, calculating whether he can move me out of the way. Hank would never hurt me—he'd toss Mitch Hambly across the room, but there's nothing I could do or say that would cause him to lay a finger on me. He's not that sort of man.

"You need to move," he says. "This is happening whether you like it or not."

I fold my arms across my chest. "I'm not moving."

"I'm taking her to the hospital," he says through his teeth. "Don't make this difficult, Polly."

"You're not taking her anywhere. She's on the mend."

"You've *got* to be kidding me."

"We'll go to jail, you know," I point out. "That's a guarantee. Is that what you want?"

"I want that girl to get the medical care she needs."

We both stand there for a moment, our eyes locked together. Hank knows me well enough to know I'm not the sort of person who backs down easily. When I want something badly enough, I get it.

Eventually.

"You can't stay there all night," he says.

He's right. I can't spend all my time guarding the basement door. At some point, I'll have to eat and sleep and use the toilet. Or else he'll go back to work and use the phone there to call for help. When Tegan first got here, the threat of imprisonment was enough to keep Hank under control, but not anymore. I have to make sure he does the right thing, even when I'm not around. He needs to recognize how serious this is.

"If you take her to the hospital," I say quietly, "I'll kill myself."

As the words leave my mouth, I realize it's not an idle threat. I mean what I'm saying. I want this so badly, and if he takes it away from me when I'm this close, I won't be able to go on. After all, I already tried it once.

It all started when I was working a shift in the newborn nursery. It was back when I was struggling with infertility and there were no adoption prospects. In other words, it was the most painful place to be. But I believed I could handle it. And for most of the shift, I was fine. I was, after all, a professional.

The next morning, when my shift came to an end, I was sitting in a rocking chair, holding one of the newborns. And I just...I wouldn't give him back. I remember one of the other nurses shaking my shoulder and telling me it was time for me to go home. But I just kept staring down at that sweet little face. I didn't want to give him up—not when they asked me nicely and not when the requests became more stern. Even when the security guard showed up, I refused to budge.

My supervisor called Hank at home. He came rushing over to the hospital, and he sat with me and coaxed me into returning the infant. Thankfully, the parents never found out what I did. If they had, there might have been criminal charges filed. But as it was, the hospital agreed to deal with it quietly. I handed in my resignation, and that night, I went to the bathroom and took every pill in the medicine cabinet.

I remember Hank shouting my name, trying desperately to wake me up. I had never seen him quite so scared. He must have called for an ambulance, because the next thing I knew, I was in a hospital bed, an IV in my arm, disappointed to still be alive. A mandatory stay in a psychiatric hospital followed, which ruined my chances of adopting or fostering a child for good.

There have been times when I was grateful that Hank saved me from taking my own life. Now is one of the times—when the prospect of becoming a mother is so real, I can taste it. But if he takes that away from me, I know what I have to do.

And this time, I'll get it right.

Hank's eyes fly open wide, and he takes a step back. He was worried about going to jail, but he's much more worried about this. "You don't mean that."

"I mean it. I promise you."

"Polly..."

"You take her to the hospital," I say, "and when you get back, you'll find me dead."

His mouth opens, but no words come out.

"And I won't mess around like last time," I add. "I learned my lesson."

I get a flashback to the terrified look on his face when he was shaking me awake after I took all those pills. I've never seen Hank as scared as he was that day. He will do anything to keep that from happening again.

At least that's what I'm counting on.

"Then you're coming with me," he says.

"Oh really?" My right eyebrow shoots up. "You going to tie me up and make me?"

He can't force me to go with him to the emergency room, and he knows it. If he betrays me, I'm going to make sure I'm gone by the time he gets back and that there will be no saving me this time.

"Please don't be like that, Polly," he manages. "I…I love you."

"I love you too." I lift my chin. "But that doesn't change a thing."

He studies my face, trying to figure out if I mean it. Whatever he sees makes him take another step back, his hands in the air. "We're going to talk about this later."

"We can talk about it all you want," I reply.

I don't add the obvious: *But it won't change my mind.*

CHAPTER 52

TEGAN

Hank's boots sound like gunshots on the floor above me.

If there was ever a chance to convince Polly to call for help, it is gone now that her husband is home. He will never allow that to happen.

The drink Polly gave me is churning in my stomach. At first, I thought if I could get on her good side, maybe she would take pity on me and let me go. Maybe I could show her that she didn't have to do what he told her to do—she didn't have to fear him. All she has to do is pick up the phone and dial 911. Hank would never even know.

But then when she told me Dennis was here looking for me, I lost it. He must be frantic by now, thinking I'm dead or worse, and the two of them lied to him. After I found that out, I was willing to do whatever it took to get out of here. I needed to go on the offensive.

But that didn't work either.

I don't know what was in that drink, but I feel terrible now. Could there have been some kind of drug in it? Polly tasted it, so it seems unlikely, but I suppose it's possible she was only pretending to drink it. My stomach keeps cramping up, and waves of nausea course through my body. The best thing I can say is at least I'm in the chair, so I can wheel myself over to the bathroom and hunch over the toilet to evacuate what is left of my lunch.

Well, whatever it is she might have drugged me with, I've now gotten rid of most of it into the toilet. And the rest I threw on her shirt.

A loud noise from right above me interrupts my thoughts. I recognize the sound immediately—it's the hinges of the basement door creaking as it swings open. And then a second later, it slams shut again. I can make out Hank's voice, which is a low roar that resonates through the ceiling.

Polly, get out of my way.

I quickly deduce what must be happening upstairs. Hank wants to come down here, but Polly is stopping him. I have no idea what his intentions are, but she is holding him back—maybe physically. She's risking her own safety by incurring his wrath in order to protect me.

If I ever doubted that she's on my side, those doubts have vanished. She's not perfect, but she's doing her best. Polly might be the only thing keeping me safe from whatever fate Hank intends for me.

My ears strain to catch snatches of their conversation. It's hard to make out any words, but Hank sounds furious. I hold my breath, waiting to see if the door will swing open again, if that giant man will come stomping down to the basement in his big, scary boots with that menacing look in his eyes.

But it doesn't happen. The door stays closed.

I have no idea what Hank has in store for me. Is he eventually planning to rape me, the same way Simon did? Or is it enough for Hank to know that I'm trapped in the basement, at his mercy? Is that what he's getting off on?

I'd like to get out of here before I find out.

It's past nine o'clock when the door to the basement opens up again. I can tell from the lighter footsteps that it's Polly, and I let out a sigh of relief. I'm not going to lash out at her again. Polly is the only person in this house who's on my side, and I need to let her know that it's okay to help me. I'm sure she's terrified of Hank's temper, but some of her hesitation must be that she knows if I get out of here, I'll report that she and her husband kidnapped me, and they would both go to jail. It is an impossible situation.

"I'll help you back into bed," Polly says softly. "I'm sure you're tired."

She's right. As glad as I was to get out of bed earlier, I'm desperate to get back into it now. I'm tired, my back is aching, and my ankle screams in pain every time I move it the slightest bit. And my legs feel like two huge blocks of cement from hanging downward all day.

We repeat the same process we did earlier to get me into the chair, this time in reverse. It's just as painful on my ankle as it was the first time, but now it's even worse, because the second I get into the bed, a monster contraction squeezes my entire midsection. The pain is enough to make a cold sweat break out under my armpits.

"Are you okay?" Polly asks.

"Yes," I gasp, even though I'm not sure I'm okay. This was not a Braxton-Hicks practice contraction. That was a real one.

What if I'm going into labor?

God, I have to get out of here. I am not giving birth in this basement.

"Please let me go," I say for what feels like the hundredth time.

"You're going to be fine," Polly reassures me. "I'm sure your husband will be glad that you're looking out for your baby."

Enough of the lies. I'm not getting out of here unless I tell Polly the truth. "I'm not married, okay?"

She arches an eyebrow. "Oh?"

"No, I…I don't even have a boyfriend." I wipe beads of sweat off my forehead. "It's just me and the baby. I'm doing this alone."

"Does the father know?"

"I…" I definitely don't want to tell Polly what that asshole did to me. "I don't know who the father is. It was a one-night stand. I don't know his name."

"I see…"

"So you have to understand…" I swipe at a sweaty strand of hair that has fallen in my face. "I'm not going to try to get either of you into any trouble. I just want to get out of here."

"Trouble?" she says dully.

"Yes." I nod. "You can't let me leave, because if I do, I'll tell the police what you both did, and then they'll arrest you. You're stuck."

Polly is silent, playing with the end of her long braid. She knows I'm right.

"But I won't tell anyone. I swear to you. And... and I don't have a boyfriend or husband who is going to be upset. My parents are both dead. Nobody cares about me."

"What about your brother?"

Damn, why did Dennis have to come over here? "We're not that close. He just feels guilty that he didn't want to come visit me. We hadn't seen each other in years."

The wheels are turning in her head. I hold my breath, hoping she believes me. It's not entirely a lie. Dennis cares about me, but nobody else does. Certainly not the father of my baby. Not even Jackson—the one person who has put a smile on my face over these last few difficult months. Simon and Jackson are probably thrilled I vanished without a trace.

"Just let me go," I plead with her, "and everything will be fine. I won't tell a soul."

There's a loud thud upstairs that startles her. She backs away from my bed. "I have to go."

I suck in a breath. "But...you'll help me?"

"Yes," she says. "I'll help you. I promise."

Before I can say another word, Polly turns and heads up the stairs. The last thing I hear is the door to the basement slamming shut.

CHAPTER 53

POLLY

Hank has barely said two words to me the entire night. He's upset about what's going on. He's upset that I threatened to kill myself if he tried to get Tegan to the hospital. He doesn't know exactly what I'm planning, but it's nothing he wants to be part of. Unfortunately, that's not how marriage works.

He's already lying in bed when I finish up in the kitchen and come to join him. I get undressed and crawl under the blankets next to him. I expect him to lean in and give me a kiss like he has every other night when we've gone to sleep together. But he doesn't. He just lies there, staring at the ceiling.

"Hank?" I say.

He doesn't answer.

"Hank," I say again. "Are you okay?"

He doesn't turn to look at me. "There's a woman imprisoned in our basement. Do you *think* I'm okay?"

My cheeks burn. "I told you not to worry about

it. We're going to let her go eventually. This will be fine."

"How will it be fine?" He sits up now, propping himself up on his elbow. "Explain it to me."

"I told you, I'm helping her. She's grateful."

"Don't lie to me, Polly." His face is red now. "She stabbed you with a fork. She threw that drink—God knows what was in it—all over you. She's not grateful."

"Just trust me. It will be fine."

"You keep saying that." This time, the crease between his eyebrows goes all the way up his forehead. "But here's the thing. I keep thinking about this over and over. And every time I think about it, I can't think of a way for this to end without us going to jail unless..."

"Hank?"

In the moonlight, his eyes look glassy. "Unless we kill her." His voice breaks. "And, Polly, I don't want to kill her."

"Hank..."

"That's what you have in mind, isn't it?" His voice is shaking now. "That's what you were thinking all along. You get rid of her, and then you take the baby." He squeezes his eyes shut. "I'm so stupid."

"You got it wrong, Hank."

"I don't think I do."

"Well..." I shift on the mattress, which creaks under my weight. "Say we did kill her..."

"Polly!"

"Just, like, hypothetically..."

"No. *No.*" He shakes his head firmly. "Not even hypothetically. This is not on the table, Polly. I mean it."

"She's all alone, Hank," I tell him. "She told me so.

She doesn't even know who that child's father is. She's been drinking whiskey from a flask in her purse. Do you think she's fit to be a mother?"

"That's not for us to decide."

"And nobody is even going to care that much if she disappears." Well, maybe her brother. I'm not sure if I believed her when she said they barely had contact, considering how upset he seemed. But I'm sure he will move on eventually. "Nobody would care if she vanished off the face of the earth."

"*I* would care."

I'm so frustrated with him, I could scream. Tegan said repeatedly that she didn't want to be a mother, that this was all unplanned. And when she told me nobody would miss her if she was gone, it was like she was giving us permission to…well, you know. And it would be so easy to get rid of her. I bet she'll weigh practically nothing once the baby is out of her.

I never imagined Hank would be my biggest barrier. Doesn't he understand that this is our opportunity to get everything we ever wanted?

"You have to trust me on this," I say. "Can you please just trust me for once?"

I look at his face in the shadows. He used to trust me. Before The Incident happened, I was at the top of my game. Hank was proud of the fact that his wife was a nurse at the hospital—he used to brag about it to anyone who would listen. And if he had so much as a paper cut, he would bring it to me. *What should I do, Nurse Polly?*

He doesn't feel that way about me anymore. Ever since that day, he thinks I'm emotionally fragile. I'm not sure he'll ever trust me again.

"If you take her away," I say, "I'll do it. I'll kill myself. I swear."

"Yes," he says tightly. "You told me."

We're both quiet, lying in the dark, staring up at the ceiling.

"Polly," he says in a low voice, "you can't hurt that woman."

"I won't."

He rolls his head to look at me. "I mean it. I don't want you to lay a finger on her."

The deep groove between my husband's eyebrows has become a crater. He's really upset, and the only way to end this discussion is to tell him what he wants to hear.

"I understand, Hank," I say. "I won't hurt her."

If it helps him to sleep at night to get that reassurance, I'll give it to him. But in the end, I'm doing this for him. For *us*. He knows it, and he'll never go behind my back. I'm all Hank's got, and he would never do that to me. Never. He's too scared of losing me.

He knows how this will end. And when it comes down to it, I bet he'll help me get rid of the body too.

Soon our family will be complete, just as my mother foretold.

CHAPTER 54

POLLY

I can't stop thinking about my conversation with Hank.

After tossing and turning for an hour, he finally drifts off to sleep, but I lie awake. I'm not worried about Hank turning me in—that's one thing he'd never do—but my head is swirling with the possibilities of all the ways this could go wrong. But the biggest problem of all is increasingly clear:

Tegan could get free.

Putting her in that wheelchair was a mistake—I see that now. I thought she'd get some exercise and it would be good for her circulation, but when she came at me with that syringe, I realized she's feistier than I gave her credit for. I won't let her back in that wheelchair, just to be safe, but that might not be enough. She might have a broken ankle and be heavily pregnant, but she's also very young and has one good leg and two working arms. And she's desperate. If she's frightened enough, she might summon the will to hop up those stairs and escape.

If the door to the basement had a lock, I'd feel better about it. But it doesn't, and it's not like Hank can put in a lock right now. He wouldn't even do it if I asked. As long as that door is unlocked, Tegan could escape at any time. At this very moment, she could be slipping out the front door.

The thought is enough to make me sit bolt upright in bed.

Hank groans in his sleep and rolls over. I'm not sure if he's having a bad dream, but he's still asleep. He's less troubled than I am by the idea that Tegan could escape under our very noses. That we could lose our family just like that.

Unless I do something to stop it from happening.

I slide out of the bed, careful to be as quiet as I can so as not to wake my husband. I start to put on my slippers but then at the last minute decide to go barefoot. I leave the bedroom, closing the door behind me.

Naturally, almost every stair makes a loud creaking noise as I step on it. Our house is as old as the hills, but we love it. And one of these days, when he's got time and a little more money, Hank will fix it up like he promised he would. But I don't expect he'll have much time in the near future, since we've got a baby on the way.

The first floor of the house is blessedly silent. I creep over to the basement door, and it's still closed. There's no sign that Tegan has escaped. No impending disaster.

I'm safe. For the moment.

The floor is ice-cold against the soles of my bare feet as I walk across the living room to the cabinet where Hank keeps his tool kit. My husband loves tools, and his kit is nearly as heavy as I am, but I manage to heave it out of the cabinet and lay it down on the floor. I pop it open and examine the contents, searching for one particular item.

A hammer.

It doesn't take me long to find because it's the biggest thing in the tool kit. It's just a standard hammer, but I swear it's bigger than any normal hammer. I can still picture Hank's beefy fingers wrapped around the handle as he pounded the nails into this very cabinet, which he built with his own two hands.

I pick up the hammer, testing the weight in my own hands. Yes, this will do nicely.

The hinges on the basement door whine slightly as I crack it open enough to slip inside. I hold my breath, listening for the sounds of Tegan stirring downstairs. But there's nothing. I can just barely make out the inhale and exhale of her breaths.

The basement is very dark, so I cling to the banister as I make my way downstairs. I don't dare turn on the lights—I slipped a small amount of Benadryl into her dinner, but she barely touched it, so I have no confidence she'll remain asleep. I try to be as quiet as possible as I descend the stairs, even when I'm fairly sure a tiny splinter has wedged itself in the heel of my right foot.

Then I'm at the bottom.

Tegan is sound asleep. Even though she didn't take the Benadryl, the sounds of her deep inhales and exhales fill the room. There's a tiny amount of light from the moon, which is enough for my eyes to be able to make out the bulge of her abdomen and the smooth contours of her face. Despite the fact that the room is a moderate temperature, she has a sheen of sweat on her forehead.

My gaze drops to her legs. She's still got that boot on her left ankle, which is almost certainly shattered. She can't walk on her left leg—that much is certain. But her right one is in good working order, albeit swollen from the pregnancy. If she managed to crawl to the stairs, I can imagine her dragging herself up them using the banister to help her. The time after the baby arrives will be especially problematic, because she will no longer have that huge weight tying her down.

And then we will be in big trouble.

But if her other leg were out of commission... Well, that would ensure she wouldn't be able to leave here until we were good and ready to let her go.

I'm not going to break her leg, exactly. I mean, I'm not a complete psychopath. Besides, I'm not sure a hammer would be strong enough to shatter the two supporting bones of the leg—the tibia or the fibula. I'll likely just chip or bruise them and then piss her off enough to spur her to get the hell out of here. No, I've got to be strategic about this.

I've been thinking about it, and the best thing to do would be to break her right kneecap.

The kneecap is a delicate bone, and the hammer will shatter it easily—there's a reason mobsters are infamous for that sort of thing. And once it's broken, she will have difficulty moving her right leg. Walking on it will be nearly impossible, especially if she doesn't have her left leg to support her.

With two broken legs, Tegan will truly be at our mercy.

I have to do this. It seems cruel, I admit, but I don't have a choice. Tegan is in a position to either give us everything we've dreamed of or else destroy my family and send me to prison. This is the only way to protect myself. I'm sorry Tegan has to suffer, but she's already in pain. What's a little more?

And really, this is a case where the ends justify the means. Tegan will be a terrible mother to that little girl, based on everything I've learned about her. What if she's drunk-driving and kills them both next time?

I raise the hammer over my head, positioning it so that when I bring it down, it will land squarely on her right kneecap. The impact will surely wake her, but by then, it will be far too late—the kneecap will already be shattered. My hands quaver, and I take a deep breath. On the count of three…

Two…

One…

Tegan stirs in the bed, letting out a low moan. She squirms in the sheets, screwing up her face for a moment. She looked young before, but in the moonlight, she looks even younger. Like she's still a teenager. A kid. Her eyelashes flutter, and she lets out a soft sigh.

Oh my God, what am I *doing*?

I relax my grip on the hammer, letting my arms fall to my sides. I can't believe what I almost did. I almost just smashed another human being's leg with a hammer—on purpose! My mother, who lay in this bed before Tegan, would have been ashamed of me. I'm a *nurse*, for goodness' sake! I'm supposed to help people get better, not…

I back away from the bed, a tight sensation in my chest. Maybe Hank had a point—maybe we have gone too far. But there's no other way out of this situation. I don't want to hurt Tegan, but what else can I do? There's no world in which Tegan remains alive and we get to keep her baby.

I swallow a lump of bile in my throat. I might not be able to break Tegan's kneecap, but at some point in the near future, I've got to make some hard decisions. I won't let this girl keep me from getting everything I ever dreamed of.

PART 4

FOUR DAYS AFTER THE CRASH

CHAPTER 55

TEGAN

I don't feel good.

That's the first thought I have when I wake up in the morning. I don't feel good. Something is very wrong.

My head feels funny. It feels like I am in a fish tank, looking out at the world through several feet of water. And I can't stop shaking. My whole body is trembling. I haven't felt good since my car slammed into that tree, but this is a whole other level of awful. On the plus side, though, the pain in my left leg seems to have subsided.

I place a hand on my belly, feeling for Little Tuna. At first, I feel nothing. But then I feel just the tiniest of little kicks. It's weak though. It's not the soccer star kicks she was giving a week or two ago. It's obvious that whatever is affecting me is also affecting my baby.

What is wrong with me?

I roll my head to the side, and to my horror, Simon Lamar is standing next to the bed. I jolt in surprise. What is he doing here? He's wearing a suit, and he has his arms folded across his chest, a smirk on his lips. He's holding a leather briefcase, and as he stands over me, he flicks it open and pulls out a sheaf of papers.

You should have taken my offer while you could. Now you're screwed. Again.

Then he takes a lighter out of his pocket—the same one that Jackson had gifted me—and holds the flame to the papers in his hand. They catch fire immediately, going up in a blaze of smoke.

I open my mouth to scream, but before I can, he vanishes. Instead of Simon, there's just a dark shadow on the side of my bed.

Oh God, I'm hallucinating.

I try to shift in the bed in an attempt to get comfortable, which is hard given that I can't stop shaking. I feel cold and hot all at once. It's a very strange sensation. I want to have something to drink, but I also feel like I would throw up if I tried to drink anything.

As I shift, I notice the pain in my left ankle is not nearly as bad as it was before. And then it hits me that I'm not feeling much of *anything* in that leg, pain or otherwise.

This is not good.

I look down at my left foot, which is still in the boot, since I wouldn't let Polly take it off. Now I wish I had let her. I try to wiggle the toes of my left foot. Are they moving? I don't think they are.

Something is *really* wrong.

"Polly!" I try to yell out, although my voice comes out in a hoarse whisper.

I pull the blankets up to my neck, but then I feel

too hot and I push them down again. I can't seem to get comfortable. My temperature is all screwy. In the back of my head, I recognize that I'm really sick, yet I can't push away the fog enough to get as panicked as I probably should be.

After what feels like an eternity, the door to the basement creaks open. Polly's boisterous voice echoes down the stairs. "Good morning!"

Through the cloud in my head, I recall our conversation last night. I made one last attempt to bargain with her so that she would get me to a hospital. She told me she would do it. I hope she meant it.

"Tegan?" She stops at the foot of my hospital bed, staring down at me. "Are you okay?"

I open my mouth, but no sound comes out. Instead, I just shake my head.

She rounds the side of the bed and places an ice-cold hand on my forehead. Her eyes widen. "You're burning up."

"I…I am?" I croak.

Her gaze rakes down the length of the bed and comes to a stop when she gets to the end, where my boot is sticking out of the covers. She walks right over there while I feebly attempt to protest. She places one hand on either side of my black fur-lined boot. And she pulls—*hard*—until it pops off.

I expected it to hurt, and when it doesn't, that's the most terrifying thing of all.

Right away, I can see how swollen and red my left calf is. Then she peels off my sock, and I let out a gasp. My foot is extremely swollen and dark red, practically purple. My foot is bent to the right at a frightening angle, and there is an open wound on the exposed side. Even from the other side of the bed, I can see thick, yellow fluid leaking out of the wound.

"This is infected," Polly says, her voice flat with shock.

Yeah, no kidding.

"Hospital," I manage. "You…you promised."

She stares down at my foot, her lips pursed together. "You need antibiotics."

Right. I do. I need to go to the hospital and get antibiotics. "Hospital" is all I can eke out.

She's quiet for a moment. "Right. Hospital."

Oh, thank God.

Polly looks down at my foot for another minute, then she turns around and goes back upstairs without another word. I hope she's calling 911 right now. Because if she doesn't, I'm not going to make it out of here alive. And neither will my baby.

CHAPTER 56

POLLY

This is all Tegan's fault.

If she had just let me take the damn boot off in the first place, I could have cleaned up the wound and disinfected it. Then she wouldn't have gotten that infection. But instead, she stubbornly wouldn't let me see it—like a *child*. And this girl thinks she is responsible enough to be a mother? What a joke. That baby wouldn't last a week.

Of course, this leaves me with a dilemma. Tegan is sick. I should have figured it out when I saw her covered in a layer of sweat last night, but I wasn't exactly thinking clearly at that moment. She's got an active infection in her foot at the very least. I'm also concerned she may have developed a blood clot in that leg from the lack of movement coupled with the fracture. I have no doubt that if I don't do something, she will die. And if she dies, our baby will die too. I could try to perform some sort of C-section to save the baby, but that's a last resort.

I've got to get her medication. *Soon.*

Hank is barely speaking to me at breakfast. I make him a plate of eggs and bacon like I often do, and he eats it without saying a word. He just keeps looking up at me with an unreadable expression on his face. It isn't until he's nearly cleaned his plate that he says, "Aren't you bringing food down to Tegan?"

"I already gave her a plate," I say.

He starts to wipe his mouth with the back of his hand, but then he stops himself, picks up his napkin, and uses that instead. He's good at not getting food in his beard at least. People look at Hank and think he's some uncouth ogre, but that's not what he's like at all. "Is she okay?"

I can't tell Hank that Tegan has an infection. If I do that, he'll insist she go to the hospital. It's like he doesn't even *care* anymore that the two of us could go to jail for this for a very long time. The only thing keeping him from calling right now is my threat about killing myself.

"She's fine," I say. "Happy as a clam."

He grunts like he doesn't quite believe me, but he also doesn't know the extent of what is going on. He knows Tegan doesn't want to be in our basement, but he doesn't know how sick she is. But I'm going to make it right. I'm not going to let my baby die.

Hanks scrapes his chair back against the floor as he stands up. He stomps into the living room, yanking his coat from the coatrack. I follow him to the front door, just to make sure he's gone before I do what I need to do next.

"Have a good day at work," I say to him. "I'll see you tonight."

He looks up at my words. He stares at me for a long time, as if struggling to figure out what to say.

"I love you, Polly," he says.

I don't know why he said that to me. He seemed furious with me all morning. It makes me a little uneasy, but I push the feeling away. "Well, I love you too." I lick my lips. "You know, I'm doing all this for you. For us."

"I know," he says quietly.

And then he turns and leaves the house without another word. Maybe he finally gets it. But I still don't quite trust him.

I walk over to the window and watch him climb into his truck and drive off. I stand there, still watching, as his truck disappears into the distance. I need to make sure he's gone. Because he can't be here to witness what I'm about to do next.

CHAPTER 57

POLLY

We have a second bedroom upstairs. We had once imagined it would eventually serve as a nursery for our first child, and Hank had even spoken of building an extension if we had more children, but things didn't work out that way. Instead, it's an office.

Not that Hank or I really need an office. Hank is a mechanic. And I am…well, right now, I'm nothing. But when I was a nurse, I didn't need an office very much either. But I did use the desk when I worked on Hank's bookkeeping for the auto shop. Or to store tax documents and important papers.

And that's what I'm looking for right now.

I sit down at the desk in our office and sift through the papers in the top drawer. I haven't used this drawer in a while, so it doesn't take me long to find what I need. I pull out a piece of paper and lay it down in front of me. Then I dial a number on my phone.

"Walgreens pharmacy," a clipped female voice answers.

"Hello." I clutch the piece of paper in front of me. "My name is Dr. Chloe Passaro. I'd like to call in a prescription for a patient."

"Sure. What's the patient's name?"

"Polly Thompson." I recite my date of birth for her as well.

"Okay then," the pharmacist says, "what would you like to order?"

"Cephalexin," I say. "Five hundred milligrams twice a day. Dispense fourteen tablets. No refills."

"Is that all?"

I hesitate. My other concern is the possibility of a blood clot in her leg, but without an ultrasound to diagnose it, I wouldn't feel comfortable giving her a therapeutic dose of blood thinner. But she should at least get a prophylactic dose. "Do you have prefilled syringes of enoxaparin?" I ask.

"Yes, we do, Doctor."

I order enough for her to get through the next month. By then, this will come to an end, one way or another.

"Thank you, Doctor," the pharmacist says. "Can I have your NPI number?"

I look down at the paper in front of me that contains all of Dr. Passaro's identification numbers for when I used to call in prescriptions on her behalf. Of course, I always identified myself as "Polly, the nurse working with Dr. Passaro." But that wouldn't work in this situation.

A pharmacist takes down Dr. Passaro's information, and I suspect that by the afternoon, I will get a call saying my prescription is ready. But the antibiotic won't be for me. It will be for Tegan. I checked which antibiotic would be safest to take for a pregnant patient with a skin infection, and that's what I have called in. Given how sick she is, I'm scared the infection has spread to the blood, which means if we were in a hospital setting, she would certainly require IV antibiotics. But this is the best I can do.

It's dicey to impersonate a doctor I haven't even worked for in several years. But then again, it's not actually that risky. I'm not calling in narcotics or anything that would raise a red flag. All I've done is ask for a week's worth of an antibiotic and a low dose of a blood thinner. Dr. Passaro will never know about it.

Now that I've got the antibiotics being dispensed, I creep back down to the basement to check on Tegan. I tried to offer her some breakfast, but she was so out of it that I was scared she might choke. I did manage to get her to drink some water.

Right now, she's fast asleep. Her eyelashes flutter slightly with each breath, and her cheeks are flushed pink. I have a thermometer in the medicine cabinet, but I'm afraid to check her temperature. Just by touch, it's clear she's running a high fever.

"Tegan." I nudge her slightly. "Tegan?"

She murmurs but doesn't open her eyes.

I pull back the sheets from her left ankle. I tried to hide my reaction from her when I first saw it, but it looks awful. The skin is bright red and shiny, and when I press my fingers against the top of her foot, I can't palpate a pulse. And that wound from the accident looks terrible. There is a fair amount of pus oozing out of it, and I'm not sure how deep the infection goes—maybe even down to the bone. If I did take her to the hospital, there's a reasonable chance she would lose that foot.

I grab the first aid kit under the bathroom sink and do my best to clean out the open wound. I run warm water over it, and I try my best to disinfect it with Betadine, even though I recognize it's far too late. When I'm done, I wrap her foot up gently in Kerlix gauze.

The most disturbing thing of all is that she barely stirs through the entire thing.

I chew on my lip, trying to figure out my next move. Finally, I walk around the side of the bed to the nightstand and rifle around in the bottom drawer. I pull out a stethoscope and stick the tips in my ears. I lay the diaphragm of the stethoscope on the bulge of Tegan's belly and close my eyes, listening.

There's a heartbeat. It's weak, but I hear it.

The baby is okay.

But she won't be for long. I've got to get that antibiotic right now, and I've got to get that baby out of her before it's too late.

CHAPTER 58

TEGAN

I've been dozing all morning.

I was vaguely aware of Polly coming in to do something with my left ankle. It hurt enough to wake me up, but I just lay there and let her do it. I didn't have the energy to talk to her. There was no point in fighting. At some point, she came in to offer me food, but my appetite was gone. She coaxed me into drinking a few sips of water, and that was all I could keep down.

I hope she's calling for an ambulance. I have to believe she isn't just going to let me die here.

But I'm not sure anymore.

My eyes finally crack open at the sound of the basement door opening and heavy footsteps landing on the top step. I've been out of it all morning, but that sound is the first thing to get my attention. I know whose footsteps those are.

It's Hank.

No, not now. Please, not now…

I close my eyes, pretending to be asleep. It was hard enough to deal with him when I was feeling halfway okay. I don't want him near me right now.

But it doesn't matter what I want. He's coming. His footsteps grow louder as he descends the stairs.

"Miss Werner?"

He's at the foot of the bed now. Oh God, what does he want from me? Can't he tell I'm seriously ill? But maybe this is the moment he was waiting for. Maybe this is my lot in life. Simon Lamar already took advantage of me, and now this giant man wants a go at me. And I am far too weak to fight him off. He doesn't even need to drug me.

He comes around the side of the bed so he's right next to me. His large hand drops onto my arm, and he shakes me. "Miss Werner! Can you hear me?"

I don't answer.

He stands there for a moment, hovering over me. I'm hopeful that he's going to leave when he realizes how sick I am. But—to my horror—he puts one arm under my knees and the other under my back. And he lifts me into the air.

"Stop!" I gasp. "What are you doing?"

He blinks at me, surprised that I'm awake. For a second, we're face-to-face. "Are you okay?"

"No, I'm not okay." My mouth feels like it's made of sandpaper, and it hurts my head just to say the words. "Please put me down right now."

He frowns. "You need to go to the hospital. We need to go now—before she gets back."

He's lying. He's got to be lying. But I'm too weak to fight him. I let him carry me up the stairs, not sure where he's taking me, but anything is better than the basement.

"Where are you taking me?" I murmur.

"The hospital," he answers patiently.

"Stop lying to me," I croak. "Please tell me..."

Hank fumbles a bit to get the door open while still keeping me in his arms. It's cold outside, but it feels good on my hot skin. The truck that brought me over here is parked in the driveway, and the passenger side door is already open. But apparently, we're not taking this journey alone. There's another man standing next to the truck, and it takes me a second to recognize who it is. When I do, my body is racked by a violent chill.

It's Simon Lamar.

He's waiting for me by the truck.

"What's *he* doing here?" I shriek.

Simon and Hank are in it together—conspiring to hurt me. Even though I didn't trust Hank, I genuinely never saw this coming. I assumed it was a coincidence that Hank came upon me that night in the snow, but it wasn't. Simon sent him to find me and trap me so I couldn't tell anyone what he did to me.

I struggle in Hank's arms, but he's got me firmly in his grasp. It barely takes an effort on his part to keep me contained. "Please don't do this!" I beg him. "He's a terrible man. He wants to hurt me."

"Who?" Hank asks.

"Simon!"

"Who's Simon?"

His voice is convincingly blank. I look back at the truck to point out his partner in crime, but to my surprise, nobody is there. Simon has vanished into thin air.

All I can see now is that dented pickup truck with the door hanging open. Simon is simply gone, like he was never there in the first place.

A wave of dizziness washes over me. Oh God, did I *imagine* him? I must have.

I really am sick.

Hank carries me the rest of the way to his truck. He's surprisingly gentle as he helps me into the passenger seat. He leans over me to buckle the seat belt, then climbs into the seat beside me and starts up the engine. I take one last look out the window, searching for any signs of Simon, but all I can see now are spots dancing before my eyes.

"Where are you taking me?" I croak.

"Roosevelt Memorial Hospital."

"No, you're not."

"I swear, I am."

"Where's Polly?"

He doesn't answer that one. He keeps his eyes pinned on the road as he drives me to God knows where. He claims he's going to the hospital, but I don't know why he would do that. Why take me to the hospital when he knows I'll turn him in and he'll end up in jail?

I place my hand on my belly. I don't feel any movement at all from Little Tuna. Even early this morning, I could feel her move. But now there's nothing. And I don't hear her voice in my ear anymore. It might be too late.

"There's something wrong with my baby," I say. Even through my haze of fever, the panic is mounting inside me. "I need to go to the hospital."

"I'm taking you to the hospital," Hank says again,

even though it's a lie. It has to be. "We'll be there real soon."

I don't know where he's taking me. It's possible I hallucinated Simon standing by the truck, but this man didn't keep me captive in his basement for four days just to drive me to the freaking hospital. He's taking me somewhere he can do what he wants with me, and Polly won't be able to stop him anymore.

"Please," I beg him. "Please don't do this..."

This time, he ignores me entirely. I can only watch him drive as my body shakes with chills.

I stare through the windshield, wondering where we're going. The strange part is that we don't seem to be going deeper into the woods. In fact, we're pulling onto a busy road with lots of cars surrounding us.

Could I get the attention on one of the drivers? Alert them that I'm being held hostage?

Hank slows to a halt at a red light. I bang on the window next to me, trying to get the attention of the vehicle next to ours. The driver is a middle-aged man who is bobbing his head to music I can't hear. "Help!" I cry in a hoarse voice. "Please help me!"

I press the button to roll down the passenger side window, and Hank's eyes widen in alarm. "Tegan!." He fumbles with the buttons on the door next to him, and the window reverses its course. "You need to calm down before I get in an accident. We're almost there."

I start to bang on the window, but he's moving again, pulling off the busy road. Have I missed my opportunity to get help? I wonder if I could somehow make a run for it the next time he stops. It seems unlikely with my broken ankle, but I have to try. I summon up every ounce of my remaining strength, but there's not much left. I take a deep breath, and for a moment, everything goes black.

And when my vision clears, there's a hospital looming in the distance.

I stare out the windshield at the large building in front of us, unable to entirely convince myself it isn't a mirage. I blink and rub my eyes, certain that when I do, it will disappear, and we'll be in front of some remote dungeon where Hank will finish me off.

But no. It's real. Hank really did drive me to the hospital, and now he's pulling up in front of the entrance.

He puts the car in park, and then he just sits there for a moment, taking deep breaths. "Tegan," he says quietly, "you need to know that Polly is a good person. She only did what she did because… Well, I don't have a good excuse for her. But if you were ever in the hospital and my wife was your nurse, you'd know what a great person she is. She was a great nurse, and she's a great wife. There's nobody better, really. And I'm just saying, this isn't her." His eyes are glazed as he stares out the windshield. "It's just… It's been a hard few years. I'm going to get her help though. I promise."

My brain is hazy, and it's hard to comprehend his words. What is he saying? Is he trying to tell me that *Polly* was the one responsible for imprisoning me in the basement?

Is that possible?

You need to go to the hospital. We need to go now—before she *gets back.*

"Anyway, what I'm saying…" His chin wobbles

under his thick beard. "All I'm saying is please don't ruin her life. Please."

I don't know what to say.

Fortunately, Hank doesn't wait for an answer. He gets out of the truck, and he flags down a man at the entrance to the hospital. Before I know it, they're loading me onto a stretcher. An oxygen mask is pressed against my face, and that's the last thing I remember for a long time.

CHAPTER 59

POLLY

I'm feeling a lot more optimistic by the time I get home from the pharmacy in the early afternoon, clutching a white paper bag containing fourteen tablets of cephalexin as well as the thirty syringes of enoxaparin. I'm hopeful this will do the trick. If it doesn't, she may need IV antibiotics, and that is going to be a much bigger pain in the neck. I'm not sure what I'm going to do if that happens, but I'll cross that bridge when we come to it.

When I arrive back at the house, I notice the front door is unlocked. I'm certain I locked it though. I remember doing it. I mean, it's not like I would have left the front door unlocked, knowing that Tegan is in the basement. I'm a lot more careful than that.

So why is the door unlocked?

The only thing I can think of is that Hank came home early. But why would he do that?

I step into the house, my stomach churning slightly.

I look around, and I don't see anybody. The house is quiet. "Hank?" I call out.

Silence.

My heart speeds up in my chest. I take long strides in the direction of the basement door. My mouth falls open when I discover that the basement door is open.

No. *No.*

I tear down the steps to the basement. "Tegan?" I call out. But of course, there's no answer. Because she's not in the hospital bed anymore.

She's gone.

"Tegan!" I scream.

For reasons I can't quite explain, I run over to the hospital bed and rummage through the sheets, as if I might discover her hiding within them. I don't. She's not in the basement. She's not here anymore.

I sprint back up the stairs, my heart thudding so hard it hurts. The police must've come in here while I was gone. They rescued her, and now they're waiting to arrest me. That's got to be what happened. There's no other explanation. After all, Tegan wasn't capable of leaving on her own accord.

I run out the basement door, preparing to run out to my Bronco. I've got to get to the auto shop and tell Hank what happened. He'll know what to do in this situation. He's good like that. He always knows exactly what the right thing to do is.

Except when I get into the living room, Hank is standing there. He's wearing his winter coat, and his hair is mussed from his hat. He must have just come in.

"Hank," I say breathlessly. "I…I was just in the basement. Tegan is… She's gone."

I expect him to react with panic like what I'm feeling. After all, the police would arrest both of us, not just me. But instead, he just stands there rigidly. "I know."

I squint at him. "You know?"

"I took her to the hospital."

His words are a punch in the gut. I stare at him, unable to believe what I'm hearing. "How could you do that?"

"She was sick. She needed to go to the hospital."

"But..." I wring my hands together. "I brought antibiotics for her. She would have been fine."

"She needed to go to the hospital," he repeats firmly.

I fell in love with Hank on our first date. He was a big guy, but he was so endearingly shy but also funny and thoughtful and ruggedly handsome, and I'd never had a man look at me that way before—like he thought I was the most wonderful human being he'd ever met. I knew on that first date—even before my mother said it—that he was the man I was going to marry someday. I never told him this, but as we were ordering dessert, I was already planning our lives together—a sweet little cottage with two children who were a perfect mix of him and me, and maybe a dog. I already loved him, even then.

Today is the first time in the twelve years since we met that I have hated him.

"How could you do that?" I scream at him. "Do you realize what you've *done*?"

Hank shakes his head. "I had to, Polly."

"She's going to tell the police what we've done!" I yell at him. "We're both going to go to jail."

"I had to. I'm sorry."

Tears prick at my eyes. How could he look at me that way? How could he not even *care*? "That was our baby, you know. That was our only chance. That was my only chance to be a mother, and you…you *ruined* it! You ruined our lives!"

My mother said that someday, our family would be complete. But she was *wrong*. I wish instead of telling me what a good man Hank was, she'd told me to run far away and find someone with a lick of common sense.

Hank tries to put his arms around me, but I shove him away. He's always been able to comfort me in the past, but not this time. I always felt like we were in this together, but I don't feel that way anymore. We had a chance to be happy together, and he ruined it. He ruined *everything*.

"Polly," he murmurs.

"Don't." I back away from him. "You need to stay away from me."

"Look, I'm going to call Dr. Salinsky…"

"*I don't need to see a shrink!*"

Hank freezes. He's not used to me raising my voice that way. He stands there like a deer in the headlights. "Polly, can we please talk about this?"

"Talk?" I snort. "We didn't talk *before* you decided to betray me. I just…I don't want to talk to you anymore. I'm done talking."

With those words, I turn around and hurry up the steps to the bedroom. I slam the door behind me, and then I lock it for good measure. I hear Hank's heavy footsteps on the stairs, followed by a knock at the bedroom door. "Polly?"

I sink down onto the bed, my hands trembling. "Go away!"

"Come on. Let me in. Don't do anything stupid."

The most maddening thing is how calm he sounds. That's my husband all over. He never gets worked up over anything. He didn't even care that much that we couldn't have children together. No wonder he found it so easy to bring Tegan to the hospital and give up our last chance for a baby.

"I want to be alone!" I say.

"Polly..."

"I said go away!"

But I don't hear his footsteps leaving. And the shadow of his body lingers under the door. "Polly, I'm really worried about you. Will you please let me in?"

He's scared I'm going to kill myself. It's a little too late for that. He should have considered that *before* he drove Tegan to the hospital. He feels obligated to make sure I'm okay, although in reality, he would be better off if I killed myself. He knows it, even if he doesn't want to admit it. Through all our fertility treatments, all the doctors said that Hank's sperm count was perfect. The problem was with *me*.

Of course, it's too late now. After what I've done, we're both screwed. The police will be knocking on our door any minute now, as soon as Tegan is well enough to tell them the entire story.

"I'm fine." I force my voice to stay at a normal volume. "Really. I just don't want to talk right now. Okay?" When he doesn't say anything, I add, "I swear I'm okay. I just want to be alone."

"I need you to open the door, Polly."

"I told you, I'm fine."

"If you don't open the door, I'm calling 911. I bought a new phone."

He absolutely means it. If he thinks I'm a danger to myself, he's going to call for an ambulance and possibly have me hauled away. And if he does that, I won't be able to do what I need to do.

Finally, I unlock the bedroom door and pull it open. Hank is standing there, still in his coat, wringing his hands together.

"See?" I say. "I told you, I'm fine."

He inspects me head to toe. He scrunches his face up like he's not entirely sure he believes me. "You said if I took Tegan to the hospital, you would..."

I wave a hand. "I was just being dramatic."

He raises an eyebrow.

"Really, Hank." I fight to keep my voice from shaking. "I'm fine. You can go back to work."

"No," he says. "I'm not leaving you."

Why is he being so stubborn? We can't afford to keep the shop closed for even a day, and he knows it.

I stand my ground, blocking his way into the bedroom. "You can't come in the bedroom."

"Fine," he says. "I'll be downstairs. I won't call 911, but I'm going to call Dr. Salinsky. And...and maybe a lawyer."

"That's fine. Go ahead."

He frowns, lingering at the doorway. "I love you, Polly."

Is that even true anymore? He used to love me. Before I lost my mind. Ever since then, he hasn't looked at me the same way. He doesn't look at me like I'm the most wonderful human being he's ever met, that's for sure. We stay together out of habit now. It was up to me to make our family complete, and I failed miserably.

"I love you too," I say, because he won't leave 'til I say it.

Hank decides to trust me. His footsteps disappear down the hallway. He's afraid to leave me alone for the moment, but he can't stay here forever. Eventually, he's going to leave this house. And that's what I'm waiting for.

I promised him I would make this right. And I'm going to deliver.

CHAPTER 60

TEGAN

"You could have died."

The orthopedic surgeon, Dr. Tewari, is incredibly blunt. She's spent the last several minutes in her rumpled green scrubs standing by my bedside, explaining what she has already done and what is still left to be done and mostly scaring the crap out of me. But I can see in her brown eyes that she means it.

"Yes," I murmur. "I know."

I gently adjust the monitor strapped to my belly to make sure Little Tuna is doing okay in there. Someone outside in the Labor and Delivery unit is monitoring her heartbeat, and I can see on the screen by my bed that she's at a steady 120 beats per minute. After they gave me some fluid through an IV, both Tuna and I felt much better. Right now, I've also got IV antibiotics running into my other arm. They gave me a small dose of morphine to take the edge off as well. I feel a bit like a pincushion, but I'm obscenely grateful for all the care they have given me in the hours since I've been here.

I think we're going to be okay, Mama.

"We washed out your foot wound," Dr. Tewari explains. "It was grossly infected, and you also have a trimalleolar ankle fracture..."

She's droning on about my ankle fracture, but what I don't know for sure and I'm too scared to ask is whether she thinks I'm going to lose my foot. It looked so awful this morning, and although it's wrapped in a thick layer of gauze now, I'm sure it looks just as bad, and I still can barely feel it. Worse, I *heard* somebody outside my hospital room say something along the lines of "might lose that foot." So it's not like I'm worrying over nothing.

I wish she would tell me, but I'm also too scared to hear the answer. Anyway, I have to focus on Little Tuna right now. As long as she's okay, nothing else matters.

"Also," Dr. Tewari says in a quiet voice, "the police want to speak with you."

This statement breaks through my haze. I stare up at the doctor. "They do?"

The police must have found out about Polly and Hank keeping me held hostage. I can't wait to tell them everything those two did to me. Honestly, I feel sick just thinking about it. If they had taken me to the hospital to begin with, I would never have gotten this sick. If I lose my foot, it will be their fault. If anything happens to Tuna, it will be their fault.

"Yes," the doctor says. "The officer said your car had been tampered with prior to your accident."

What?

I thought I couldn't possibly feel worse than I feel

right now, but there it is. Someone *tampered with my car* and caused my accident? How could that possibly be? Who would do something like that?

Of course, that is a stupid question. I know exactly who would do something like that. A man who did not want me going to the police. A man who would have been happy if I died in that accident. If my baby died.

"I told them you're not up for it right now though," Dr. Tewari says. "I sent them away for now, but whenever you're ready, you can speak with them."

I definitely need to speak to the police. And after we talk about the car, I'll tell them all about the couple who held me hostage for four nights. Even though I felt for Hank when he was telling me about his wife's mental health problems, it doesn't matter. That woman almost killed me and my baby. She ought to be locked up forever. And her husband should be locked up too for letting her do it.

"But there's a family member asking to see you," Dr. Tewari tells me. "If you feel up to it. He says he's your brother."

I haven't seen any familiar faces since I arrived at the hospital, and my heart leaps at the idea that Dennis is outside asking to see me. "Please send him in."

When my brother peeks his head into my room, rapping softly on the open door, I almost burst into tears. "Teggie?"

"Dennis!" And now I really do cry. It's just been too much the last few days. Too awful for words. "You're here!"

"Of course I'm here." He looks terrible. He's got dark shadows under his eyes and a few days' growth of a sand-colored beard on his chin. His fingernails are bitten to the quick, like they always are when he's anxious about something. "I've been driving here every day since they found your car to look for you and harass the police to get off their asses and find you."

"Yeah." I wipe the tears from my eyes. "It's been a rough few days."

He collapses into the chair by my bed. "Where *were* you?"

"I..."

I want to tell him the whole story, but I can't. It's too horrible and too humiliating. *A couple kept me in a hospital bed in their basement and wouldn't let me leave.* Even after the trauma of what Simon Lamar did to me, when I close my eyes, it's that basement room that I see. I'm afraid to go to sleep because I'll have nightmares about it.

I'll save it for the police.

"Teggie?" He picks up my hand, and I realize how ice-cold I must be, because he is so much warmer. "Are you okay?"

I can only shake my head no.

"We'll talk about it when you're ready." He gives my hand a squeeze. "Also, you should know that there's a man named Jackson Bruckner in the waiting room who has been asking to speak to you. He says he's a good friend."

I'm surprised to hear that. "Jackson is here?"

Dennis nods. "He arrived here right after I did. Is he...your boyfriend?"

I flinch, remembering my completely inappropriate fantasies about Jackson before I knew what he was really like. "Hardly. He was helping me with the contract with Simon Lamar. And I don't want to see him."

I suddenly feel completely exhausted. Dennis doesn't have any idea that Simon raped me. I need to tell him everything, but this is not the time. I am too emotionally spent, and I still feel physically awful. Maybe in a few days, we can sit down together, and I can explain to him why I said no to all that money. I'm sure I'll still be in the hospital by then.

Oh God, how am I going to pay for this hospitalization? And my delivery? And the rest of my life?

A sudden contraction squeezes my stomach and brings tears to my eyes. For the first time, I wish I had just lied and pretended Simon never did what he did to me.

CHAPTER 61

POLLY

Hank raided the medicine cabinet while I was out at the drugstore.

Everything is gone. Every last bottle of pills has vanished, stored in an undisclosed location. He even took the razor I use to shave my legs and the scissors he used to use to trim his beard before he let it go wild.

Clearly, he took my suicide threat seriously.

But right now, the true danger isn't me taking my own life. We kidnapped a woman. And if she is still alive—which is not a given—she will certainly tell the police everything about what we did to her, if she hasn't already. We will almost definitely both go to jail for this.

Unless I do something about it.

As promised, Hank doesn't leave the house. Not only that, but every hour, he comes upstairs to knock on the bedroom door. If I don't answer right away, he calls out my name. I have to answer at that point, because if I don't, he will break the door down.

My chance comes in the early evening, when Hank goes out to the backyard to chop more firewood.

I knew he would do this. We used up most of our wood during the storm, and we use the fireplace in the evening in place of heat to save money. He assumes I'll be down for dinner, and he wants to have the fire going.

Little does he know I won't be here when he comes to fetch me for dinner.

I have a very short gap of time to make this happen. I used to work at Roosevelt Memorial, so I know that seven o'clock is the change of shift. Change of shift happens when the nursing staff from the day shift signs out all their patient information to the nurses coming on for the evening shift. When that happens, there's about thirty minutes of chaos. The nurses are deep in conversation, and no meds are handed out. It's a brief window of time when just about anything could happen.

That window will be my opportunity.

I search through the bottom dresser drawer in the bedroom, which is where I keep my scrubs. I used to wear them to work every day, but now they're just sitting there at the bottom of the drawer, neatly folded, mocking me. I pick up a nondescript flower-print pair from the top of the drawer and change into them. I wrap my braid around itself until it becomes a neat bun. Then I look at my reflection in our bedroom mirror.

I look just like I used to when I went to work every day. Before everything went down the toilet.

I walk down the steps to the kitchen, taking them as quietly as I can so Hank doesn't notice me coming down. But no—he's distracted by chopping wood in the backyard. I can just barely see him out the back window, wearing only a flannel shirt despite the cold because he always works up a sweat from chopping. The sight of my big, strong husband chopping wood in the backyard is as familiar to me as my own face—he has done this every winter since we got married. He has always made sure that we don't run out of wood for our fireplace. That we're always kept warm.

I turn away from the window. It's time to go.

It hits me that I never brought over lunch for Sadie today. I start to grab some tinfoil to make her a quick sandwich to drop off on my way out, but then I see out the window that Mitch's truck is in their driveway. If he's home, I need to stay away.

I linger at the kitchen counter for another few seconds. Hank raided our bathroom, but he stupidly left behind all the knives in the kitchen. My eyes rest on a pair of kitchen shears that we keep in our knife block. I grab them out of the block, testing their weight. Then I drop them into the pocket of my scrub pants.

I hope Sadie will be okay without me. Because after this, I don't know if I'm ever coming home.

CHAPTER 62

TEGAN

Dennis excuses himself to go grab some food from the cafeteria before it closes. I don't want him to leave, but at the same time, I'm exhausted. I could nap while he's getting food.

My eyes are starting to drift shut when the door to my hospital room cracks open. Suddenly, I am completely alert again.

"Hello?" I call out. I wonder if it's the nurse with more pain medication. Not that I can have much while I'm still pregnant.

But it's not the nurse. It's *Jackson.*

Unlike my brother, who looks like he slept in his clothes the last three days, Jackson is wearing a crisp white shirt and tie, and his black hair looks relatively neat given that it's the end of a long day. Only his eyes look slightly bloodshot behind his thick glasses. They rake over me, from my swollen belly to my gauze-covered foot and ankle, and they widen slightly even though I can tell he's struggling to hide his reaction. I'm sure I look shockingly awful.

"How are you doing?" he asks stiffly.

The question tugs on my nerves. I can't believe the nurse let him come in here. "I'm absolutely wonderful."

He has the good grace to look embarrassed. "I know. I'm sorry. I'm just glad you're okay."

Is he? *The officer said your car had been tampered with prior to your accident.* Who would have the motivation to tamper with my car? Simon, of course. But he would never do it himself. He would get somebody else to do it. A lackey who has been driving out for the last couple of months to *handle* the girl he knocked up.

"Listen." He drops into the chair by my bed. "We need to talk."

He is uncomfortably close to my bed. Did the nurse really let him in here? I was clear that I didn't want any visitors besides my brother. But I've gotten to know Jackson pretty well recently. He's a jerk for not believing what I told him about Simon, but I genuinely can't imagine him hurting anyone.

The officer said your car had been tampered with prior to your accident.

"I'm too tired to talk," I say. "I…I'd rather you leave."

"This will be quick," he promises.

"Jackson…"

"No, let me say this." He levels his gaze at me. "The other day, when you said that stuff about Simon and what he did to you, I was really surprised. My job is to protect Simon, you know?"

"Uh-huh…"

"And I handled it horribly." His light-brown

eyebrows scrunch together. "I always heard stories about women having the courage to be honest about what happened to them. That's what you did, and I reacted in the worst possible way. Worse, I covered for Simon. I'm so ashamed of my behavior."

I frown. "Are you?"

"I really am." He fixes his eyes on me. Are his pupils dilated, or am I just imagining it? His eyes suddenly look darker than usual. "I'm really sorry things turned out this way, Tegan. Truly. You of all people don't deserve it."

Jackson is making me really nervous now. I don't know why, but it feels like something isn't right here. Jackson's apology feels off somehow. I mean, it's hard to believe he's sorry after what he said to me. I wish Dennis would hurry up and get back from the cafeteria.

There's nobody outside my room that I can see. I push down on the red call button to contact the nurse. The last time I called, the nurse appeared almost instantly. But now it doesn't seem like anyone's out there.

"Did you call for the nurse?" Jackson asks. Damn, I didn't realize he saw me do that. "They're signing out for the next shift right now. I doubt anyone is coming for a bit." He pauses. "It's just you and me."

I feel like I'm going to be sick. "Oh..."

"But I can help you." There's a glint in his eyes that sends a chill down my spine. "Tell me, Tegan. What do you need?"

"Nothing," I say quickly. "I'm fine."

"But you hit the button for the nurse."

"It was a mistake."

Jackson considers my words for a moment. He

glances at the door, verifying that we're still alone here. We are. "Listen, Tegan..."

I squirm in the bed. "Jackson... I... I'm really tired..."

"I'm sure you are." He leans in closer to me. Too close—I can smell his aftershave. A minty smell, much different from Simon's cologne. "But there's something you need to know..."

CHAPTER 63

POLLY

I haven't set foot in Roosevelt Memorial Hospital since the day of The Incident.

It was so humiliating. I didn't even do anything that bad. It's not like I was going to hurt that newborn. I knew I couldn't *go* anywhere with him. I was just *holding* him. And I was definitely going to give him back *eventually*. I just wanted to hold him a little bit longer.

I didn't need to be escorted out by security.

Today when I march into the hospital, I leave my coat in the car so that everybody can see my scrubs, and I'm wearing my old badge. They confiscated the badge I was wearing on my last day, but I have an extra from when I thought I had lost it and had security print off a new one. It won't get me into the med rooms, but I don't need it for that. It's just for appearances.

And it turns out I hardly need it. The security guard barely looks up as I walk past. It's still visiting hours. I grab a surgical mask from the front desk to conceal my face, just in case.

I stride purposefully in the direction of the elevators. I check the directory on the wall to verify that Labor and Delivery is still on the third floor, and then I wait patiently for the elevator to arrive. There's a man next to me who is about my age, and he's clutching a stuffed elephant in one hand and a box of chocolates in the other. He notices me looking at his possessions and smiles.

"My wife just gave birth to our first," he says with a touch of pride. "I know the baby is too little to appreciate this but… Well, my wife will enjoy the chocolates."

My lips feel rubbery as I try to return his smile. "I'm sure she will."

I wonder what Hank would have brought me if I had ever managed to get pregnant. I imagine him roaming through the aisles at the supermarket, trying to pick out a treat for me that I would enjoy. And then stopping at a toy store after. Whatever he got, the animal would surely be wearing a baseball cap.

That will never happen now.

The elevator doors swing open. The man next to me is a gentleman, and he waves for me to go in ahead of him. My eyes swim with tears as I press the button for the third floor and the elevator slowly starts to rise. I reach into my scrub pocket, and my fingers close reassuringly over the handle of the scissors that will ensure Tegan will never tell anyone what we did to her.

Soon, this will all be over. I won't have to smile and pretend to be happy for people having babies. I won't have to watch Hank pretending to be satisfied with the life he's stuck with because of me. He can have the fresh start he deserves.

Hank will be frantic when he notices the bedroom is empty and my Bronco isn't in the driveway. He'll search the house, looking for me. Then he'll get in his truck and drive around, trying to find me. Eventually, he'll think to come here.

But by that time, it will be far too late.

CHAPTER 64

TEGAN

Teggie? You okay?"

Whatever Jackson was about to say or do to me gets interrupted by Dennis standing at the entrance to my hospital room. Jackson rotates his head to look at my brother and gives him a dirty look.

"Tegan and I were talking," Jackson says irritably.

"Actually, we were done talking." I flash Dennis a look to let him know that I need Jackson out of my room ASAP. "And I'm really tired."

Jackson's clean-shaven jaw twitches. "Tegan..."

"She's had a long day, Jackson." Dennis shoots Jackson a hard look. "Time to head out, man. Whatever it is, you can talk tomorrow."

For a moment, I'm worried Jackson might refuse to leave and that things could get ugly between him and my brother. I'm relieved that Dennis has arrived to defend me at least—after everything that's happened to me, it's nice to have someone in my corner. But then Jackson lifts himself off the chair and gives me one last, long look. "We need to talk tomorrow, Tegan," he says. "First thing."

All I know is I'm not giving him another chance to be alone in a room with me.

Finally, Jackson turns and trudges into the hallway. I had expected to feel the tension drain out of my body with his exit, but somehow I still have an uneasy feeling I can't seem to shake, like there's still danger on the horizon. I put a hand on my belly, and Little Tuna gives me a reassuring kick.

"Jesus," Dennis says as he settles back into the seat that Jackson vacated. "What was *his* problem?"

Truer words have never been spoken. But the weird thing is that the two of them almost seemed like they already knew each other. Dennis even called Jackson by his name. Which is really strange, because how could they know each other? I never mentioned Jackson in my conversations with Dennis, and earlier, he acted like he didn't know who he was.

"If that lawyer comes back," Dennis adds, "I'll make sure to tell him you don't want to see him."

I nod, although I'm not certain all of a sudden. When Jackson was by my bed, I wanted him gone. But there was something he wanted to tell me. And the look in his eyes—it wasn't menacing. It was something else.

It was fear.

"Are you okay?" Dennis asks me for what feels like the millionth time.

I squirm on the mattress, trying to get comfortable, which is almost impossible with my broken ankle and giant belly. "This pain is awful."

"Yeah, I know." He frowns. "I broke my leg in three places when I got into that car accident. Remember?"

"Of course I remember." I had been so worried about Dennis when I got the call about his accident. He was my only family left at that point, and I couldn't bear the thought of losing him. I hate that I put him through much worse over the last few days. "It was similar circumstances too, wasn't it? An icy road?"

He nods, his gaze growing distant for a moment. "Right. There had been a snowstorm the night before, but that guy you were dating—Brian, was it?—broke up with you, and you were so hysterical on the phone, I had to come."

I remember Brian breaking up with me, although I didn't ask Dennis to drive out—he had insisted. Except now there's a slight edge to his voice, like he's upset with me for having forced him to drive in a snowstorm.

He doesn't blame me for that crash, does he? The accident brought his career as a professional skier to a screeching halt, sure, but he always seemed happy with his life as a ski instructor. He isn't like our father, who was obsessed with achieving more and more success in his career. And when he failed, it killed him. Dennis is different. He's content with what he has, and he cares about me more than anything else.

"It wouldn't be so bad," I say, "if I had a way to pay for all this."

"What about your insurance?"

I glance over at the IV dripping medicine into my vein. "My insurance is terrible."

"What about the money from Lamar?"

Despite everything, I feel a surge of irritation. I never

told Dennis what Simon did to me, but I explained in no uncertain terms that I wouldn't be accepting that money. "I told you, I can't take that money."

"Yes, but circumstances have changed." He looks pointedly at my broken ankle. "Maybe you should reconsider."

He has a good point. Things were bad enough before my accident, but my situation is much worse now. God knows how long I'll be unable to work because of my broken ankle and infection. I'm falling deeper into the hole than I've ever been. And despite the fact that Simon ripped up that contract, I have a feeling if I came back to him, he'd been more than willing to draw up a new one for me to sign.

Except that's not going to happen. No way. I will not take hush money from that man. He did a terrible thing to me, and I won't keep my mouth shut and let him do it to other girls.

"No," I say with forcefulness that surprises me. "I'm not taking his money. Never."

Dennis opens his mouth as if to argue with me, but then he shuts it, and his shoulders sag. I feel guilty that he's the one I'm going to have to rely on to help me after the baby comes, but he'll be there for me. He always has been.

"Anyway," he says, "don't think about it right now. You've been through enough, and you look wiped."

He's right about that. I have been through far too much the last few days, and even though I told Jackson I was tired in order to get rid of him, my eyelids suddenly feel like lead. Now that my pain is under better control, I can get a decent night's sleep for the first time in days.

"You should take a nap," Dennis tells me. "You're safe now. There's nothing to worry about anymore."

"Maybe I will," I murmur. "Just for a little while… just to…"

And before I can even finish the sentence, my eyes have drifted shut.

CHAPTER 65

POLLY

The man with the chocolates and the teddy bear steps aside to let me get out of the elevator first. But while he walks toward the maternity ward, I linger behind. My stomach is churning, and I feel like I might be sick.

I'm losing my nerve.

But I can't. If Tegan talks to the police about me and Hank, it's all over. This is the only way. I can't save myself, but I can save Hank.

As I'm about to walk toward Labor and Delivery, a tall, skinny man with thick glasses and a rumpled suit brushes past me, his shoulder jolting mine. He had been absorbed by something on his phone, and when he knocks into me, he looks up in surprise. "Sorry," he mumbles, although he goes right back to looking at the screen.

My phone vibrates in my pocket. I pull it out. Unsurprisingly, there's a text message from Hank, who must have finished chopping wood and discovered I was gone:

Where are you?

And then a second later:

You're not in the bedroom. Where did you go?

And then:

Please come home right now!!!

I want to write back to him. I want to tell him that I'm sorry about what I'm going to do, but it's the only way to save him.

But if I write anything, he's going to freak out. So I stuff my phone back in my pocket.

Goodbye, Hank.

Time to do this.

I keep my hand in my pocket, gripping the shears. In my scrubs and with the ID badge strapped to my chest, I know nobody will stop me. I'm able to walk right into Labor and Delivery, and just as expected, the nurses are huddled together, passing off their assignments from the morning shift to the evening shift. Nobody questions me, because I look like I belong here. I blend right into the scenery. I am invisible.

The names aren't on the doors, but I know they keep a list of who is in every room at the nurses' station. As casually as I can, I slip into the nurses' station and locate the list lying on the keyboard of one of the computers.

Werner. Room 308.

I'm gripping the scissors in my pocket so tightly, my

fingertips are tingling. I walk briskly and with purpose down the hallway. I pass 301, 302, 303…

Am I really going to do this? Do I have it in me to harm another human being? I couldn't even break her kneecap, and this is far, far worse. But it's the only way to keep my husband out of trouble.

304, 305, 306…

My phone is ringing now. Hank is calling me. I pull my phone out of my pocket and press a button to reject the call. Then I switch the phone to silent.

307, 308…

And here I am.

I see her right away. Tegan. She's lying in the hospital bed, her blond hair limp around her face. Her belly is jutting out, and her left ankle is wrapped in a healthy layer of white gauze. Her eyes are shut, and she's sound asleep, which will make this a heck of a lot easier.

Except then I realize she's not alone in the room. There's a man standing at her bedside. It takes me a second to recognize him as the man who was at my house looking for Tegan. The man who said he was her brother.

Except he's not just visiting with Tegan. Something else is going on in this room.

The man has a syringe in his hand. And he's trying to hook it up to Tegan's IV, but he's fumbling a bit. I may not have worked as a nurse in years, but I very much doubt the rules have changed enough that a random family member is allowed to inject whatever they want into a patient's IV line. This man does not have good intentions.

I stand in the doorway, frozen. Tegan's brother is

trying to hurt her. I came here to keep her from turning me and Hank in to the police, but this man is doing the job for me. All I have to do is back away, and this entire nightmare will be over.

"What are you doing?" I blurt out.

The man jerks his head in my direction. His eyes grow large at the sight of me. He drops the IV, which is now leaking fluid. He pockets the syringe. "Sorry," he says. "Are visiting hours over?"

I release the scissors in my pocket and plant my hands on my hips. "I asked you what you were doing."

Tegan's brother opens his mouth. Even though I recognize him from when he came to my house, he is likely unable to place me in my scrubs and surgical mask. He surely just thinks I'm a floor nurse. I stand there, waiting to see what story he will concoct about what he was just trying to do. But instead, he surprises me. He starts running, nearly knocking me down in his desperation to get out of the room.

Tegan's eyes crack open at the commotion. For a second, our eyes lock. "You!" she cries.

I don't have time to deal with her right now. I turn around and run after the man, who has a considerable head start. "Stop him!" I shout.

My sneakers pound against the linoleum floor as all the staff turn to stare. A few of them start moving, but I'm in the lead. It's up to me—I've got to stop that guy. It's all I can think of.

I'm not fast enough to catch him, but I manage to hook my fingers on the collar of his ski jacket from behind. It doesn't stop him, but he stumbles and loses his balance, taking a second to right himself. The stranger

I'd seen earlier—the one with the thick glasses—is waiting by the elevator, and he rushes over at the sight of the chase. Without any hesitation, he grabs Tegan's brother and shoves him hard against the wall, holding him in place with his elbow to his neck. That man is stronger than he looks.

The stranger glances over his shoulder at me while Tegan's brother squirms under his grasp, gasping for air. "What did he do?" he barks at me.

"He was trying to inject something into her IV," I say breathlessly.

The bespectacled stranger doesn't even look surprised. I can hear him hiss in the man's ear, "I *knew* it! I knew you did it, you piece of shit!"

A security guard joins them, and I quickly explain the situation. Because I look like a nurse, everything I say is taken very seriously. The guard nods like this isn't even the wildest thing he's seen today. I almost believe it.

Then the guard fishes the syringe out of the man's pocket. I wonder what was in it. Nothing good, I suspect.

"Thank you, Polly," the guard tells me when I'm done with the whole story.

I open my mouth, shocked that he knows my name. Then I remember. I'm still wearing my ID badge. "Oh" is all I can say.

I've got to get out of here. It's only a matter of time before they figure out that I don't actually work here as a nurse. And if anyone remembers what I did two years ago, that's not going to look good for me. I could wind up going to jail along with Tegan's brother. So the second the guard turns his head, I slip away as quietly as I can.

I came here to kill Tegan Werner, to stop her from sending my husband to jail. But the truth is I never could have done it. I didn't have it in me after all.

So instead, I saved her life.

CHAPTER 66

TEGAN

Jackson has to explain it to me five times, and I still can't wrap my head around it.

"I'm so sorry, Tegan," he keeps saying. "I know this is the last thing you need right now."

I have allowed the police to enter my room. Well, *one* police officer. A detective named Maxwell is here, and he has been the one investigating my car accident. And it turns out he has also been investigating Simon Lamar.

"We found a man that Lamar paid off to tamper with the tread on your tires the night before your accident," Detective Maxwell tells me. "They knew the tires wouldn't be able to maintain traction in a snow storm, and that's why your brother suggested driving out to see him."

"But why would Dennis..." I can barely say the words. My brother was my whole universe for a long time. Why would he do something like this to me?

"Your brother and Lamar were business partners," Maxwell explains. "Lamar was financing a bunch of new ski resorts with your brother. This was a huge deal for him. And Lamar was very clear that if you went to the police, the deal would not happen."

It was actually when I was visiting my brother at the resort where he works that I met Simon Lamar at a bar. Apparently, he had just finished a meeting with Dennis.

I always thought of my brother as a laid-back guy who was happy with his career as a ski instructor, but as it turned out, he had more in common with our father than I thought. When he realized the deal he'd been arranging was slipping through his fingers, he was willing to do whatever it took to make it work.

It turns out Dennis was never as okay as I thought he was with losing his chance to go pro. I never realized he blamed me for the car accident that took him out of commission. It pains me to think of the simmering resentment he'd felt for years.

Jackson puts his hand on my shoulder. "I was trying to tell you about it, but then that bastard came back. I didn't think there was any chance he'd be bold enough to try anything while you were in the hospital, or else I never would have left you alone." He squeezes his eyes shut. "I never should have left. I'm so sorry, Tegan."

"It wasn't your fault," I tell him, and I mean it. I was the one who sent him away.

"I meant what I said before," Jackson says. "I'm so ashamed and sorry for my reaction when you told me what Simon did to you. I...I couldn't believe I said all that stuff to you. After I left your apartment, I contacted another woman who I knew Simon paid off, and

I discovered it was the same story. He drugged her too, but she took the money to keep her mouth shut." He flinches. "When I called you right before your accident, when we had that bad connection, I was trying to tell you that I wanted to help you, and I was going to the police to tell them what I knew about Simon. I wanted to back you up when you came forward and make sure he would never do anything like that ever again."

"Well," Detective Maxwell says, "he definitely won't be doing that again. We have Lamar in custody, and we intend to hold him accountable for everything he has done."

I look at the detective. "What was in that syringe?"

"We think it was morphine." Maxwell pauses. "You were already getting morphine, so the lethal dose could have been chalked up to a nursing error."

Lethal dose? Jackson looks about as rattled as I feel. I can't believe my own brother would do something like that to me. I have never felt so alone in my entire life.

I'm still here, Mama. You've got me!

I do still have my daughter. The one blessing is that she made it through this, still okay.

"We're trying to figure out who that nurse was who stopped him," Detective Maxwell says. "She was at your door and kept your brother from giving you the morphine. But she was wearing a mask, and the other staff members didn't recognize her."

I flash back to the moment I woke up. To the woman standing at the door to my room and those green eyes staring back at me over the top of the mask.

Polly.

Polly showed up here tonight. I don't know what

her motivation for coming was, but she stopped Dennis from killing me and my baby. I hate her for what she did to me, but I also realize that if it weren't for her and Hank, I would be dead right now. They have saved me twice over. I am only here right now because of her. I owe her.

But I'm still not sure it's enough.

CHAPTER 67

POLLY

The first thing I see when I exit the hospital is that familiar green pickup truck.

Hank.

When he sees me, he jumps out of the driver's seat, leaving his truck behind, even though this is not a parking zone, and in another thirty seconds, someone will come over and tell him so. But right now, he couldn't care less.

"Polly!" he cries. "What are you doing here?"

He looks really freaked out. His hat is lopsided, and his coat is unzipped, revealing his oil-stained flannel shirt. When he reaches me, he grabs me by the shoulders like he's afraid I'm going to run away.

"Everything is fine," I say. "I promise."

"But—" His eyes dart around the entrance to the hospital. "Why are there so many cop cars around here?"

"Don't worry. They're not here for me."

He inspects my face, not sure if he should believe me.

"I promise," I say. "I'm free to leave. But my car is in the lot."

"Leave it overnight," he says. "We're going home in my truck."

I can't blame him for not wanting to let me out of his sight. And truth be told, I'm not excited about trekking back to my car without my coat. So I obligingly climb into the passenger seat of his truck.

Hank revs up the engine, and I rub my hands together to stay warm. The kitchen shears jab me slightly against my thigh, and I shiver, thinking about an alternate reality where I went through with my misguided plan. In that reality, I would either be dead or on my way to prison right now instead of riding home in a warm truck with my husband. I'm glad I'm living in this reality.

"I think you're right," I say. "I should make another appointment with Dr. Salinsky."

Hank glances over at me. He doesn't say anything, but he puts his hand on my knee and gives it a squeeze.

"I love you, Hank," I say.

"I love you too, Polly." His deep voice breaks. "More than anything."

And then I rest my head against his big, broad chest, and he puts his arm around my shoulders, holding me tightly like everything he cares about is right here in the car, in the seat next to him. Every pore of his body radiates love for me.

Someday, your family will be complete.

I've spent so many years of my life focusing on the child I wanted so badly. But Hank is my family, and he's given me more love than I would have gotten from a dozen kids. It took almost losing everything to realize how blessed I am.

A year after her death, I finally see the wisdom in my mother's words. I've got Hank and he's got me, and our family is complete. And now we're going home together to have a nice quiet night, just the two of us.

"Let's go home," I tell him.

He nods and puts the car in drive.

Except a quiet evening is not what the night has in store for us. Because after Hank drives us back to our house, I see the police lights flashing before we even reach our driveway.

Tegan told them what we did. It's all over.

They're here to take Hank and me to jail.

CHAPTER 68

POLLY

"What's going on?" Hank blurts out.

It takes me a second to realize that the police lights aren't around our house. The police are surrounding Mitch Hambly's house. There are a whole bunch of them.

Oh no. Sadie.

If Mitch hurt her, I swear I will make good use of those kitchen shears.

Before Hank can stop me, I leap out of the truck. I am dressed completely inappropriately, with no coat and only sneakers on my feet. Within a second of stomping through the snow, my feet are wet and cold. But I keep going until I get to the other house, which is surrounded by yellow police tape.

"Excuse me, ma'am," a young officer says as I approach the tape. "I'm going to have to ask you to step back."

"But this is my neighbor!" I cry. I point to our own house. "I live right over there."

"I'm sorry. I'd recommend you go on home."

"But...the little girl...is she all right?"

The officer isn't listening to me though. He is talking into a police radio.

A second later, Hank comes up behind me. He grabs my elbow as his gaze darts around the scene before us. "Polly, this is police business. We shouldn't be here."

"But what about Sadie?" I fold my arms across my chest. "I'm not leaving here until I make sure she's okay."

Hank could very easily pick me up and throw me over his shoulder to bring me back to the house. But instead, he shrugs off his heavy coat and rests it on my shoulders. "Put this on before you freeze."

"Aren't you going to be cold?"

"Are you kidding? You know I'm a furnace." As he says it, though, his teeth chatter slightly.

"It's way too big," I grumble, but I wrap the warm coat tighter around me. It smells like oil and wood chips and Hank.

I crane my neck to see what's going on. The officer is talking into the radio again. I can only catch snatches of what he's saying. *Forty-six-year-old male...blunt head trauma...*

And that's when I look down in the snow in front of the house. And I see drops of crimson.

"Hank!" I grab my husband's sleeve. "Look! There's blood in the snow."

Hank blanches when he sees where I'm pointing. He looks like he's making up his mind about something, and finally, he walks up to the yellow tape and clears his throat loudly. I follow close behind.

"Excuse me," he says to the young officer. "My wife

and I live next door. We have a right to know what's going on in our backyard. I need to know if we're safe."

The officer spends a moment taking in my husband's six-foot-four-inch frame. Finally, he says, "Nothing to worry about, sir. Looks like your neighbor was drunk and took a bad fall down his front steps and got knocked unconscious. Then he suffocated with his face down in the snow."

Mitch is *dead*? I always got a feeling that his drinking would be the end of him. But I didn't expect it to end so soon. "And what about his young daughter?" I ask. "Is she okay?"

"She's okay," the officer assures me. "We're going to find a place for her."

"But she doesn't have any other family..."

"Don't worry, ma'am. We've got it under control."

Hank puts his arm around my shoulders. I lean my head against him, and as I feel his heart beating against me, I make a vow to myself that no matter what, I will make sure that little girl comes out of this okay.

CHAPTER 69

TEGAN

Tia Marie Werner.

Five pounds eight ounces.

And absolutely perfect.

I cradle my newborn daughter in my arms, staring down at her impossibly tiny face. She had a brief stay in the neonatal ICU, but they have cleared her to spend her days in my own hospital room, now on the maternity ward. And I spend most of the time just staring at her and thinking about how lucky I am.

After all, I came perilously close to losing her. Twice.

How could a human being be this small? Her entire foot is about the size of one of my toes. Her nose is the size of a little tiny button. And her eyelids are paper thin, almost translucent. Every time she takes a breath, it's like a little miracle.

"You did it, Little Tuna," I tell her. It's going to be difficult making the transition from calling her Tuna to calling her Tia. "You got born. That's going to be the hardest thing you'll ever have to do. It's all easy from here."

Tia blinks up at me with her clear blue eyes. She doesn't look like she quite believes me, but that's okay, because it's a damn lie.

Ever since Tia's birth, I haven't heard her talking to me in my head anymore. The baby voice went away entirely. But when I look at her tiny face, I know what she's thinking. Even though the umbilical cord got cut, we still share a connection that we'll have forever.

After all, she was the only other person with me down in that basement.

It's hard not to keep thinking about those days I spent down in Hank and Polly's basement, even though I've told the police that I can't remember any of it due to the knock on my head. It's ironic that I'm pretending not to remember something that I'll carry around with me for the rest of my life. Detective Maxwell has given me his personal cell phone number, and a dozen times a day, I pick up the phone to call him and tell him what happened. But I never make the call. I still haven't given anyone their names or admitted what they did to me.

There's a rap at the door to my hospital room, and I know who it is before I even hear the familiar voice behind the door: "Tegan?"

"Come in," I call out.

After a brief hesitation, the door swings open, and Jackson is standing there, like he has every day since I've been in the hospital. He's wearing his same rumpled dress shirt, and his eyes look tired behind his glasses. But he's got a smile on his face.

I haven't left the hospital since I was admitted for

sepsis, and Jackson has been practically the only person who has come to visit me. My parents are gone, the father of my child is in jail, and so is my brother, both awaiting trial. So it's just me and Tia. But every evening, Jackson is here.

"Tegan," he says. "How are you doing?"

"Good," I say. "Tia drank a whole bottle."

I always wanted to breastfeed my daughter, but with the number of medications circulating in my bloodstream, it's safer not to. I try not to focus on it though. What's important is that she's healthy and happy.

"I brought you something." He pulls out a little pink teddy bear he had been hiding behind his back. He holds it up to show me. "Tia's first teddy bear!"

I laugh because the teddy bear is almost as big as she is. It seems like every day, Jackson shows up with a new surprise for us. He is desperate to make it up to me for not believing me when I first told him what Simon did. I don't know how I could have ever thought he would hurt me.

"Also," he says as he settles into the chair by my bed, "I'm making arrangements for when you get home."

"Arrangements?"

He nods. "You're going to need a lot of help given that you've got a new baby and you're still healing. So I'm booking a physical therapist to come to your apartment every day, and I've got a list of nannies and housekeepers that I'm interviewing."

My face flushes, and I hold Tia close to my chest. "I can't afford that."

"Yes, you can," he says firmly. "I talked with Simon, and he has signed papers to pay you child support starting immediately."

My mouth falls open. "How did you get him to do that?"

One corner of his lips quirks up. "I am very persuasive. Meaning I have access to a lot of dirt about him that would make his case even worse. And it's already bad enough."

I don't want to know the other dirt about Simon Lamar. What he did to me is bad enough. I'll always hate him for it, although I recognize that if not for him, I wouldn't have this tiny little miracle bundled in my arms. It's complicated, to say the least.

Jackson picks up the pink teddy bear and places it on the dresser across the room, which, like the rest of the room, is covered with flowers from what seems to be pretty much every person I've ever sat down next to over the course of my life. Jackson lingers at the dresser for a moment, smiling down at something. "Hey," he says. "You already have a teddy bear."

"I do?"

He lifts up a brown teddy bear clutching a red heart. There's a little card strung around the teddy bear's wrist. He opens it up and reads, "Dear Tegan, I wish you and your daughter all the happiness in the world. Love, Polly."

I freeze, my heart sinking into my stomach. *Polly*.

She sent me a gift.

"Cute teddy bear." He looks up to smile at me. "Who is Polly?"

I open my mouth, but no words come out. This is the perfect opportunity to tell him everything. To tell him how that evil woman kept me hostage in her basement for four nights while I begged to go to the hospital. How she nearly cost me and my baby our lives.

How she is sick and deserves to be locked up, maybe forever.

But somehow, I can't say any of that.

Hank pulled me out of my car when it was stuck in the snow. If he hadn't done that, I would have frozen to death. And if Polly hadn't stopped Dennis from injecting morphine into my bloodstream, I would have gone into cardiac arrest.

If not for Hank and Polly, Tia and I wouldn't be here right now. And that's worth something.

That's worth everything.

I gaze down at my daughter's face. *What do you think, Tia? What should I do?* And as always, I don't get an answer anymore. She just stares up at me with her big, trusting eyes. This absolutely perfect baby who I almost didn't get to hold in my arms, if not for that woman and her husband.

"Tegan?" Jackson says.

"I don't know who Polly is," I finally say. "I never heard the name before in my life."

EPILOGUE

TEGAN

ONE YEAR LATER

As I look around the living room of my three-bedroom townhouse, I feel a sense of deep satisfaction. For the first time in a long time, I have a place to call my own.

The town house was a fixer-upper for sure. I had some money from Simon, but not tons. Fortunately, Jackson volunteered for Habitat for Humanity after college, and he was excited to help me get the place fixed up. We have spent the last year working on it, but I'm proud of my new home.

I hear footsteps coming down the stairs. Jackson is coming from the second floor, where he's been working on what I hope will serve as a playroom. His hair is disheveled, and he wipes a smudge of dirt from his forehead. "I took measurements, and I can go buy the carpet today," he says.

"You don't have to buy me carpet for the playroom," I say. "You don't live here."

"Considering how much time I spend here, I feel like I should be on some sort of rent payment plan."

That's not false. Jackson has spent so much time at my house, I have let him sleep in the extra bedroom several nights. After all, Tia is still sleeping in a crib next to my bed. I can't quite let go.

A wail echoes from the corner of the living room, where Tia has face-planted on the carpet. She has been learning to walk recently, but she falls more often than she stays on her feet.

I can sympathize. A year ago, I could barely walk due to my broken and infected ankle. And I didn't for quite a while. It was a long process, progressing from the wheelchair to a knee scooter or crutches, then a cane, and now nothing at all. But I have a limp that Jackson swears is not noticeable, and my ankle still aches in bad weather.

"It's okay, Tia!" I rush over to my sobbing daughter. "Mama is here."

"Mama!" She holds her little hands out to me. "Mama!"

It was her first word and is still her favorite.

I pick her up off the floor to comfort her, brushing away her downy yellow curls. She clings to me, and I can feel her heart beating rapidly against my chest. It frightens me sometimes how close I came to losing her. And how close she came to losing me.

I learned to stop blaming Hank and Polly Thompson for what they did to me. Simon Lamar was the one who messed with the tires on my car and caused the accident that almost killed me. Hank and Polly, on the other hand, saved my life. Twice.

So no, I never told the police what they did. I couldn't make myself do it. But I do hope Polly got some help. Somehow I think with Hank by her side, she'll end up okay.

As for my brother, I don't feel nearly as kindly toward him. He is currently serving ten to fifteen years in a federal prison for attempted murder. He's written letters to me, begging me to forgive him. He claims that he never believed the faulty tires would kill me. He just thought an injury from a car accident would put things in perspective and that the hospital bills might persuade me to reconsider Simon's offer. That's why he had me bring his flask, knowing its presence would make it look like I'd been driving drunk. It would discredit me. I also suspect that after blaming me for his own accident years earlier, he thought this would be karmic retribution.

But even if I could forgive him for the accident, there's no mistaking what he was trying to do with that vial of morphine. He saw the look in my eyes and knew I was never going to take Simon's money. He was out of options, and he meant to kill me just to ensure his deal with Simon would go through. How can I ever forgive him for that?

I still don't understand how he could've done that to me. I loved Dennis more than anyone else in the world. I thought he felt the same way about me. It was the kind of betrayal that you can never bounce back from.

"What do you want to put in the playroom once it's finished?" Jackson asks me.

"Well," I say, "we should have a little table for arts

and crafts. We can put a play kitchen down there. And a giant doll house. And what do you think about a ball pit?"

He laughs. "A ball pit?"

"Why not?" I bounce Tia on my hip. "What do you think, Tia? Do you want to play in a tub full of multicolored balls?"

Tia, who is in a serious oral phase right now, just sticks her hand in her drooling mouth.

"I'd say she wants to *lick* a tub full of multicolored balls," Jackson says, laughing.

"I just want her to be happy." I plant a kiss on my daughter's forehead. If I'm holding her, I end up kissing her roughly once every sixty seconds. "After all, she doesn't get to have a dad."

Not that I ever want her to meet her real father. Simon Lamar drugged and raped me, and as it turned out, he did the same to many other women and will be spending most of the rest of his life in prison as punishment.

Tia can never know who her father is.

"She might have a dad," Jackson says. "Someday."

"Hmm. That would involve me going on a date at some point." Between single motherhood, my rehabilitation from the accident, and the therapy appointments to deal with the trauma of everything I have endured, dating hasn't been on my radar. And I'm still working to save money for nursing school—my plan is to go when Tia enters kindergarten. Seeing how capable Polly was as a nurse made me even more determined to go. She inspired me.

He raises an eyebrow. "And you going on a date is unlikely because..."

I meet his eyes. The best part of the last year has been the frequent visits from Jackson. For a long time, I was grateful that Jackson was respectful enough not to make a move, because I didn't think I could handle a relationship after everything that happened to me. And eventually, I assumed the two of us had settled firmly into the "friend zone." But now that I'm looking squarely into his eyes, I'm not so sure anymore.

"I don't know," I finally say. "I guess it hasn't come up."

"And…uh…" He scratches his scalp until his hair sticks up slightly. "Would it bother you if it did?"

We stare at each other for at least five seconds. A little tingle goes through me, and I realize how long it's been since I had that feeling. I'd forgotten how *good* it felt.

"No," I say. "It wouldn't bother me at all." I raise an eyebrow at him. "You staying for dinner tonight, Jackson? I'm ordering in Chinese food."

He grins at me. "I wouldn't miss it."

I'm not in any rush, but maybe my love life isn't completely over. Maybe tonight, after dinner is over, he'll suggest we prolong the evening by watching a movie together on the sofa. And then when I finally walk him to the door, he'll lean in for a kiss. And then I'll kiss him back.

Jackson is a good man. I wasn't sure if they existed, but if they do, he's one of them. He cares about me a lot, and one of these days, he'd make a great father to my little girl. And I know that if I ever told him anything again in the future, he would believe me without question.

Which is why I will *never* tell him what happened those four nights after the crash.

POLLY

I love bedtime.

We have a routine now. After the three of us have dinner as a family, Sadie gets in the shower. It used to be a bath, but after she turned eight, she decided she wanted to have showers. She's becoming more independent.

Then when the shower is over, Sadie wraps herself in the light-pink fleece bathrobe we bought her, and I brush out her hair and tie it into two identical braids. Then she takes my hand, and we walk together to the room that used to serve as my office but is now her bedroom, where she waits for her bedtime story.

Right now, we are reading *Matilda* by Roald Dahl. Monday, Wednesday, and Friday, I read chapters to Sadie, and Tuesday, Thursday, and Saturday, Hank reads to her. We alternate Sundays.

It's cold tonight, and Sadie climbs under the down comforter in her bed, tucking herself all the way up to her little chin. She loves being read to. It's one of her favorite things, even though she's gotten to be quite a good reader. She reminds me of Matilda a bit in that way.

"This is my favorite book so far," she tells me.

I smile as I crack it open to the dog-eared page. "Even better than *Charlie and the Chocolate Factory*?"

She considers my question. She is such a thoughtful little girl. I always thought she was a nice kid, but now that she's living here, I've gotten to learn how amazing she really is. "I think it is."

We were lucky to get Sadie. After her father died, she went into foster care since she had no relatives willing to take her in, and it was discovered that her biological mother had died of an overdose. I had been wallowing in self-pity after our adoption fell through and then The Incident, but I knew I had to pull myself together if I was going to help Sadie. The fact that we already had a relationship with the girl helped in the process, but there was nothing quick about it. I got a note from Dr. Salinsky though, testifying to my excellent mental health, and eventually, we were approved to become foster parents for Sadie. She's lived here ever since.

I read three chapters from the book as Sadie's eyes drift shut. She usually can't make it past the third chapter without falling asleep, but even so, just as she does every other night, she asks me, "Will you read one more chapter, Polly?"

She calls me Polly, but after we officially adopt her, I'm hoping she'll call me Mom. She's never really had a mother, so I'd like to give her that. And I want her to be my daughter so badly it hurts. She did have a father, so I'm not sure if she'll call Hank her dad, but I wouldn't rule it out. She never mentions her father, and she absolutely adores my husband.

Our family was complete before. But with Sadie, our cups are overflowing. I would do anything for her. Hank and I both would.

"You done reading?" Hank asks from the doorway.

I start to nod yes, but Sadie pleads, "One more chapter."

I poke her in the arm. "You're going to fall asleep before we even finish the next page."

"I won't!"

"You definitely will, missy."

Before I can protest again, Hank speaks up. "Let me read to her, Polly."

Hank was never much of a reader, so it surprises me how much he enjoys reading to Sadie at night. Then again, he's dived headfirst into everything about being a father. He gives Sadie way too many piggyback rides, he's had no fewer than a dozen snowball fights with her this winter, and they built the most impressive snowman I've ever seen (it was as tall as Hank). And he says as soon as the weather turns nicer, he's going to build her a clubhouse in the backyard.

He also tells me he would be happy to keep an eye on her if I want to try to find some sort of work outside the house. It's an idea I've thought about more and more, but I'd like Sadie to be completely settled in first. And Hank's shop is doing well these days, so we can make do without the money.

"All right." I rise from the chair and hand the paperback book over to my husband. "All yours. But she's going to be asleep in the next sixty seconds."

Hank grins at me. "I'll take my chances."

He kisses me before I leave the room. He holds me in his arms for just a little bit too long, but that's okay, because I don't want to let go either. He's the best husband I could ask for.

And I'm so happy that he kept me from making a terrible mistake one year ago. You know you've got someone really special when they are able to save you from ruining your own life.

I tiptoe out of the room while Hank settles into the chair that I vacated so he can read that last chapter to Sadie. As I close the door, I notice that he isn't reading from the book. Instead, he's leaning close to her, speaking in a hushed voice.

And she's answering back in the same hushed voice.

I see them doing that from time to time. Whispering to each other. I don't know what they're talking about. But I suppose it couldn't be anything that important. If it were, Hank would tell me. After all, we don't keep secrets from each other.

HANK

I've gotten to love Sadie like she's my own.

I never thought I would. I never imagined becoming so attached to the child we took into our home. But after only a short time, I can't imagine life without this little girl. Polly was absolutely right.

But that's not the reason I allowed her to foster Sadie, against my better judgment at the time.

My wife has issues. God knows, I love her. But the years of infertility did a number on her. I thought she needed more years of therapy before we considered bringing a child into our home. But this wasn't just any child.

"Hey, Sadie," I say after Polly leaves the bedroom.

She blinks up at me with gigantic blue eyes that seem to take up half her face, although they don't look quite as huge now that she's managed to put a little meat on her bones, thanks to Polly's cooking. "Yes?"

"Look out the window," I tell her.

She rolls her head to look out the window next to her bed, where huge snowflakes have started to fall from the sky. "It's snowing!"

"That's right."

"Is it going to be a blizzard?" Her voice is almost fearful as she poses the question. "Will we be snowed in?"

My stomach churns, remembering another blizzard that happened only a year ago. I wonder how much Sadie remembers of it. I'd hoped she'd forgotten it, but I'll never forget. Or what I did in the wake of the blizzard that changed our lives.

It was the same day I brought Tegan to the hospital. Polly begged me not to, but when I realized that girl was being held in our home against her will, there was no question of what I had to do. Afterward, Polly was furious, and I was debating if it was safe to leave her alone in the room, but I knew I'd be right downstairs. I made an appointment with Dr. Salinsky for the next morning and checked on her every hour, but I was going out of my mind with worry, so I decided to go out to the backyard to chop some firewood that we badly needed for our fireplace.

Big mistake.

When I finished chopping the wood, I went upstairs to tell Polly that I was going to get some dinner started. When she didn't answer, I was ready to bust down the door, but then I tried the doorknob and found it unlocked. She was gone. I ran downstairs and discovered her Bronco was gone too.

Even though her car was missing, I thought there was a chance maybe she'd gone over to see Sadie. So before I got back in my truck and started driving around town searching for her, I went to Mitch Hambly's house and knocked on the door.

When Mitch opened the door, he stunk of alcohol. It was only six o'clock in the evening—a little early to be stumbling drunk if you ask me—but that was his business. I asked him if he'd seen Polly, and he laughed in my face. *Can't seem to keep track of that wife of yours, can you, Hank? She's a real nut job.*

I didn't care if he insulted me or my wife. I needed to find Polly, and that was all that mattered. And if all he did was toss a few insults my way, I would have turned around and gone back to my truck.

But at that moment, Sadie appeared behind Mitch in the hallway. And her little face was all black and blue. Maybe if this had happened on any other day, I would've done things differently. Or maybe not. What kind of terrible excuse for a human being does something like that to a little girl? Just the thought of it still sends my blood pressure through the roof.

So I grabbed Mitch by the collar. It felt good to take that son of a bitch and hurl him down the steps of his front porch as hard as I could. He landed face-first in the snow, which was a softer landing than he deserved. I could have beaten the living daylights out of that bastard, but then I noticed Sadie watching me from the front door with those big blue eyes. And I stopped myself. I didn't want her to see me beat her father to death.

I leaned in to talk to her. *Your dad shouldn't hurt you that way,* I told her. *If he ever does it again, you come get me right away. Got it?*

And she nodded.

She shut the door behind her, and I started to walk away. I couldn't worry about Mitch right now—I had to find Polly. But then I saw Mitch starting to get back up in the snow. His beefy face was bright red, and his right hand was clenched into a fist, and a single word passed through his lips like a growl: *Sadie.*

He was angry that I threw him into the snow. And if I walked away, he was going to take it out on his daughter.

If I came back later that night, she might be dead.

I had never killed anyone before, but I didn't even think about what I did next. I shoved Mitch's face back into the snow, ignoring his muffled shouts and protests as he struggled for air. He was a big, strong guy but not bigger and stronger than me. There was a point when I could have stopped and let him go—no major harm done—but I wasn't about to let him go back to Sadie after I had pissed him off like that.

After a minute or two, he stopped struggling so much. A couple of minutes after that, he wasn't moving at all.

I got back to my feet, the knees of my blue jeans soaked with melted snow, shocked by what I had just done. But I wasn't sorry—it was the only way. I did what I had to do, and I hoped when he was found, the police would assume he'd passed out drunk and suffocated. But that's when I turned around and saw her:

Sadie. Standing before me, not saying a word, just staring up at me with her big eyes.

She saw everything.

You better call 911, I choked out, knowing that once the police came, Sadie would tell them what I did. I'd spend the rest of my life in prison for murder. It wasn't what I wanted, but I did what I had to do to keep that little girl safe from that monster, and once I made sure Polly was okay, they could take me away.

But then a funny thing happened. Sadie never told the police a thing about what I did. The only story they heard is that he fell down the stairs while drunk and that she found him, dead.

She kept my secret.

I've been hoping she would forget that night. But when I see the fear in her eyes as she looks out on the snowy night, I suspect she still remembers.

"Do you remember any other blizzards?" I ask her.

"Maybe," she says evasively.

I clench my teeth. I shouldn't push her. The last thing I want is to remind her of the terrible thing I did. But how could she forget? How could she forget the night her father was murdered?

"So you *do* remember," I say.

She blinks at me. "Remember what?"

"Remember...your dad? And...what happened to him..."

She looks at me for a long time. She remembers—it's all over her face. I wonder if she's mad at me for what I did. She knows I killed him. She knows I'm the one responsible for taking her father away from her.

She must hate me, at least on some level. Wouldn't she have to? She doesn't understand why I did it. She doesn't understand what I felt when I saw that man was beating up on a defenseless little girl.

"I don't know what you mean," she finally says. She tilts her chin up to me. "*You're* my dad, Hank."

I stare back at her in the dim light of her bedroom. "That's right," I say. "I am."

I reach out and take her tiny hand in mine as we watch the snowflakes falling from the sky. She might not have forgotten, but she understands. My daughter will never tell a soul what I did for her. We will both keep this secret.

Keep reading for a look at another Freida McFadden thriller, *The Boyfriend*!

PROLOGUE

TOM

BEFORE

I am desperately, painfully, completely, and stupidly in love.

Her name is Daisy. We met when we were four years old. I've been in love with the girl since age four—that's how pathetic I am. I saw her at the playground feeding bits of her sandwich to the hungry squirrels, and all I could think was that I had never met any living creature as beautiful or as kind as Daisy Driscoll. And I was gone.

For a long time, I didn't tell her how I felt. I couldn't. It seemed impossible that this angel with golden hair and pale blue eyes and skin like the porcelain of our bathroom sink could ever feel a tenth of what I felt for her, so there was no point in trying.

But lately, that's changed.

Lately, Daisy has been letting me walk her home

from school. If I'm lucky, she lets me hold her hand, and she gives me that secret little smile on her cherry-red lips that makes my knees weak. I'm starting to think she might want me to kiss her.

But I'm scared. I'm scared that if I tried to kiss her, she would slap me across the face. I'm scared that if I told her how I really feel, she would look at me in sympathy and tell me she doesn't feel the same way. I'm scared she might never let me walk her home again.

But that's not what I'm most scared of.

What I am most scared of is that if I lean in to kiss Daisy, she will let me do it. I'm scared that she will agree to be my girlfriend. I'm scared that she will allow me into her bedroom when her parents aren't home so that we can finally be alone together.

And I'm terrified that the moment I get her alone, I will wrap my fingers around her pretty, white neck and squeeze the life out of her.

CHAPTER 1

SYDNEY

PRESENT DAY

Who is this man, and what has he done with my date?

I'm supposed to be meeting a man named Kevin for dinner tonight at eight o'clock. Well, it was supposed to be drinks at six o'clock—drinks are easier to escape from—but Kevin messaged me through the Cynch dating app that he was running late at work and could we push it to dinner at eight?

Against my better judgment, I said yes.

But Kevin seemed really nice when we were texting. And in his photos, he was cute. *Really* cute. He had this boyish smile with a twinkle in his eye, and his light-brown hair was adorably messy as it fell over his forehead. He looked like a young Matt Damon. I've been on a lot of bad dates through Cynch, but I was cautiously optimistic about this one. I even arrived early at the restaurant, and I have spent the last ten minutes eagerly waiting at the bar for him to arrive.

"Sydney?" the man standing before me asks.

"Yes?"

I stare at the man, waiting for him to tell me that Kevin was killed in a tragic taxi accident on the way to our date, because this guy is definitely *not* Kevin. But instead, he sticks out his hand.

"I'm Kevin," he says.

I don't budge from my barstool. "You are?"

Okay, let's be real here—nobody looks as good in real life as their dating-app photos. I mean, if you're looking to score a date, you're not going to snap a photo of yourself when you're rolling out of bed with a hangover. You're going to doll yourself up, take about fifty different shots from every conceivable angle and with a dozen lighting options, and you're going to pick the very best one. That's just good sense.

And hey, maybe that one perfect photo was taken ten years ago. I don't agree with this logic, but I understand why people do it.

But this guy…

There's no way he is the same man as in his Cynch profile. Not ten years ago—not *ever.* I just don't believe it.

Even though it's an obnoxious move, I grab my phone from my purse and bring up the app right in front of him. I compare the boyishly handsome man in the photo to the man standing in front of me. Yeah—nope.

My date for the evening is at least ten years older than the guy in the photo and bone thin, bordering on gaunt. I think his eye color is different too. His blond hair is badly receding, but what's left of it is long and pulled back into an unkempt ponytail.

This is not the same man as in the photo. I'm even more sure of that than I am of the fact that I enjoy long walks through Central Park and bingeing Netflix.

"Yes, that's me," Fake Kevin assures me. (Although really, the guy in the photo is Fake Kevin. Maybe the photo really *is* of Matt Damon. I'm starting to think it might be.)

I begin to protest that he doesn't look anything like the photo, but the words sound so superficial in my head. Okay, yes, Kevin looks vastly different from his profile photo. But does that really matter? We have been texting through Cynch, and he seems like a nice enough guy. I should give him a chance.

And if it's not going well, my friend Gretchen will be calling me in twenty minutes with a manufactured excuse to get me the hell out of here. I never, *ever* go on a date without a planned rescue call.

"It's really great to meet you in real life," the real Kevin says. "You look exactly like your photo."

Does he expect me to say it back? Is this some kind of test? "Um," I say.

"Come on," he says. "Let's get a seat."

We snag a booth in the corner of the bar. As we're walking over there, I can't help but notice the way Kevin towers over me. I tend to like tall men, but he badly needs a little meat on his bones. It feels like I'm walking next to a broomstick.

"I'm so glad we are finally doing this," Kevin tells me as he slides into the seat across from me. Why is his ponytail so messy? Couldn't he have at least combed it before our date?

"Me too," I say, which is only slightly a lie.

He rakes his gaze over me, an approving expression on his gaunt face. "I have to tell you, Sydney, now that we're actually meeting in person, I genuinely feel like you are the perfect woman."

"Oh?"

"Absolutely." He beams at me. "If I closed my eyes and imagined the perfect girl, it would be you."

Wow. That's...sweet. Possibly one of the nicest compliments I have received on a date. Thank you, Real Kevin. I'm starting to feel glad that I stayed. And like I said, I do like tall men, so even though he looks vastly different from his profile, I get a tiny tug of attraction. "Thank you."

"Well," he adds, "except for your arms."

"My *arms*?"

"They're kind of flabby." He wrinkles his nose. "But other than that, wow. Like I said, you're the perfect woman."

Wait. My arms are *too flabby*? Did he really just say that to me?

Worse, now I am straining to surreptitiously examine my bare arms. And why did I wear a sleeveless dress tonight? I have only two sleeveless dresses in my closet. I could have worn something with sleeves that would have concealed my apparently hideous arms, but no, I chose *this*.

"Can I get you two something to drink?"

A waitress is standing over us, her eyebrows raised. I pry my gaze away from my monstrous arms and look up at her. "I...I'll have a Diet Coke."

"A Diet Coke?" Kevin seems affronted. "That's boring. Get a real drink."

I never drink alcohol when I'm on a first date with a man I've met on Cynch. I don't want to impair my judgment in any way. "Diet Coke *is* a real drink."

"No, it's not."

"Well, it's a *liquid*." I glare at him across the sticky wooden table. "So I would call it a drink."

Kevin rolls his eyes at the waitress. "Fine, I will have a Corona, and she will have a *Diet Coke*." Then he winks at the waitress and mouths the word *Sorry*.

I glance over at my purse next to me. When is Gretchen going to call? I need an escape route.

But maybe I'm not being fair. I've only known Real Kevin for five minutes. I should give him more of a chance. That's why I told Gretchen to call twenty minutes into the date after all. Five minutes is a snap judgment. If I can't give a guy more than five minutes, I'm going to be having first dates for the next twenty years. And now that I'm thirty-four years old, I don't have that luxury.

"Hot damn," Kevin remarks, following the path of the waitress with his eyes as she goes to get our drinks. "She has *really* nice arms."

Gretchen, where are you?

READING GROUP GUIDE

1. Tegan ends up choosing her morals over money. Is there an amount of money that could make you turn against your morals?

2. If you were lost in an uninhabited area with no cell signal, do you think you could navigate yourself safely to where you want to go, or would you be lost without the internet?

3. Both Tegan and Polly make a lot of assumptions about each other and about other people. How can our assumptions hurt our relationships? Why is it difficult to recognize the assumptions you've already made?

4. How trusting in general are you of strangers? How trusting would you be if you were in a compromised state, like Tegan?

5. Do you think Polly tried to handle Sadie's situation in the correct way? Was she helping Sadie or putting her in more danger?

6. Hank chooses to take Polly's side throughout much of the novel, despite his misgivings. Do you agree with his decisions? How much would you do for the one you love?

7. How much do Polly's mother's words about having a "complete" family influence her actions? Why do you think she feels incomplete? What do you think makes a complete family?

8. Are Hank and Polly ultimately good people? Do you think they will make good parents for Sadie, given everything we learn about them in the book?